KT-592-033

Comment by Julia Siboney, author of 'Children of Light': *I love it when I find a book so touching as yours. The story itself is the force of it all, you capture human emotions going against real life obstacles. It's been a beautifully haunting read.*

Comment by Isabel Lopez, author of 'Isabel's Hand-Me-Down Dreams': *Beyond Nostalgia is a story told with such tenderness and depth that it will break your heart. Though not sappy-sweet in sentimentality, it is warm and loving. It evokes our own fragile memories of that true and eternal love that happens but once in a lifetime and of making choices that will sometimes haunt us forever. It reaches out and grabs the hopeless romantic in all of us. The vivid imagery of his New York neighborhood and the memories of an unforgettable bygone era will touch many of his readers, but in the end, it will be the moving story of two young lovers and the heartbreaking cards they are dealt that will have readers reaching for the Kleenex and reminiscing about the one that got away and took their hearts with them. Powerful in its simplicity and honesty.*

Comment by K.C. Hart, author of 'Summer Rose': *I absolutely love your story. The place, the pacing, the sweet youth of Theresa and Dean, you have captured it all, the language. I have no idea why, but I kept thinking about Eddie and the Cruisers all through the story, and I don't even remember what that movie was about.. Dean's voice (your writing) is so perfect. I feel him peeling off the shells of the protective coating he's layered to protect himself and her. This is about more than love it is about intimacy, opening your heart and soul.*

Comment from Barbara Mayo-Neville, author of 'The Sea Pillow': *I have to admit that I am dumbfounded to read such a lovely, haunting and relational story from the hands of a man! There are a few men who can write in such a way--it is wonderful.*

I was dancing near the gym's center court line when, as it does so often in the city, trouble erupted. Fueled by a six pack of Rheingold Beer, I was feeling right, getting into the Shing-a-Ling with Debra Kennedy, a cute little blonde I knew. We were dancing real well together to The Rascals' hit 'Lonely too Long' and soon, after seeing what we could do, most of the couples around us started giving us a wider berth on the hardwood floor. By now I was feeling cool, real cool, like Travolta must have a few years later in Saturday Night Fever.

But there was somebody in the crowd who didn't think I was all that much, or maybe he did, and that's why he started in. All I know is this guy who had been dancing next to me, a real tall oriental dude with a greased-back Elvis hairdo, suddenly slammed an elbow into my kidney. Instantly, I saw stars, an entire galaxy, and my eyes glazed over just as fast. I hunched over, grabbed my side, tried real hard to squeeze away some of the pain. Then, just as quickly, I spun back up and around, aimed real high, and nailed the troublemaker with a good one to the cheekbone.

Fists were flying, a flurry of rights and lefts, hard punches, and I was getting the better of him. But it didn't last long. Mere seconds elapsed before two chaperones grabbed me; big burly blue-collar types in ill-fitting sport coats and mismatched polyester ties. They yanked me off the instigator and started dragging me, no questions asked, toward the principal's office.

"Lemme go," I shouted, "he started the whole thing!" But it did no good. My captors wouldn't say a word, or listen to one either. They continued to strong arm me out of the gymnasium then down a long empty hallway. One beefy hand cuffing each of my skinny arms, I felt like Lee Harvey Oswald just before he ran into Jack Ruby.

After successfully transporting me to the principal's office, my captors paused for a moment and eyeballed the long row of empty metal folding chairs lining the wall just inside the doorway. "Let's put 'im over there," one of them finally said, jutting his square jaw toward the farthest chair from the doorway. They marched me over, plopped me down, and gave me two nasty looks that said *Don't even think about making a run for it*.

They then strode across the linoleum to where this very old nun, a tiny woman the size of a pixie sat behind the biggest desk I'd ever seen.

She couldn't have been an ounce over eighty pounds. Translucent skin stretched across her forehead and tiny cheeks tight as leather on a bongo. With only that tiny face and miniature black habit visible behind that huge mahogany desk, she looked like something you'd see on "Laugh In". But that's where the humor ended. The chaperones surely didn't think anything was funny. With their backs to me now, both of them facing the toy nun, their heads bowed like altar boys, they began murmuring to her.I leaned this way and that, but their voices were too low. I couldn't discern one word of my indictment.

At first I wasn't overly concerned about the whole thing. There had been other times my friends and I had been in fights, and all anybody ever did was kick us out. Our only concern on those nights was how many guys might be waiting for us outside. But this thing was beginning to drag on a bit too long. I was getting antsy. I thought, 'Shit man, maybe they don't play around here at Saint Agnes'. Then, when one of the chaperones pointed to the telephone and I thought I heard him say something about the police, I really started getting uptight. Even with the buzz still going on in my head I realized things could get real serious, real quick.

A minute or so went by. I looked out into the hall and considered making my break. Ten, fifteen feet, and I'm out of here, wouldn't take but a second or two. I could do it so fast they wouldn't know what was happening. I'll haul ass outta here, go down the hall right to the coatroom. Then I'll ... Right there my scheming ended. That's as far as I got. Boom! Poof! It simply shut down, just like that. Because standing outside that doorway, on the far side of the hall, off to one side, apparently trying to remain hidden from everybody else in the office, was the most beautiful girl I had ever seen. And her dark, alluring eyes were locked on mine.

Holy Christmas! What a knockout! She's got to be the prettiest girl this side of the G.W. Bridge. A little on the hood or hitter side maybe, like the kind of girl who's into guys with greased back hair and leather jackets, but still, what a fox!

I felt like I was in Westside Story, one of the 'Jets' checking out one of the forbidden 'Sharks' girls. This girl was utterly captivating - no, beyond captivating. Forget that she wasn't all that tall or overly busty, that she didn't dress collegiate like me and my friends. She had this rare beauty that was as subtle as it was striking. Wrapped tight in a sleek, black dress with spaghetti straps, I'd have been content just to stare at her bare shoulders all night.

But there was so much more to take in. Her hair, blacker and silkier than her dress, cascaded from a perfectly centered part like two dramatic stage curtains, framing her face like a masterpiece. A teenage Cleopatra with eyes so dark, so mysterious, they almost looked oriental, like sideways drops of dark coffee that looked into you rather than at you. And talk about lips - full, sensual, all-female lips coated ever so carefully with a sexy flesh-tone gloss. Lips that somehow seemed familiar but, of course, weren't.

She lifted her chin just a bit, arched her feline brows and slowly brought an index finger to those lips. "Shhhh!" Then she lowered her hand from her mouth and pantomimed a word, just one word, system … or assistant … something like that. I wasn't sure. She straightened her dress, cleared her throat, twice ran her fingers through her hair, and strode into that office looking like the queen of Queens. Exuding an air of confidence that nobody alive could put on, she marched directly over to the nun and chaperones, and began talking to them.

With her back to me, I couldn't hear a word she was saying.

A few moments later, she and the chaperones turned toward me. The toy nun looked my way too. I noticed the girl's forehead was a bit crinkled, as if she was perturbed at something. Forcing what felt like some goofy innocent expression onto my face, I wondered *what the hell is going on here now?*

Then my jury turned back around to resume their deliberation. But before the girl turned away she snuck me a quick wink and an assuring smile.

A moment later they finally broke their huddle, and all four heads bobbed in agreement. A few more words were spoken, then the mystery girl strode over to me. She said, "Come on. We're going home."

Side by side in Saint Agnes' hallway, both of us stepping quickly, our eyes connected once again. It was then that we shared our first smile.

Who is this dream girl? I wondered. Why did she come to my rescue? *Have I met her before?* Nahhh, I would have definitely remembered.

Without breaking stride, I peeked over my shoulder, back toward the office, making sure no one was in sight or hearing range. Then I looked at her again and asked quizzically, "Do I know you?" My beer buzz not yet totally worn off, my words came out louder than I'd intended and ricocheted off the narrow hallway walls.

"Shhh ... " my new friend said, " ... wait till we get outside."

Even her voice was intriguing, a bit deeper than I'd expected...

"But, I've got to tell my friends I'm ... "

"No ... you can't," she whispered forcefully. "Those men see you back inside there, it'll be all over. They told me to take you directly out of the building. We'll get our coats, then we have to leave."

Oh well, I figured, no big thing. Plenty of times before, me and the guys had split up when we met girls. Times when we took them home, or took whatever they'd give us in apartment building basements or on their rooftops.

It seemed very strange, but as we descended the steps outside the school, thoughts of making sexual advances didn't even enter my mind. Usually by now I'd be conjuring where to take a girl, but with this one it was different. Somehow it felt special just to be with her. I was not only flattered by what she had just done for me and intrigued by her beauty, but also dumbfounded by how unpretentious she was.

We took a stroll beneath a starry sky, she sensibly dressed in a knee-length, quilted coat, me under-dressed in my lightweight varsity jacket. A log burning in a nearby fireplace filled the night air with a pleasant richness, but it was getting colder by the minute, and I shivered as I dug a chilled hand into my pocket for my Kools.

"Want one?" I asked, holding out the pack.

"No thanks. I have my own."

From her purse she extracted a Marlboro, the hitter's cigarette of choice. But this small cultural difference didn't bother me either. Somehow it made her even more appealing, sort of like being with the enemy's woman during wartime. With my brushed-metal Zippo, I lit her smoke first. I did this the conventional way, not the cool way I always did when with the guys, jerking it back and forth across my thigh in two, quick, well-practised motions, one to open the hood, the other to activate the flint wheel.

"How'd you do it?" I asked, holding the windblown blue flame to the end of her cigarette. "How'd you get me outta there?"

"Easy. I just told Sister Carmella that you were my brother."

So that was what she had mimed to me from the hallway, not system, or assistant, but sister.

"I also told her that I saw that other boy start the fight ... which I did." Then she smiled, a small bashful smile that warmed my heart when she admitted, "I was watching you dance."

I drew on my cigarette meditatively then exhaled. Mixing words with smoke, I said, "Thanks a lot, but why'd you do it? You don't even know me."

"I do now!" she said, looking at me with those eyes, her lips evolving into a most captivating smile. "I thought you were cute!"

That's what I'd suspected, hoped anyway. Now she'd admitted it. Hearing it come from that lovely mouth made the moment seem like a wonderful dream.

Our eyes still embraced in the darkness, I smiled back at her shyly. Totally disarmed by her beauty, I was forced to admit to myself something I'd never dare tell anyone else, that no way could such a perfect creature possibly be interested in me. In just - what, ten, fifteen minutes? - this living, breathing doll had stripped away every ounce of all that thin bravado I was so used to flaunting. Of all the girls I'd met in my young life, this was the only one who seemed too good for me. I didn't much like the feeling, yet still, I ached with desperate desire. With no mask to hide behind now, I could only resort to acting like my true self. And it's a lucky thing I did, because whether I realized it or not at the time, frankness and honesty form the very foundation of all true romances.

"By the way, my name's Dean ... Dean Cassidy. What's yours?"

"Theresa Wayman," she said. Then she paused for a couple of strides, her eyes searching deep inside my soul's blue windows.

I knew she liked what she saw when she said, "I'm glad I met you tonight, Dean Cassidy."

Suddenly, I no longer felt cold. I actually felt warm inside. The warmth of her words had gone straight to my heart and pumped throughout my body.

Though Theresa lived just a few blocks from Saint Agnes, she and I walked all over College Point that night. We strolled up and down quiet side streets where unbroken chains of parked cars buffered sidewalks alongside interminable rows of two-family homes. We spoke easily about the things that newly-acquainted teenagers do: school, music, movies, likes and pet peeves, favorite aftershaves and perfumes. We inventoried our friends to find out if any were mutual. A few were. We talked about our families, but only briefly. I said nothing of my mother's mental problems or my father's vile temper. All she said about her family was that she and her mother lived alone. Since she didn't volunteer any information about her father, I didn't push the issue.

As I said before, I wasn't about to try any funny stuff. No way was I going to jeopardize her apparent fondness for me. As a matter of fact, she made the first show of affection.

She put her arm around my waist. It happened on Broadway when we were oohing and ahhing in front of an unlit jewelry shop window. Well, really, I was sneaking glances at her reflection in the plate glass more than I was surveying the trove of gold and silver behind it. We had been walking for some time now and it had gone from chilly to downright cold. If I hadn't been broke, I would have taken her to the all-night diner and warmed us both up with coffee. But all I had in my pockets besides my Zippo, and maybe some lint, was twenty cents for bus fare home. I strained to hide my shivers the best I could. But Theresa was sharp. She quickly picked up on the tremor in my hand when I pointed to a real spiffy, Florentine-finished ID bracelet behind the glass.

It was then that I felt her arm slide around the small of my back. Nothing pretentious about the gesture, just a heartfelt, benevolent reflex meant to help warm me up. Talk about being in heaven! This was it. Looking down at her, directly into those dark exotic eyes, I lowered my shivering hand and laid it gently around her slender waist. For a second or two we held this pose, then, slowly, allowing her ample time to pull away, I leaned to kiss her.

She let me. It was nothing passionate, just a meeting of young lips, pressing gently, yet eagerly. Right then both our lives took on a whole new meaning. Instantly, my old world transformed into a totally different place. A wonderful alien place, saturated with new hope.

It was nearing 1 a.m. when we finally arrived outside Theresa's house. She pointed across the dark, deserted street, to a two-story house that was exactly the same as all the rest on the block. "That's where I live," she said, "on the first floor." The happy glow that had been in her voice and on her face all night disappeared, replaced now by concern and disappointment. She focused intently on the front window. A pale light was on inside, and there was music playing, sad music, depressing bluesy stuff that kids our age definitely were not into.

Still arm-in-arm as we stepped between two parked cars to cross the narrow street, I looked at her again and asked, "What's the matter, something wrong?"

"Ohhh, nooo … nothing." She managed a melancholic smile. "It's just that I … I can't ask you inside, and I feel bad about it." Then we stepped onto the sidewalk and she turned to face me. "I'm sorry," she said. "I wanted to invite you in, let you get warm, make you a cheeseburger or something."

Seeing the disappointment intensify on her face, I put my hands on her trim waist. Not having a clue as to what was troubling her, I said, "It's OK, I understand." Then I forced a smile, "Can I call you?"

"Of course! You better!" she said, as she hurriedly fumbled through her purse for something to write with.

In the time it took her to dig out a pen and a matchbook, she had twice glanced at her front window.

"Please call me, Dean."

"Tomorrow, I promise."

Rising to her toes, she slipped her hand on the back of my neck and kissed me once again. God, she knew how to kiss! She eased her tongue inside my mouth, slowly sweeping it over my teeth and gums, exploring for a moment before bringing it to meet mine. Holding her in my arms, I felt through her coat the swell of her breasts as they pressed against my chest. I wasn't shaking any more. Our tongues now sliding against each others, I cheated a little. I opened my eyes, just a bit, to see if she was into this as much as I was.

What I saw was upsetting. A single tear had spilled from where her eyelashes met. I pulled away, gently.

"What's wrong?" I asked. "Is this something I can help with?"

She bit her lower lip then said, "No. It's nothing major … I'll explain another time."

She sniffled, then smiled for my benefit and said, "I won't go anywhere tomorrow. I'll wait for your call … Dean Cassidy." Then she kissed my cheek, turned quickly, and went into her house.

I can no longer bring the feeling back, but I still remember how ecstatic I was waiting for the bus outside Bogart's Bar on Broadway that special night so many years ago. Looking up at the night-time city sky, I saw new stars, brighter stars, more stars than ever before. I even recall the misty stream rising from my mouth as I muttered to the heavens, "God, please, let there be many more nights that I'll wait on this bus stop."

Chapter 2

As usual, when the city sun rose Sunday morning, it was obscured from our first floor apartment. Secondhand rays delivered light to our bedroom but there were no visible horizons anywhere outside it. We never saw the sun down there until late morning, when it finally rose above the surrounding rooftops.

Shortly after it had risen somewhere out in the burbs, the sun's indirect light managed to penetrate the urban grime coating the outside of our bedroom window, waking me up in the process. As the backs of my eyelids went from black to red, my first thoughts of the new day were of Theresa Wayman and the night before.

Squinting across the room, seeing my parents' bed empty and rumpled, I sighed in relief.

Yes, I was sharing a bedroom with my parents. Here I was, crowding my eighteenth year, a starter on Flushing High's basketball team, had my own part-time job and all, and I had to sleep in the same room as my parents. All because my father was too damn cheap to spring for a place with two bedrooms.

Thank God! I thought. *Privacy!* Well, almost. As usual, the door was wide open. It had been that way for a long, long time. I must have been about eight when its hinges pulled from the wooden jamb, and it had laid to rest against the wall ever since.

I used to wonder, still do once in awhile, how such a beautiful, ornate French door with so many glass panes ever wound up inside our sixty-year-old, rent-controlled tenement. But, really, that didn't matter. What mattered was that it never got fixed. I'd rationalized this was because my father, like most New York apartment dwellers, wasn't much with tools. But deep down I knew his lack of aptitude had nothing to do with it. Even if he had been handy, he wouldn't have bothered to fix the thing.

Dad had already gone off to drive his cab that morning. As for Ma, I heard her loud and clear, already going hot and heavy with her rosary beads. You see, excessive praying was just one facet of my mother's merciless mental illness. Every day she'd spend hours at a clip down on her knees in front of her makeshift altar rattling off her Our Fathers,

16

Hail Marys, and whatever that other prayer was. But still, crazy as this was, I had to give her some credit. She'd actually fashioned our bargain basement chrome and glass tea cart into a first rate religious shrine complete with holy relics and pictures. There were a bunch of statues (two with halos), two crosses, and about a dozen flickering red candles just like the ones at Saint Leo's Church – the ones they charged you fifty-cents to light.

Ma always prayed in a slow, deliberate, cantor that drove me absolutely nutso. Lord, it was so depressing. But not to her. To her way of thinking it would be irreverent, her all loving and forgiving God would surely get her, if she ever rushed through her prayers. No sir, not my mother. She'd get this long, rhythmic cadence going. A resounding chant so loud I believed if Jesus Christ himself was up on the roof, six flights up, standing right there on 'Tar Beach' (where me and the guys used to get our suntans), he'd hear her prayers, without turning on his super powers.

Even my flat-assed, played-out pillow pulled tight over my head did little to muffle Ma's haunting chants as they rushed through the open doorway like an eerie draft. But, used to this as I was, my mind transcended her religious racket, and I was able to recollect all the wonderful events of the night before.

I ran a mental chronology of the evening, playing it all back best I could on my mind's screen, that first heavenly vision of Theresa, all the walking and talking, her putting her arm around me, that first kiss, the last one. And I thanked God it wasn't all just some cruel, wonderful dream.

Next I pondered when to call her. I wanted to do it right away but obviously couldn't so early on a Sunday morning. *Come on!* I thought. *You must be out of your mind! You don't want to come across as too eager. Shoot, even if you weren't worried about your ego, and it was the middle of the afternoon, you still couldn't call her from here.* You see, our telephone was in the foyer, right off that dungeon of a living room where Ma was praying like a lunatic to be cured from a cancer she didn't even have.

The decision was easy. I'd call Theresa from Cy's Candy Store. Cy's was where the guys and I holed up when we skipped Mass, which we were then doing with increased frequency. It had been five or six weeks

"Yeah, I'm gonna call her, if that's OK with you."

"Geez, De Cee," Jimmy Curten said now, "lighten up a bit."

Of course, Donny had to get in one more zinger as we shouldered our way through the legions of faithful souls crowded outside the church. The jerk lifts his arm straight up, points down at my head and yells in front of all these people, at the top of his lungs, "This boy's in love! Don't mess with 'is woman!"

As always on Sunday mornings, Cy's Candy Store was mobbed inside. Customers clutching The Daily-News and The Star-Journal lined up by the register. Diners packed the food counter, some working on eggs and bacon, others wolfing down bagels and cream cheese. Behind them stood a row of soon-to-be-diners waiting patiently, chatting with friends, reading The News. All four booths along the wall were occupied, but at one, three guys were getting up to leave, guys we knew, though only casually, and wanted to keep that way. Hard-core dopers in their twenties who, true to form, were way overdressed for such a fine spring day. All of them were in their trademark junkie coats - knee-length, baaad-looking black leather jobs. Beneath those coats, they each wore hugely-contrasting frilly tab-collar shirts, lavender, yellow and white. These guys were some messed up hitters still trying to hold onto the doo-wop days.

When they brushed by us, alongside the counter, we all nodded at them, just the smallest hint of recognition. We knew not to ignore them, but not to be overly friendly either. These messed-up dudes were probably doing six maybe seven bags of 'H' a day. They were exactly the type of bad actors the streets, and our parents, always taught us to stay away from. But they knew us from the neighborhood, and this small hint of familiarity might just prevent them from jumping us some night, unless of course, they happened to be strung out.

As I slid by the short one, the one with the deadest, yellowiest eyes, the one they called 'Apache', I heard him mutter "fuck" under his breath. Once they passed I turned to see what had pissed him off so much. It was Father Bianchi, the youngest priest in our church. He had just entered the store. Good old Father Bianchi with his olive skin and greased-back DA haircut always looking more like a wise guy than a man of God. But forget book covers. This man was one of the most caring human beings I've ever known, anywhere.

Father B's prime concern in life was looking after the young people of Saint Leo's Parish, and he was damn good at it. And he always seemed to take a particular interest in us guys. Sure, he knew our fathers, but that had nothing to do with it. Unlike most adults we knew, he truly liked us. He cared about where our lives were heading, and he showed it. Countless times, on his days off, this selfless young man who'd been reared in Hell's Kitchen (a place most people wouldn't stop to defecate in), would take us to different fun places. You know, the old 'get the kids out of the city for a while' routine. He'd sometimes take us fishing to Little Neck Bay or a Mets game up the street in the nosebleed section of Shea Stadium. Other times he took us to 'The Garden' to see the Knicks, or swimming out in Rockaway Beach.

Paying for his newspaper and Lucky Strikes at the register now, Father Bianchi nodded and smiled at the three junkies. He said something to them, then he turned to watch Cy count his change into his hand. These hard core addicts (dope fiends who didn't care about themselves, their own mothers, living or dying) shared an exasperated look, but they remained right where they were alongside Father B. A moment later the four of them stepped outside to talk.

Sliding into the booth, knowing well and good that Father Bianchi would soon be back for his morning coffee and to socialize with the parishioners, we huddled over the table, hurrying to get our alibi straight. If he asked, we'd tell him we already went to church. Eight o'clock Mass we'd say. Then I'd really pour it on by voluntarily telling which priest said the Mass. You see, ever since Father Bianchi had gotten me a part-time job at the rectory's office that past December, I'd had privy to the priest's Mass schedules. I knew this week the eight o'clock had been assigned to 'Father Speedy'. Yes, I know, Father Speedy is a weird name for a priest, but that's what we guys called old Father Toomey. Time and again he earned the nickname! He may have been getting on in his years, but he could still say Mass faster than any priest half his age. The reason Father Speedy had such a swift delivery was no secret in the parish. Everybody knew. You'd have to be living under a pew not to know that Father Toomey was a heavy boozer. The general consensus was that the octogenarian priest always rushed mass so that he could get back to the rectory for 'a hair of the dog'.

Finished with the druggies now, Father Bianchi came back inside and *finds out that my mother is nutso, so out of it that she constantly threatens to kill herself.* Maybe, maybe, maybe. I continued this self-inflicted torment until I reached Theresa's front door.

There were two bells alongside the door, one on top of the other. I rang the bottom where 'Wayman' had been scrawled with a ballpoint pen on a sliver of masking tape. Directing my eyes to the door now, I found myself nose to nose with one of three small windows that lined the top of it. There was that haunting reflection again. Vague as it was, what with a doily-like, white curtain backing the windows, I began toying with my hair nervously, patting it down low, strategically low, on my forehead with my finger tips. Still hung up on that pimple, I arched my brows high as they'd go, which in turn wrinkled my forehead. Then I rolled up my eyes. If I could see my hair up there, it might be hanging just low enough to conceal that disturbing zit.

Good news! I glimpsed at my hair. *Maybe if I walk around with my forehead crinkled up all day, she won't notice the damned thing!* I was giving this strategy serious consideration when suddenly the doily jumped aside and Theresa peeked out. Seeing her face again, albeit just a half-view of its loveliness from behind the curtain, instantly eradicated all my negativity. It was as if a long, violent storm had suddenly ended and the most brilliant sun you'd ever seen had broken through the clouds. And when she opened the door, looking oh so curvy in a sleeveless, burgundy v-neck and skin-tight blue jeans, she looked at me as if I was the special one, I knew instantly why I had I had come to see her.

After exchanging hellos, purse in hand, she asked, "Want to come inside, or would you rather go out for awhile?"

Being in no hurry to meet any parents yet, even though she lived only with her mom, I said, "Didn't you say there's a park around here?"

"Yes. But, you must want a drink or something to eat first?"

"No thanks, I'm not real hungry," I lied.

Out on the sidewalk anguishing over whether or not to take her hand, she took mine, as if she had read my mind. Then she leaned her head against my shoulder, looked up at me, smiled, and said, "I'm so glad I didn't have to wait until Friday to see you."

It was a colossal understatement when I said, "Me too, Theresa."

For the longest time, we sat on a park bench down by the water.

Out on Long Island Sound, not far offshore, a small fleet of boats were anchored, fishing for spring flounders. A father and two small children flew box kites high in the spring breeze. Pairs of lovers, alone in their own worlds, strolled hand in hand along the pathways. Other couples lying on the new green grass whispered the world's only words to one another. An old lady talked to her Chihuahua as she coaxed it along on a delicate leash. When they got a little closer and the dog squatted to take a dump, I quickly deflected Theresa's attention to a huge cabin cruiser pushing east toward the Throggs Neck Bridge.

Conversation came easy, just as it had the night before. Time quickly stole away. By late afternoon, having gotten all prerequisite small talk out of the way, we started talking about something much larger. A subject I never discussed much with my friends let alone a girl, the future. Heck, up to this point in time, my perception of what lay over the horizon never transcended the next party, dance or basketball game.

But talking with Theresa was much different than it was with most kids my age, boys or girls. She was one of that rare breed of bright kids who, without being a bookworm, had skipped a grade at school. Just turned seventeen, and already she was finishing her senior year in high school. She was just that smart. Already she was thinking about ten years down the road, about goals and financial security and things like that. But, high as such things were on her list, I could see they were not at the very top. What was paramount to Theresa was having roots. She'd have her own place. "Maybe out on the Island or maybe somewhere else," she'd said, "but I'll have that home. It blew me away when she emphasized that it had to be a home, not just a house, that a house was nothing more than wood, brick and glass, whereas a true 'home' actually has a soul. I considered this to be the most profound piece of thinking I'd ever heard come from another teenager, though at the time I had no idea what 'profound' meant.

When she began explaining why roots and security were so important, her voice became very intent. I could tell by that tone change and the seriousness in her mahogany eyes that I was about to hear some pretty heavy stuff.

"You see, Dean, my father died eight years ago. And since then, we've moved eight times."

Man, I thought, she must like me an awful lot to be telling me this stuff already.

Lifting a windblown lock of raven hair from her face, she went on, "It would have been bad enough had we moved around the block or across town all those times, but we didn't. We relocated, went to different states. Dean, we have lived in Florida, New Jersey, and North Carolina, twice ... and, every time, we wound up coming back here, to where we started in the first place."

Suddenly, a dark damper was cast on our relationship's potential. My heart felt like it had dropped out of my ribcage. The afternoon sun seemed to have lost much of its brightness. Each of my words, saturated with concern, I asked, "How come your mother keeps moving you guys?"

Sliding to the edge of the slatted bench, looking deeper into my eyes, she took my hand in both of hers. "Please, don't get mad at me, Dean. But, that's something I just can't explain to you just yet. When I do tell you, you'll understand why. I like you ... very, very much. I liked you the minute I first saw you last night. And now ... now that I'm getting to know you, it's really important to me that I keep on seeing you."

Then she leaned toward me, put both her arms around my neck and drew me close. She kissed me, long and hard. Her shampooed hair lifted lightly in the breeze, feathering my cheek, tickling it. The subtle fragrance of just enough perfume added to the essence of this wonderful kiss. Her lip gloss lubricated both our lips, as hers massaged mine. It was as if she wanted to consume me. And, she did.

When our lips separated, our faces remained close, and she held my eyes with hers. Her breath, quickened from the exchange of passion, was sweet and warm on my face. But she didn't say anything. Silently, she waited for my reaction to her pleas for patience.

When I smiled and said, "Fine ... take your time, Theresa. Tell me about your family when you're ready," her desperate look vanished, her mouth widened into a gleaming smile, and she pecked me on the lips, twice. And on that park bench, that glorious spring day so long ago, Theresa and I became one. After that, when we were apart, separated at school, at home, or anywhere else, no matter the distance, we were still together. Nothing would ever separate us, ever. Or so I thought.

By the time I walked Theresa home late that afternoon, the sun's rays had lost much of their heat. Sparrows chirped and hopped on lawns no bigger than area rugs. Small children played on sidewalks, while bigger kids had a stickball game going, out in the street. Their working-stiff fathers sat on stoops like urban kings, drinking Rheingold beer with neighbors, waiting for their wives to finish cooking dinner. And what dinners, scrumptious Sunday meals we could smell wafting from so many open windows, a cornucopia of delicious aromas that intensified my hunger, and surely Theresa's, too. Boiling corn beef and cabbage, kielbasa and of course, from the Italian kitchens, the ambrosial all-day sauce, drifted out on to the street.

Not saying much now, just taking in the sights, sounds, smells of her neighborhood, our bellies empty but our young hearts full, Theresa and I strolled ever-so contentedly toward her place. But my half of this peaceful, easy feeling quickly vanished, when I recognized a guy from school coming up the sidewalk toward us. It was Mike Trueblood, disgustingly-handsome, Mike Trueblood. Just what I needed, when things had been going so well with Theresa. Every girl at Flushing High had a crush on him. Not only was he a terrific looking guy, but he also worked out with weights and had the super physique to prove it. It was bad enough that he had all those attributes, but he was conceited as all hell on top of it. Trueblood was forever peeking into mirrors, windows, hell probably even puddles. Anywhere he could cop a reflection of himself, he would. It was almost comical. He'd stop any time he thought somebody might be watching, dig on himself awhile, then run a comb through his impeccable, beach-boy-blonde hair, all the while tensing his goddamn phenomenal biceps for affect. I knew who he was alright, but I didn't know him. Never wanting to give him the satisfaction the slightest gesture of recognition might bring, I'd always gone out of my way not to even make eye contact with him.

As he approached us, a most excruciating silence seemed to separate Theresa and I. This creep, Trueblood, had desecrated the greatest day of my life in a matter of seconds. Heat rose in my face as it flushed. You can't imagine how much I hated myself for this. For sure, Theresa would swoon over the sight of Trueblood now, just like all the girls at school. Maybe she'd make a comment after he passed, maybe the uncomfortable silence between us would simply linger. Maybe she'd loosen her grip on my hip. Surely she'd show some sign of being zapped by *the* Michael Trueblood's genetic gifts. I felt like an intruder. For one gut-wrenching, ego-mortifying moment, I felt more inadequate than ever before. Like an idiot. Like some lame poser with a huge zit on his head who had just realized he'd been a fool to think he could ever have had a future with a girl so far out of his league.

With Trueblood only three struts away from us now, I braced myself for disappointment, inevitable, monumental disappointment. Prepared for the annihilation of all my pride, battling the true pull of my emotions, trying my best to hide my humility, my eyes met Mike Trueblood's.

I wanted to disappear, just wither away, somehow dissolve into the cement sidewalk.

But the weirdest thing happened. Trueblood actually nodded at me, said, "What's happenin'?" It was the first time either of us had ever shown the other any sign of recognition. He acted like he respected me, like we knew each other. But that wasn't all. What happened next really blew me away. Trueblood shifted his eyes to Theresa, and he said, "How ya doin' Theresa?"

Holy cow! I thought. *They know each other!* How could it be? How could two such extraordinarily good-looking kids know each other and *not* hook up. *Hate to admit it, but he's the goddamn best lookin' guy in school. And Theresa, shit, she's the best-looking girl I've ever seen. They're made for each other.*

But Theresa tightened her hold on my waist. Her head a little higher now, obviously proud to be with me, almost like she was showing me off, she greeted Trueblood. Her tone casual, yet polite, almost like an adult speaking to a child, she said, "Fine, Michael. How are you?"

His trademark confident smile seemed actually bashful now. I swear! And his face reddened too! Even Mike Trueblood, my school's biggest playboy, every girl's dream-guy, was stupefied by Theresa's beauty. Let me tell you, I felt like King Kong. Had I been on a basketball court at that moment, I could have dunked two hands backwards. My biceps felt two inches bigger than Trueblood's and I was a full foot taller. Lord, I was wild about this girl. What guy wouldn't be? Hell, everywhere we'd gone that day, the park, the ice cream parlor for Cokes, walking down Broadway, as well as all those side streets, male eyes of all ages had ogled at Theresa.

Long shadows trailed us as we approached her front steps. She asked me inside for the second time that day. Again, I had to pass. It was already crowding six o'clock and I was running late for my job at Saint Leo's rectory. On the front stoop, we shared a long goodbye-kiss, a smile, and then two quick pecks. When I said goodbye, though a brick hunkered down in my gut, I was ecstatic; ecstatic about having found her, ecstatic that my eighteen-year solitary confinement had finally come to an end. I was more alive than I'd ever been.

two book-carrying friends, I took over his space. Leaning back, one foot up against the rail, trying to look cool, I fired up a nervous smoke with my Zippo, as I continued to watch the Friday-frantic rush of humanity before me.

But my expectant eyes kept pulling to the other side of Main, to the empty bus stop in front of a coffee shop over there. Each time I dragged on my cigarette, my anxious eyes clicked from the clock overhead, to the coffee shop, back to the clock. I could have sworn the minute hand was creeping backwards.

But finally, at seven-thirty-five, an orange bus labored to a stop across the street, and I watched a dozen faceless people climb out before I spotted Theresa. She strode to the corner and joined a small herd of pedestrians already waiting for the light to change. As they cheat off the curb, they're all painted red by the neon light outside the Main Tavern. Theresa doesn't see me yet but I see her, standing out from all the others like a perfect diamond. I'm thinking again just how lucky I'd been to have met her, when it suddenly becomes clear what Eileen Dolan had been hinting about. Theresa had on a new outfit, collegiate clothes, all of it brand new--a burgundy, man-tailored shirt, its button-down collar rising high from the v-neck of a white tennis sweater and a pair of female-tight, beige jeans. She even had on cute little shoes, scaled-down versions of the size eleven chukka boots on my own feet. WOW! She'd actually gone out and bought all these clothes, just to make me happy. Hot-damn!

When the light turned green, traffic stopped and the cluster of people on the corner scurried, urban-cautiously, across the wide street. The closer the group got, the more conspicuous Theresa became. She looked like a starlet making an entrance on Oscar night. She held her head high, delicate chin uplifted just a bit, not cocky by design, just an innate display of confidence and stand-offishness, mandatory deportment for someone so young, so pretty, so oh-too-sexually alluring for her years.

Stepping toward the curb in her queenly gait, she saw me through the passing throngs in fractured glimpses. Her natural defenses simply melted away, and she beamed like the school girl she was.

"Hi handsome," she said, coming up to me, reaching out for both my hands. I gave her a quick peck on the lips.

34

Knowing that every man on this crowded intersection had to be watching, envying me, made me more than a little self-conscious, but I loved it. I relished it. Although just a boy, I now had something that grown men ached for but could never have. I could see it in all the passing, straying eyes. Theresa was something to look at alright. A rare beauty who commanded unwanted attention from the opposite sex, and jealousy from her own, everywhere she went. I was enjoying it now, but because of my own jealous nature, I would in the future have problems dealing with all the male attention Theresa attracted.

Standing on the bustling corner, people darting every which way like so many worker ants, I asked her, "Where do you wanna go, the Keith's or the Prospect?"

"Gone with the Wind is playing at the Keith's," she said. "Everyone says it's terrific. It starts at 8:05. But, if you want, we can check out the Prospect first and see what's playing there ... we have enough time."

Now, I knew that all the girls were flipping out over 'Gone with the Wind', so I figured it had to be some mushy, frilly love story. Nevertheless, being as crazy about Theresa as I was and thrilled just to be with her, not realizing I was about to take in the greatest film classic ever produced, I was more than willing to make an uncharacteristic sacrifice. Nobly, I offered, "Gone with the Wind sounds good to me, if you want."

"Oh, Dean, that'd be fantastic," she said, knowing well and good how most boys who hadn't seen the movie felt about it.

Arm-in-arm we headed up Main Street to where it runs out smack in front of Keith's RKO Theater. The shared excitement of being together propelling our steps, we walked faster than we realized. When we were about halfway there, striding past Hardy's Shoe Store where I always bought my four-dollar penny loafers, I told Theresa I liked her outfit. In the glow of the store's lights I could see her face had flushed a bit. For a few steps she didn't say anything and her confident smile turned bashful. But then it widened and she said, "It's just a little something I bought during the week." It wouldn't be until a couple of weekends later that she'd admit she bought the collegiate outfit, and several others, to impress me, that she had taken almost a hundred hard-earned dollars from the small college fund she'd saved from her part-time earnings at a College Point book store. money she had been putting away for her all important education, for two years now, since she'd been back in New York, this time.

Unlike me, Theresa was a planner. And as time went on, that would prove to be one of our few differences. She looked to the future, while I only lived for the here and now, a philosophy that, in the not too distant future, I would pay dearly for.

Once inside the theater, we climbed the carpeted stairs and I led Theresa past a green-lighted loge sign into the darkness of the balcony. But not all the way up. It was common knowledge that to take a girl to the last row on the first date was presumptuous. A guy had to show he respected his date by avoiding the last row of seats. But it was a huge sacrifice since you knew damned well that's exactly where you wanted to be, the most private place in the entire theater. As we tentatively toed our way into the darkness, up the balcony steps beyond the mezzanine, this unspoken rule flashed in my mind. But now it was irrelevant. Theresa was different than all the rest of the girls I'd dated, and just being with her was enough for now. I wasn't going to rush intimacy this time. When the time was right for both of us, I'd know it. But still, I wanted us to have a little privacy so I lead her to two end seats, next to the wall, three rows from the top. By this time, 'Gone with the Wind' had been playing for three straight weeks and attendance at the Keith's was beginning to wane. The flick was no longer attracting sellout crowds, and that was good. It turned out that nobody would sit in our immediate vicinity, nobody next to or behind us. We were so far up there that, when the volume dropped during the romantic scenes, we could hear the rapid-fire clicking from the projection window high on the wall behind us.

It was during one such romantic scene, well after the intermission that we began to kiss along with Rhett and Scarlet. When Theresa snuggled closer to me, I figured it might be some sort of sign, a signal maybe. So I kissed her, tentatively at first, not knowing how she'd react, just a benign meeting of our lips. But soon, once we'd gotten a good taste of each other, our desires overshadowed any inhibitions we might have had. Arms locked tightly around one another, fingertips in each other's hair, massaging, we eased naturally into that ancient primeval ritual. We kissed away the rest of the theater, the whole rest of the world. Other than our two throbbing hearts and the cells of our bodies, nothing existed. For the moment, we were Adam and Eve. Everything else had gone extinct, or better yet, not yet been created.

A hundred and nine pounds of solid gold in my arms, my chest firm against her breasts, only the arm rest separating us, our breathing quickened and deepened. Then Theresa surprised me. She slid to the edge of her seat, pivoting sideways, and laid her leg over the top of my thigh. Deep in my stomach a strange wonderful feeling stirred. I felt like I was going to lift-off, right out of that velvet chair, when ever-so-gently she pulled her lips from mine, pecked them twice, then went to work on my neck. Her face brushing inside my high-boy collar, she slid her open mouth along the thin sensitive skin on my neck, occasionally pausing, kissing it, warming it with the heat of her rhythmic breath.

My response to all this stimulation was purely natural, not contrived or mechanical like it had been with all those nameless girls before Theresa. I slid my hand, slowly, from the long wispy hairs on the nape of her neck down inside the front of her tennis sweater and shirt, intentionally telegraphing the movement, giving her ample opportunity to stop me if she wanted. But she didn't stop me. Unchallenged, slowly, my hand found its way beneath a bra cup coming to rest on her bare breast. Ever so delicately I began to massage her.

Slowly, but deliberately, she withdrew her face from where it laid nestled in my neck. Raising her half-closed eyes to mine, she brushed aside a tress of hair. *Oh no*, I thought, *here it comes. She's going to stop me and I'm gonna feel like an A-1 jerk.* But, she didn't. Again she didn't say a word, but her bedroom eyes cried out to mine. They told me, "It's OK, Dean, but you better be who I hope you are, who I think you are. Please ... please be for real."

Then, as I held her in my palm, feeling the hard swell of her nipple against my fingertips, she kissed my mouth again, lustfully and for a long time. Right then and there, in the Keith's balcony that spring night in 1967, Theresa Wayman sequestered my heart. I knew then I was deeply and irrevocably in love with her.

Chapter 5

Two weeks after 'Gone with the Wind', I had the displeasure of meeting Theresa's mother.

It was late at night, May fifth, my eighteenth birthday. I was wearing Theresa's gift on my left wrist and had been stealing glances at it ever since she'd given it to me earlier that evening. She'd gone out and bought me that ID bracelet I liked, the one I was eyeing in the jewelry store window the night we met. One could only imagine how much it meant to me.

My arm around Theresa's waist, the ID resting on the heel of my hand, it was just about midnight when we turned up her street. We'd had a super time at a small get-together at her friend's house and were now cracking up as we relived some of the night's funny events. I remember our laughter echoing loudly in the night-time quiet and Theresa putting a hand over her mouth, and then one over mine, as we traversed the row of sleeping households on her block.

But a moment later, two doors from her place, all our light-hearted merriment came to an abrupt end. As if someone had thrown a mood-switch, Theresa's smile vanished and her face slackened.

"Shhhhh," she said. "Listen."

For a moment there was only the sound of our slowed steps. But as we got closer to her stoop, we both heard what Theresa had dreaded; that sad bluesy music. The volume was lower this time, but it was the same sad sax that was playing the first night I took Theresa home after the dance.

I was more than surprised when her voice suddenly became contemptuous. After seeing her for three weekends now, I didn't think she was capable of such ill feelings. "Well Dean, she's home. I guess you're going to meet her this time." Drumming the door with her fingernails, her other hand on the knob, she turned to me then and said, "Thank God, her man of the evening must have left by now. She's turned down the stereo, the fireworks must be over." Then she unlocked the door. "We might as well get it over with Dean. You might as well meet her."

We stepped into the blackness of the common hallway, and I fired up a nervous smoke. I kept the blue flame of the Zippo alive so Theresa could see the keyhole. The dim light it cast danced eerily on the door.

Theresa sighed as she unlocked it, and I followed her into the dusky living-room. The only pale light came from a cheap plastic lamp, a sorry Tiffany knock-off standing forlornly on a tiny end table. The walls were bare except for one that cordoned off the kitchen. On it was a tarnished star-burst clock and, to the left by the doorway into the kitchen, an eight-by-eleven black and white photograph. From where we stood, I couldn't quite make out who was in the picture, but I did take in the rest of the room's shabby appointments. The sparse furnishings were old, mismatched furniture that my friends and I would call "early depression era." Even the room's focal point, the sofa, was years overdue for the trash heap, a hulking old celery-green monstrosity with a frazzled fringe skirt and permanent ass-impressions on the two end cushions. The coffee table, one of those cheap pecan colonial jobs, was covered with tattered old issues of Silver Screen, Modern Romance, and True Confessions, most with coffee rings on their covers. There was also a Ronson table lighter, a glass ashtray with a cigarette butt mountain rising out of it, and two, near-empty wine glasses, one with cherry-red lipstick on the rim. I figured Theresa's mother and her date had probably abandoned the latter during a soulless romantic moment. Against the opposite wall, a vinyl-covered portable stereo sat uncertainly atop a metal snack tray, still playing that God-awful, depressing music. The rug felt paper-thin beneath my feet. In the swarthy light, I could only tell that it was brown.

The place looked like it was moved into yesterday after a ten minute, fifty-dollar shopping spree at the Salvation Army. Nevertheless, except for the mess on the coffee table and all the furnishings being so shoddy, the place was actually clean. I knew without being told it had to be Theresa, not her mother, who kept it that way.

Hearing the muffled growl of a flushing toilet from behind a door somewhere off the kitchen, Theresa and I just looked at each other. She asked me to sit on the sofa. Before I did, I whispered to her that this wasn't going to be any big deal, to relax.

Still, she looked so grave in the dim light, like a war-weary soldier preparing once again to do battle. Without saying anything, she emptied the ashtray for me then came back and took the wine glasses

toward the door. Over her shoulder she hollered again, "I HATE YOU, MOM! I HATE YOU! I HATE YOU! I HATE YOU!"

The last words her mother slurred before Theresa slammed the door behind us were, "You always were one selfish little bitch."

Hurrying down the hallway we could hear the locking of chains and deadbolts and her mother yell, "AND DON'T COME BACK EITHER CAUSE I AIN'T LETTIN' YA BACK IN."

Out on the sidewalk, the chilly night air seemed heavier now, like it might rain. "Come on, Theresa, let's go. I've got to call home. There's no way I'm leaving you alone tonight."

But still, she broke down. The hurt from her mother's betrayal poured from her eyes. All she wanted was for our meeting to go well. It had been so important to her. I put my arms around her, snuggled her close. Her body was tremoring and lurching so I held her tighter and rocked her gently. Beneath the street lamp's glow, we did this silent dance for what seemed a very long time. Then that bluesy music started up again and I said, "Come on, Theresa, let's find a phone. I've got to let my mother know I'm not coming home."

I hated like hell to have to call her, to deal with my own dysfunctional mother at a time like this. I knew she'd make a big deal about my not coming home. It would be doubly difficult now that she'd developed her newest delusional kick, her newest in a long litany of unfounded fears, the Mafioso. She believed they were after our family, even though none of us had any kind of a relationship with any such people. She also believed that, except for Father Bianchi, everyone with black hair was a mobster, even her shrink, Doctor Santangello. She was certain that the medicine he'd prescribed for her condition was in reality designed to slowly kill her.

Theresa and I scrunched inside the phone booth at Bogart's Bar and I called home. told my mother I'd be sleeping at Jimmy's house but, just as I figured, she wasn't going to let me off the hook all that easy. Not without first hammering me with a battery of peculiar questions, "Are you alright? Is anyone hurting you? They won't let you come home, isn't that it? What was that noise? Did you hear it? Someone's on the line! They're tapping the phone!"

I rolled my eyes to the booth's ceiling, left them there for a moment before looking down at Theresa beneath my arm. Her head rested against my chest and both her arms were locked around me. I put the phone in the crook of my neck and caressed the top of her head. She looked up to me with pink waterlogged eyes and I felt something tear deep within my chest. *Damn it,* I'm thinking, *why do I have to put up with this shit now?*

But still my mother went on, "Them bastards hurt you ... " she said, in the hardest, most threatening voice she could muster, just in case The Don or one of his soldiers were tapped in, " ... I'll go right to the F-B-I, and, oh yeah, I just happen to know an assistant DA from Queens," she threatened. Only after I ran off a succession of assurances that I hadn't yet gotten the kiss of death did she finally let me off the phone.

With nowhere better to go, Theresa and I drug heels all the way down to that park by the water where, for a long time, we sat in the darkness on two damp swings and talked. Did we talk! We opened up to each other and talked our way to, through, and beyond the next step of our spiritual communion. But it wasn't all easy teenage conversation. A lot of it was weighty stuff. I told Theresa about my mother's mental problems, and then she told me about her own personal tragedy. When she did, it shocked me. I had always thought that beautiful people like herself always led easy, tidy lives. But I learned different that night. I learned that beauty may help deflect some of the smaller bumps in life's rough road, but it does nothing to smooth the potholes. Nobody, no matter what they look like, is exempted from random, fate-dealt heartache. And Theresa was no exception. But she was still very young. Her personal pain hadn't surfaced on her face or in her eyes like it had on her mother's. Dreams were still in Theresa's eyes. You could see them. But they no longer existed for her mother. Although you could still see shades of beauty in her mother's face, her eyes were tired, most of their brightness gone from too much booze. But, as I was about to learn, it wasn't just her excessive drinking that had hardened her.

Thankfully, Theresa had not been ruined by her past, but the pain of it shrouded her words when she told me about her father's death. A breeze had come up out of the north-west, sending a cutting chill across the Sound that our light jackets were no match for. Both of us shivering, our shoulders hunched and tight, we walked from the swings to a scarred wooden bench. There we held each other for warmth and to help give Theresa the strength to tell her story.

Chapter 6

Lifting her head from my chest, Theresa looked inside my eyes. Reading the authentic concern there, she prepared to open up.

She shook two cigarettes from her pack, handed me one, and I fired them both up with my lighter. Along with changing her style of dress for me, she'd also switched to Kools.

She took a deep hit, exhaled a long stream of mentholated smoke, then said in an almost poetic way, "Dean, I want to tell you who Theresa Wayman is ... "

Her tone was mournful but there was also a hint of relief in it.

" ... better yet, I want to tell you where I've been. Someone famous once said 'You are your past', so I guess it's all the same. Anyway, I'll begin with my father. He died when I was nine years old ... I think I told you that already. But it wasn't a heart attack or cancer or even an accident that killed him." She drew a long breath, let it out real slow. "He was killed, Dean! Murdered! That's why my mother is the way she is."

I became all buggy-eyed from this shocker. "My God ... what happened?"

"We were living in Bayside at the time, in an apartment. My parents were in the process of buying their first house ... out on Long Island ... in Smithtown. It was like two weeks from the closing, and we were all so excited. My parents had already started packing our things. I still remember all those cardboard boxes stacked to the ceiling in the corner of our living room. They ... my parents ... were like twenty-eight or twenty-nine, and they had been doing without, scrimping and saving for the down payment on a house since they first got married, something like eleven years."

Theresa dropped her cigarette in the new grass, ground it out with the toe of her shoe. She left her eyes down there and sighed. She was trying to be strong but couldn't prevent the shake in her voice. I took her small cold hands in mine and squeezed them reassuringly.

"Go ahead, Theresa."

She went on with her story carefully, meticulously, wanting to get it all right. ·

"I can still picture that little house, an adorable little Cape with a white fence and a garage. It had a finished basement, too. I remember that because I thought it was going to be such fun playing in it with all the new friends I planned on making. And then there was that weeping willow tree ... in the front yard. It was just a tiny thing, about as tall as I was. The people who lived there must have recently planted it ... right in the middle of the lawn. Anyway, over the years, my mother and I have driven by the place a few times. Every time we moved back here, once we got settled in, we'd go back there. She still had a car back then, so we'd drive out to Smithtown, just to see that house. Each time that weeping willow was bigger. Last time we were out there it was taller than the house itself."

Dreamily, she paused for a moment, looking out to the black water before us, collecting her thoughts. The biting night wind had now strengthened and was whipping our hair. We shivered in spasms, the fits coming steadily and at shorter intervals. Along with its biting cold, the wind brought two blasts from a solitary tug offshore in the blackness. Small whitecaps began breaking on the pebbled beach as the Sound's mood grew fouler.

Returning to the moment, Theresa shifted her gaze from the roiling water to my face. She could see the deep concern in it.

"It was summertime and, for some reason, my father had gotten off work early that day. After supper he thought it would be nice if we all took a walk ... to get Italian ices. I remember it was a beautiful summer evening, still light out by the time we got to the candy store up on Northern Boulevard."

Anyway, on the way back, we're licking our ices and I'm on cloud nine listening to my parents talk about how it's going to be in the new house and all."

She paused then and smiled. She's back in time, a little girl again.

"God, we were sooo happy! I felt so secure seeing them hand in hand, planning our future. But Dean, in the next few seconds everything changed, our lives, our dreams, everything. We had come up to Bohack's supermarket ... do you know where it is?"

"The one near Bell Boulevard?"

"Yes, that's the one. Anyway, we're maybe thirty feet from the entrance when, all of a sudden, we hear these loud pops, gunshots,

45

three of them, coming from inside. Then, two men with stockings over their heads come running out. They're heading our way, so my father starts pushing me and my mother off the sidewalk, between two parked cars. I remember dropping my ice then and everything going into slow motion. My mother had me by the hand, waiting for a break in the traffic so we could run across the boulevard. We both turned and saw my father looking back again. He was right behind us, still on the sidewalk when those guys come running past us. Both of them had guns and were carrying these heavy canvas bags."

At this point, sobs accentuated Theresa's words. "They ... they were so scary looking with those stockings over their faces. There was no way we could make out their faces. All we could tell was that they were black. We could never have identified them. There was no way we could have been witnesses or anything."

She took a Kleenex from her purse and blew her nose.

"But it didn't matter to those ... those bastards. One yanked the stocking off his head and started shooting at my father when he ran by. Twice he missed but the third bullet ... the third bullet, Dean ... went into his left eye. It came out the back of his head. We saw it happen. The vision of him like that is something I've fought to keep out of my mind ever since. It hasn't been easy. I've dreamt about it hundreds of times."

I put my other arm around her now, cupped the back of her head with my hand and drew her face close. Cheek to cheek, her tears warm on my face, I felt so weak and helpless. My words seemed so inadequate, so understated when I said, "My God, Theresa, that's horrible."

"It's the worst when I'm asleep, when I can't control my thinking. I still dream about that day so often. I sometimes dread going to sleep."

"I'll bet it's been hell for your mom too, huh?"

"Yes, it's no wonder she's like she is. That was when she started drinking, when Dad got killed. Oh ... she drank before that, you know, socially, at parties, weddings, things like that, but after my father died is when it got the best of her."

"She must've figured it was the only way out," I said.

"Yes, exactly ... and I don't really blame her. But, you see what she looks like. She was beautiful once."

"I can see she's worn, but you can tell she was a good looking woman. It's obvious where you got your good looks from."

Theresa managed a small ironic smile, then she kissed me, twice. Her lips firm against mine, lip kisses that conveyed more affection than any passionate kiss could possibly have at that particular moment.

That was when, for the first time, she told me. She said those words that propagate our species, slowly, deliberately, "Dean ... I-love-you." Looking through my eyes, into my soul, she tilted her head, just a bit, shook it slowly and said, "I-love-you-so-much."

I had only known Theresa Wayman for three weeks, but for eighteen years my own innate need to love and be loved had been growing, intensifying, waiting for this person and this precise moment. I had loved her all that time. There had been a place in my heart reserved for her. I just hadn't met her yet. I could not, nor did I want to, keep this feeling bottled up any longer. My declaration of humanity's most powerful emotion simply gushed from within me now. "I-love-you-too, Theresa,"

Then we embraced. We held that pose and those emotions for a long moment and, in the face of the blustering wind, we became warm. But then the rain came, hard and cold, pushed by the new wind from Canada. Hand in hand, heavy drops beating on us, stinging our faces, we ran out of the deserted park.

Four blocks later, we ducked inside the first apartment building we came upon. Two radiators in the lobby of the five-floor tenement hissed and clanged, bringing up heat from the basement boiler. After stripping off our dripping jackets we sat, side-by-side, atop one of the radiators. All was wee-hour-quiet in the lobby, but we knew we couldn't stay there. Five floors, half a dozen apartments each, someone was bound to come home late on a Saturday night. If we were discovered, we'd surely be chased out. Stealthily, like two cat-burglars, we climbed the stairs of the old walk-up. Being a city kid, knowing all about apartment buildings, I knew that where the staircase ran out, one flight above the top floor there would be a landing next to the roof entry.

It was warm and dry up there. We could have some privacy if we kept quiet. Our inside-out jacket-pillows, mine rolled up hastily, Theresa's folded ever so neatly, added a semblance of comfort to the hard tile floor. Still wet from the rain, we laid there holding each other.

Sharing our body heat, feeling the beat of each other's heart against our chests, Theresa thanked me again for staying the night with her. Then an ancient urge swelled within us both. Cheek to cheek, body to body, our pulses quickened and so did our breathing. Heavy breaths against young necks aroused us with a heat that fueled our desires. This undeniable feeling suddenly erupted into an irrefutable passionate craving. Our lips met, and our tongues pulled to each other. None of it forced, everything coming so beautifully, so naturally. Instinctively, we wrestled out of our clothes. The rain pounding on the roof muted our labored breaths and pleasureful moans as we explored each other's flesh. When I entered her, Theresa withdrew her tongue from my mouth and whispered, "I love you, sooo much."

When it was over, we dressed, shared a smoke, and fell asleep in each other's arms. What we had experienced atop that tenement stairwell, couldn't have had more meaning if the act had taken place in the finest Park Avenue penthouse or the stateliest Hyde Park mansion.

Chapter 7

At about eight the next morning, we awoke to the slam of a door in the hallway below. Someone was leaving their apartment, probably going to church, the bakery, or to pick up the Sunday paper. As the heavy galloping footsteps of a man descended the stairs, we quickly straightened ourselves up the best we could. Still, we looked like what we were, two kids who'd spent the whole night out. Yet, Theresa, despite her damp rumpled clothes, lack of make-up and disheveled hair, was still beautiful. It boggled my mind that she actually loved me as hard as I did her, that she had given me everything she had to offer. Something, I had learned that night, she had never given to anyone before. I wanted this small moment to last forever.

Theresa said it would be safe to go back to her house by now. We could clean up, get something to eat. By this time her mother would be at 'The Point Diner', waiting her tables. We would be able to get inside. She couldn't possibly chain and deadbolt the door when she left for work. As we made our way to her house, neither of us said much. I hoped it was only fatigue from spending the entire night out, but I feared she might be regretting what we'd done on the stairwell. Maybe that wasn't even it. Maybe she was worried about the confrontation she'd surely have later with her mother.

As soon as we got in her house, Theresa put on coffee, then she asked me, "You don't mind if I take a quick shower, do you Dean?"

"No...Sure... go ahead."

While waiting, I smoked a cigarette and tried to recapture a vision of her lovely body. I couldn't. No man's memory can ever recall the clear splendor of a lover's body. It's always far, far better when he actually sees her again, when he loves her again. Like pain, shades of color, or scents, you simply can't bring them back into your mind as they truly are.

I punched out my smoke, ambled across the room to where that picture hung on the wall. The room daytime-brighter now, I could see it was a black and white of a little knobby-kneed Theresa in an adorable white dress, standing in front of her parents. The way Mrs. Wayman stood, her head tilted onto her husband's shoulder, reminded me of the way her daughter did that to me. She looked so different then. Mister Wayman appeared somewhat uncomfortable in his baggy suit, like a handsome, hulking tradesman who couldn't wait to get back into his jeans, like a small boy who'd been forced to wear short pants.

A few minutes later, sitting on that sofa's middle cushion, I again worried that Theresa might resent what we had done on the stairwell. That's when she came back out wearing just a white terry cloth robe. I was surprised by this new-found familiarity but at the same time relished it. But wait. Maybe my clunk-headed, testosterone-driven male ego was taking it out of context. Maybe Theresa simply figured she was covered and it didn't matter with what, and that's really all there is to it. Regardless, I thought it utterly marvelous that she'd now come out in front of me with a robe on, maybe nothing else. It was tough, but I did a pretty fair job of acting like the whole scenario was no big thing.

"Why don't you take a shower?" she asked. "There are clean towels in the bathroom."

"Nah, that's OK."

"No, really, you'll feel better," she said, massaging her scalp briskly with a pink towel.

"You sure it's alright?"

"Sure. My mom won't be home till mid afternoon."

Just the thought, of being naked in someone else's shower, made me feel vulnerable. What if Theresa's mother came home? But I was real funky, as you could imagine, so I went ahead and did it. I can't honestly say I didn't worry about her coming home as I quickly soaped, lathered, and rinsed myself, but she was only on the fringe of my consciousness. All I could really think about was Theresa standing naked in the very same tub just minutes before. Both my imagination and my hormones were again in high gear. The small tiled room was damp, the window and mirror still steamed up, her bare feet were right where mine were now. I found it all quite erotic. I longed to hold her naked in my arms again. "Forget it," I whispered to myself while toweling off, "what's important now is that she isn't hurting, that I didn't put her on some kind of guilt trip."

Safe once again after toweling off and dressing, I stepped out into the kitchen to the aroma of the fresh coffee. On the counter two ceramic cups stood next to the percolator. In the middle of the small room, an old yellow-Formica table with chrome legs was grouped with its only two surviving chairs. Where yellow tape was peeling off the vinyl cushions; brown cotton-like dashes of padding were plainly visible.

"Theresa," I called, after peeking into the empty living room.

"I'm in here," she answered, her voice sounding distant behind a closed door. "Come on in, Dean."

Instinctively, I just had to glance out the living room window. The coast being clear, I padded into the kitchen and across the linoleum. The bathroom door was open and so was the one to her mother's bedroom. I knew it had to be hers, because it was a mess.

"You in there?" I asked the only closed door.

"Yes," Theresa giggled, "come on in."

The little room was immaculate. An antique white dresser and mirror stood against one wall and a twin bed with a matching headboard was opposite it. Theresa was on the bed, lying on her back, still in her robe, her head propped on a frilly pink pillow.

Patting the mattress, smiling, she said, "Come here, Dean."

Absolutely bewildered, I took one more nervous glance through the kitchen and out the front window, then, obediently I did as I was told. Stepping uncertainly toward Theresa, her wide bright smile began to fade. Just lips now, a different kind of smile, much more serious. I thought I saw desire in it but how wasn't sure. Slowly, as if entering sacred ground, I sat on the edge of the mattress.

She raised her hand to my face and, in a gesture that seemed almost maternal, she stroked my cheek and told me "I love you, Dean Cassidy."

I felt the corners of my mouth slowly rise, then I said "I love you too, Theresa. I don't want us to ever end."

We held each other's eyes for a long moment, then, slowly, I dropped my gaze from hers. I couldn't help it. I just had to. I'd noticed in the outer boundaries of my vision a movement, a movement that for lack of a better word embezzled my attention. Theresa was ever so delicately opening her robe. I watched now as the soft material fell alongside her naked young body. It was like petals parting on a most lovely white flower. Like a lone, white cloud in a blue sky had separated, revealing the kingdom of heaven and all its promise.

grievous look she shot at me after I got up and opened the shade over the dark room's only window. Of course, she was sly enough not to let Theresa notice, but I picked up on it. I knew exactly what Ma was thinking: *Are you crazy! Why'd you do that? God knows what germs you just picked up by touching that dusty thing.* I saw her open her mouth to say something about my mindless, surely fatal, gesture but managed to catch herself.

We went on making small talk the best we could, but still there were uncomfortable breaks in the conversation. Eventually I got up and turned on the television, hoping a little noise might fill the holes in our forced, hollow conversation. Then as I started fiddling with the rabbit ears, the door opened and in came Dad. That's when Ma stopped holding back. That's when it really hit the fan!

Ma refused to believe that this man walking into our living room was Dad. Theresa or no Theresa, she totally lost it. It happened that quickly! She insisted on inspecting the back of my father's neck with her germ-scrubbed hands, appendages all red, raw and shriveled from hundreds of daily scalding washings. She needed proof, demanded to see the scar on his neck, the one he'd gotten years before when he'd had a carbuncle lanced. She truly believed my father was an imposter, somebody in disguise, some mafia capo who'd undergone a series of painful operations just to trick her.

Though I'd forewarned Theresa to expect anything, she couldn't believe what was happening.

I tried to lighten the outrageous predicament. Feeling like an asshole, acting like everything was going just peachy, I said, "Dad, I want you to meet Theresa."

"Hi honey," he managed, in a fatherly tone unfamiliar to this son's ears. "Nice to meet you."

"It's very nice to meet you, Mister Cassidy."

Then Mom butted in again, as if Theresa wasn't even there, "This isn't your father, Dean. Who the hell ARE YOU? You're not Frank."

My heart back-flipped one time, then buried itself deep inside my gut.

Theresa looked at me.

"He is so," I said. "It's Dad, Ma."

"No-he is-not," she said in that characteristic, all-knowing tone of hers. Then she rose to her feet. "Come here, YOU." she ordered this imposter, this murderer, this mobster.

Standing there, about to pop an artery, Dad said "Felicia, don't start this shit now, OKKK? I'm warnin' ya."

"I want a better look at your neck, BUDDY. Come here in the light."

That's when my old man really lost it.

"Shit, man ... (When he started a phrase with that you knew the rest was going to be profound, it was time to get out of his way) ... I told you not to start in, now." He would have stormed out of there right then, empty stomach and all, hauled ass up to Saint Leo's, if it wasn't for Theresa being there, shifting and squirming next to me on the sofa.

When my sweetheart's grip tightened on my shoulder, I glanced at her face. I saw apprehension, fear, embarrassment, shock, an entire gamut of miserable emotions, and I became enraged. The bad blood I'd inherited was boiling in my veins now. Realizing that we'd reached the point in this scene where it was too late to turn this ugliness around I said, "Welcome to the Cassidy's happy fucking household, Theresa."

"Oh my God, DEAN, don't talk like that," Ma pleaded. And, hoping she could intercept my words on their heavenly flight, she followed up with a lightning-quick sign of the cross.

"Come inside, Goddamit!" Dad said to Ma, relenting to her sick hunch now.

She'd worn him down. That was her way. My mother could wear down anyone. She probably figured she could wear down Jesus Christ with her prayers, and I wouldn't be surprised if she was making progress. Anyway, she followed Dad into the bedroom, her eyes not budging from the back of this phony's neck.

Alone at last, I asked Theresa if she wanted to split. "We could just run out the door, not have to deal with this shit anymore."

"I'd love to Dean. But we can't."

For two or three minutes, we sat in silence, listening to the indiscernible angry whispers in the next room. Then I told Theresa that with Dad's short fuse it defied all logic that he'd been able to hold back like he had, and that he actually submitted to Ma's sick demand, even with a guest in the house, had to be the world's eighth wonder.

Eventually Mom finished her probe and, reluctantly, told us to come on in and eat.

Nobody spoke at the table. It was a typical, atypical breaking of bread at the Cassidy place. Theresa and I ate little, and we ate quickly. I saw the fear grow in Ma's eyes with each bite we took. When Theresa and I both passed on desert, a packaged frozen pie, she was visibly relieved. Again I knew exactly what she was thinking. Anybody could have poisoned that damn thing, a disgruntled worker, some delivery clown, a hit man! Yeah, that's it, a hit man must have infiltrated the plant where they bake the damn things. The lengths those sneaky bastards will through to get you!

I wasn't about to hang around for an after dinner smoke. I stood to leave and Theresa followed suit. I almost popped a gut when she thanked both my role models for having her then told Ma that the food had been very good.

A minute later, when we stepped out of the apartment into the hallway, I yanked the door closed, and instantaneously all hell broke loose inside. The slam of the door had the same effect as a starter's gun as Saint Leo's 'Man of the Year' began screaming and cursing his way out of the state of grace. Talk about disgusting words! My dad knew them all. And being a creative sort of guy, he made up some pretty darn good original ones too. His booming profanities, both the clichéd and the copyrighted, thundered throughout the first floor hallway and probably could be heard all the way up on the fourth.

I swore I saw the foot thick plaster walls undulating as Theresa and I hustled, speechlessly, she wide-eyed, down the three hallway steps. Man, were we relieved to be the hell out of there.

But then, just when I thought the worst was over, I freaked.I leaned on the building's behemoth entry door and saw through the glass a bunch of our neighbors, most of them parked on lawn chairs, right outside our kitchen window. As my luck would have it, the spring evening was flawless, clear and balmy, and for the first time that year half the damned building's tenants were camped out there.

Old Mrs. Frankle, the self-perceived matriarch of our building, sat stoically on her webbed chair watching life pass by on Sanford Avenue just as she'd done for the past forty-six summers. The De Fillipos from 4D were there too, along with Donny Sculley's mother and nosey old Mrs. Jacoby. Mrs. Strunk was the only one standing. Of course her husband, Mister Strunk, wasn't there. Surely by now he'd be struggling to keep his balance atop a barstool at Paddy Q's, one of the old man's bars down on Bowne Street.

With Theresa in tow I laid a group hello on all the busybodies. Then I had another stroke of bad luck. Before they could return my greeting, Dad's booming, hoarse profanities erupted onto the avenue. For some reason they had moved their shouting match into the kitchen. My father was yelling so loud you could hear the panes vibrating on the kitchen window just six feet behind the crowd. Old lady De Fellipo was so shocked she nearly flipped her lawn chair. The profanities coming out of Dad's big mouth were so loud they momentarily drowned out all the other city noises, kids yelling and carrying on, the cooing of soot-gray pigeons up on the third floor fire escape, all the traffic racing by, even the music blaring from the Mister Softee truck across the street by the schoolyard where a swarm of little kids pushed and shoved in line. From where we were, none of this racquet, nor all of it, came even close to competing with Dad's nicotine-stained lungs.

Embarrassed as all hell, hyper-humiliated once again, I dropped my jaw, turned my head the other way and rushed Theresa past the neighbors, not bothering to introduce her. My Father's disgusting words chased us down the sidewalk, "YOU SLUT, WHAT'D YOU FUCKING START THAT FOR? YOU CRAZY-ASSED PIECE A SH ... "

Head down like a halfback, dragging Theresa in my wake, I picked up yardage fast. We skedaddled as quickly as my Converse hightops could lead us, short of breaking into an all-out run.

"There he goes, Theresa! Listen to him! Saint Leo's finest at his best!"

Finally, down near the corner where the sidewalk slopes toward Parson's Boulevard, we were out of earshot. Theresa and I slowed down. A relieved smile now wide across my face I asked my sweetheart, "Well...all things considered, what do you think went smoother, my meeting your mother or your introduction to...to June and Ward Cleaver?"

"I'd say it was close. Maybe we should have a run-off, do it all over again some time."

We shared a long hearty laugh and, as we continued down the avenue, I leaned over and kissed my new soul-mate on the forehead.

Chapter 9

The second Saturday in June was to be Theresa's prom night. And, I was well prepared. For a week and a half I'd been selling the baptismal certificates that I helped myself to while working at Saint Leo's. Just like Theresa, a good number of the girls graduating from Catholic and public schools throughout Queens would not yet be eighteen, so they'd need phony proof. You see, back then it was customary for New York City kids to go night clubbing after their proms ended, and although most clubs were pretty lax with the kids on their big night, they still had to produce some kind of proof. Everybody wanted to get into the big name Manhattan places such as the Latin Quarter and the Copacabana, so I accommodated them. Every day after school, at Kress' soda fountain, I was raking in anywhere from five to twenty-five bucks, tainted bucks. And, don't think it didn't bother me. It bothered the hell out of me that I had to get 'the root of all evil' the way I did, but for me there was no other way. To this very day it bothers me. But nobody I knew was going to give it to me, or even lend it to me for that matter. Anyhow, by prom night, I had put together almost a hundred and a half, enough to take care of the tux rental, Theresa's corsage, my share of the limo rental, and a night of partying at the Copa, that famous hangout of gangsters and celebrities.

When the big night arrived, I somehow convinced my father to give me a lift to Theresa's in his Ford Falcon. The only other time I'd ever ridden in it was the day he brought it home from the dealership, six months earlier. He had to borrow twenty-three hundred to buy that car. It was the only new one he'd ever owned. Unfortunately, a few short months after the prom, he had to sell it and buy a jalopy because the debt was overwhelming his budget. At any rate, I was thankful for the ride that night. I would have felt really lame taking the bus on such an occasion. I could just imagine all the passengers gawking at me in my blue tux, frilly shirt, and cummerbund. I don't think so!

During the twenty minute drive over to Theresa's that night, Dad and I barely exchanged a word. But when he dropped me off in front of Theresa's place, I thanked him for the ride, popped the door open, and was about to step out when he said, "Here ... take this. You might need it." It was a ten dollar bill. I opened my mouth, was about to tell him thanks anyway, I have enough money, but caught myself. I realized my refusal would have ruined for both of us this rare benevolent fatherly gesture. For this was one of the few times in my life I'd felt anything other than indifference toward my father. I took the money and I thanked him. Maybe, I thought, we were finally making some sort of father and son connection. I climbed out of the white Falcon feeling a brief pang of optimism for our relationship. I thought maybe now that I'd turned eighteen, was graduating high school, becoming a young man, we just might have more in common. But it was just another short-lived hope. A few short weeks later, with everything back to abnormal, I realized it was nothing more than a spur-of-the-moment thing. And I felt like a sap.

When Theresa opened the front door, I was dumbstruck. She looked absolutely elegant, like a woman, better than any woman I had ever seen on the cover of Cosmo. She looked so different, so much more mature. In her French curls, high heels, and that green gown with its low neckline, she was enough to make any red-blooded male howl like a coyote.

"Geez, Theresa, you look great!" I understated.

She smiled wide, did a couple of cute little poses and a pirouette. Then, checking me out, she said "Oh, Dean, look at you! You look sooo handsome." She gave me a mischievous look, pointed a manicured finger at the corsage in my hand and asked, "And what do you have there, Mister Cassidy?"

"Oh yeah … this is for you … and you know it. Now come here." I took the flowers out of the clear plastic container and clumsily slipped them over her wrist.

"Thank you, sweetie," she said in a teasing tone, her eyes transmitting immeasurable joy. Then she leaned forward, kissed me on the cheek, and I noticed gleeful tears welling in her eyes.

But all of our joy quickly went to hell. Our tender moment was cruelly raped when from the kitchen her mother's hoarse grating voice lashed out, "Where's that goddamned camera?" She stormed into the living room, not realizing I was there. "You idiot, I told you ta … " Seeing I had arrived, she stopped mid-sentence and said, "Oh … hello." The dejection in her voice was so apparent she might just as well have said, *Oh it's youuu, how you doin', asshole?*

"I think the camera's in my room, Mom," Theresa said, trying to force her voice to hold its jubilant tone, not having much success.

"Well, come on and help me look for the godamned thing," Mrs. Wayman slurred.

"Be right back." Theresa said, extending her upright palm toward the battered sofa, smiling sadly. "Have a seat."

Sitting stiffly in my tux, I lit a smoke. Three hits later I heard the witch's hushed voice from two rooms away. She spoke louder than she realized but probably wouldn't have given a shit if she had, since she was all juiced up again. "I knew you'd lose that fuckin' camera!"

Shit, why doesn't she leave her alone? It's her daughter's godamned prom night. I fished the pint of Bacardi's from my jackets inside pocket, broke the seal, took a hot swallow, and put the bottle back in my pocket.

Then, thank God, Theresa found the camera. "Here it is, Ma ... right here in the closet."

SLAP! The impact of hand against Theresa's face carried through the kitchen clear into the living room. I shot out of the sofa, caught myself, and sat back down. Somehow I fought off the urge to run in there and kick her skinny ass.

"Why'd ... why'd you do that?" Theresa cried, her voice straining with emotion.

Hearing this hurt in her voice, I just about crushed the sofa's armrest in my bony grip. I clamped my jaw and ground my teeth with more force than an enraged great white could possibly muster.

"Ah'm lookin' all over the place like an idiot, and you hid the goddamned thing in your closet."

Theresa was sobbing now, pleading in a low voice, "Please Mom, stop ... it's my prom night."

A hushed moment passed. Then they came back into the living room, together. Theresa was crushed.

Her mother stuck a finger toward the door and ordered us both to stand by it. "Go on ... both of ya."

I wanted to spit in her miserable face, but I didn't. I just stood up, snuck her a hateful look, and waited as Theresa came to me. Together, we dragged ourselves to the door where Theresa rested her arm around my waist. I felt it trembling. I looked at her face more closely now. Her left cheek was a deep red. A coursing tear-track had cut through the fine dusting of powder on it. Only once before had I seen her so sad. I snuggled her waist as reassuringly as I could as we grudgingly posed for the demon on the other side of the camera.

Just as the flash popped, a horn honked outside. Thank God! It was Theresa's friends in the limousine.

Mrs. Wayman made her way unsteadily across the room. She handed her daughter the camera, and then, as if it were a mandatory matriarchal duty, she began straightening her daughter's dress and corsage. Staring smack into Theresa's devastated eyes, she snapped as if being held at gunpoint, "Have a nice time." Saying any words that remotely resembled even a token of benevolence was next to impossible for this tormented, tormenting, broken woman. Those few words she had managed, "Have a nice time", came across as a lame attempt to retract her vodka-fuelled behaviour. Nevertheless, it was an attempt.

"Let's go." Theresa said, as she slowly eased her eyes from her mother's.

Out on the street, the chauffeur held open an outsized black door for us to join our four waiting friends. Standing behind Theresa as she climbed in, I heard that sad bluesy music starting up again.

Chapter 10

Theresa and I worried for weeks that Sister Carmella might be going to the prom. Although her attendance had always been questionable because she was so frail, so up in age, there had been no guarantee she wouldn't be going. If she did, we would not have been able to. You can imagine our relief when a few days before the big night Theresa heard through the grapevine that the diminutive principal's doctor decided it would be better if she did not go. All the loud music and excitement could prove to be too much for her. This revelation, plus the fact that there'd be no chaperones other than some of the nuns and faculty, added to our relief.

The prom was held at a posh catering hall out in Great Neck. I've long since forgotten the name of the place but still remember its huge glowing chandeliers, massive cut-glass works of art that looked like exploding glaciers bursting from the towering ceiling. There was a spacious staircase too. Bigger, wider, plushier than the one at the Keith's Theater, it gracefully swirled up to the second floor banquet rooms. Decked out as I was, promenading up these wide elegant steps with my arm around Theresa's waist, I felt like blockade-runner Rhett Butler must have when he climbed Tara's stairs with his beloved Scarlet Tara during their happier times. So swollen with pride was I, it's a wonder I didn't pop my cummerbund.

Despite the damper Mrs. Wayman had cast on our big night, young and resilient as we were, we had a ball. The prom turned out to be one of those extra special good times that you hated to see come to an end, like a good book or a good movie. It seemed to wrap up before it ever fully got under way, long before we'd had enough. But the night was young and there was still plenty ahead.

Outside the catering hall, we all six piled into the limo. Theresa and I had knocked off the Bacardis on the way to the prom and now went to work on the beer and wine the driver had on ice for us. The driver seemed like a real nice guy even though I'd caught him stealing glances at Theresa. If he hadn't been, I would not have fought back the nagging urge I had to tell him to keep his God damned eyes on the road. Anyway, after he drove us to Regina Skow's house to pick up her boyfriend's car, we gave him a nice tip and thanked him.

Regina's boyfriend (I think his name was Eddy), who was a bit older than the rest of us, had a Plymouth Duster. He was a sophomore in college and also our designated driver for the night. I felt bad for him as the rest of us partied all the way into Manhattan, but he didn't seem to mind. Anyhow, we all had another terrific time at the world-famous Copacabana. The Supremes were there and put on one heck of a show. Diana and the girls banged out one mega hit after another. When they finished up the show with 'Someday We'll Be Together', Theresa and I decided then and there it would be our song.

After leaving the Copa, prom night being the marathon it was, we took a ride on the Staten Island Ferry. We all thought it was cool as hell when Eddy drove his car right into the belly of the thing. As soon as he killed the engine he, Regina and the other couple rushed right up to the observation deck. Theresa and I stayed behind telling them we'd be up in a little while. We talked for a few minutes but, as soon as all the other cars were parked, we went right to it, hot and heavy in the back seat. And it was kind of strange, as if we'd already been in the middle of the act and, after a brief interruption, jumped right back where we'd left off. As if some imaginary switch had been flipped, we instantly returned to more torrid, more passionate heights than we'd ever reached before, like two lost lovers who had finally found each other after a very long and painful separation. But that wasn't the only strange part. As frantic, desirous, enthralled and cramped as we were, I still remember hearing the long eerie drone of a ship's fog horn somewhere off in the dark distance. I know it's weird, but the moment I heard that horn I thought it was telling me something. Sure, I'd had a lot to drink, but that wasn't it. That blast from somewhere out in the late-night harbor cut right through my alcohol induced haze. This was something different. Deep inside my consciousness I simply knew there was a message, a sign, maybe a premonition traveling through the darkness with it. Never one to believe such stuff, always the first to discount such thinking as hokey, I was absolutely certain this incident had some kind of meaning. Although I wasn't about to stop the act Theresa and I were about to culminate, I was dead certain that blast had something to do with our actions. It would be a long, long time before I'd come to realize exactly what that message was.

The next morning, after just two hours sleep at Regina's place, the six of us drove out to Jones Beach. Talk about some played-out kids. All of us were exhausted and, except for Eddy, terminally hung over. As soon as we spread Theresa's blanket on the sand, I passed out. For hours I slept as the hot afternoon sun beat down on my back and legs. I was roasted like you wouldn't believe, but Theresa fared far better. She slept right alongside me the whole time but had sense enough to wear a long man-tailored shirt over her swimsuit.

About four that afternoon she came to. Moments later I awoke to the feel of soft kisses on my neck. "We've been sleeping for hours," she said feathering her hand across my back.

I stiffened up, and she said, "Oh Jeez, I'm sorry, Dean. You look like a boiled lobster. Put your shirt on right now."

"Yeah, I'll bet I do,." I said, ever-so-gently wrestling into my tee. "Are you OK?"

"Sure. I had my shirt on. I'm just a little burnt on the back of my calves."

I rolled over, gave her a peck on the lips, then rose to my elbows surveying the beach. When we arrived earlier, the place had been packed. Blanket to blanket, it looked like one gargantuan patchwork quilt spread as far as you could see. It probably covered every grain of sand all the way out to Gilgo. But now most everybody was gone. The wind had really picked up and breakers were crashing in the surf. The only beachgoers left were a handful of young folks scattered here and there trying to stretch the weekend.

Theresa asked me to take a walk with her, so we left the others still sound asleep, still entwined in each other's limbs on their blankets.

We shared a smoke, our hair whipping this way and that, taking in the landscape as we trudged hand in hand across the sand. We made our way maybe a hundred yards up the beach when Theresa surprised the heck out of me. She started leading me away from the water, back toward the sand dunes, the desolate sand dunes of Jones Beach. If you're from 'the city' or Long Island, there's a good chance you know where they are. It's a place, not all that secluded, where, for generations some of New York's more daring young folks have given in to the ancient pull of their hyperactive libidos. I thought it strange that Theresa would even consider fooling around back there. But after we climbed down the backside of the first dune, I quickly realized she had no amorous designs. Sitting face-to-face in the sandy trough, neither of us saying a word for a few seconds, she looked deep inside my eyes, through them and beyond. Instantly, I knew something was wrong, seriously wrong. When I saw the tears start to well up, I couldn't take it any longer.

"Dammit Theresa," I demanded in a tone just short of a shout, "What the hell's the matter?"

"I wanted us to be alone for a little while," she said. "I need to talk to you, Dean."

A single tear then dripped from her eyelash, streaking the side of her face. I leaned forward, put my hand on her shoulder and asked in a much more gentle tone, "What is it honey? Something I did?"

"No, no," she assured me, "things couldn't be any better. I'm happier than I've ever been in my life ... but I'm worried. I didn't tell you last night because I didn't want to ruin our good time anymore than my mother already had."

"What are you so worried about? Tell me."

She drew a deep breath, dabbed her cheek with a shirtsleeve, sniffled again and said, "Dean, I'm afraid she might want to move us again."

"No way. What gives you that idea?"

"Remember I told you about my father?"

"Of course."

"And how my mother has been moving us from state to state ever since?"

"Yeeeaahhh," I said, as a hollow feeling inside my chest started to swell.

"Well, my father's murder had a lot to do with our moving back and forth. No ... it had everything to do with our moving. You see, Dean, my mother testified against those men who killed my dad. The police caught them that same night and she picked them out of a line-up. When it came time to prosecute, they had plenty of evidence, the guns, fingerprints, witnessess to the robbery. But my mother was the only adult who'd actually seen the shooter's face. Sure, as I told you before, I saw it too, but I was just a child and they weren't about to drag me in on it. They didn't have to anyway. It was pretty much an open and shut case. My mother's testimony alone was enough to put that … that one bastard away. But, before that, even before the trial began, we started getting all kinds of phone calls, threatening calls … scary calls."

"Don't tell me they were out on bail?"

"No, no," she said waving off the question, "of course not, they weren't going anywhere."

She paused a moment, alone in the gloom of her recollections, then she came back, "They were locked up alright, but they had friends, relatives, whatever. We got calls from a man, twice, and one from a woman, all in one day. They threatened to kill my mother, shoot her, and me too. Of course we disconnected the phone immediately. We were scared like you wouldn't believe, but then the police gave us round-the-clock surveillance. That helped a lot. Since the phone calls stopped, we thought that part of our nightmare was over, but we were wrong, almost dead wrong."

"Dead wrong, what do you mean?"

Theresa paused, took a Kleenex from her purse and dabbed her pink eyes. I slid closer, laid my arm around her shoulders, and she went on with her dreadful story, "The worst part came three weeks after they buried my father. It was night time, my mother and I were in our first floor apartment watching TV. I actually remember some Disney special was on. Anyway, when a commercial came on, I went to the bathroom and my mother went to the kitchen to make us some popcorn. All of a sudden there was this tremendous explosion in the living room. Dean, it scared the living daylights out of us. Somebody had thrown a Molotov cocktail through our front window."

"Oh my God, you can't be serious."

Theresa slowly nodded and said, "Yes, I am serious. The entire living room caught on fire instantly. There were flames everywhere. My mother and I had to climb out a bedroom window. Obviously, we got out OK … with no physical damage that is. Anyway, now you know why my mother drinks the way she does, and why we move all the time."

"Yeah, but that was nine years ago. With your phone number always unlisted and all the moving you've done those people couldn't possibly find you."

"You're preaching to the choir Dean. Of course I know that. Tell it to my mother and try to make it stick. It's the same as you trying to convince your mother she doesn't have cancer, or that the Mafia isn't after her family. Anyway, no matter where we lived, be it New York, Florida, or North Carolina, whenever something she perceives as weird happens, she panics. Anything, no matter how slight, involving a black person can set her off. It can be something as harmless as somebody asking her for the time, or directions, or just glancing her way for a second or two, she'll have us packed and ready to move the next day. She's done it! Why do you think we live in College Point and she works there, because it's all white! We've lasted there almost three years now because she's felt somewhat safe. It's a record for us, and it makes me very nervous."

She stroked my hair, pushing it back off my forehead. "I wanted to tell you all this because I love you, Dean, more than I ever dreamed I was capable of loving anyone. You are my life now, and I don't want us to ever be apart."

She then brought her lips to mine. One thing led to another and, despite the risk involved, that Sunday afternoon in 1967 we made love in the sand dunes of Jones Beach.

As they always do in northern climes, the summer months flew by as if they had wings. Fortunately Theresa's mother did not try to uproot her, but that fear certainly stayed alive. A lot of things happened during that 'Summer of Love'. A hundred thousand people flocked to Haight-Ashbury. Elvis married Priscilla in Vegas. Some of the worst violence in U.S. history erupted in places like Newark and Detroit. I started growing my hair long. Theresa and I both got into bellbottoms and smoked a little grass. Like I said, it all moved so quickly. Before we knew it, autumn arrived and temperatures started to drop. So did the leaves on Sanford Avenue's few trees. But, at about the same time those leaves died, something else was born. Another legitimate fear began festering inside me, and it was growing all too quickly. It had to do with a place called Vietnam. The catastrophe taking place there was becoming worse than ever. The War was escalating. Already four young guys I knew from Flushing had come home in body bags, guys who had earlier registered for the draft in the very same building as I did. Before the smoke would clear, and all the power games were over, tens of thousands more would be gone forever, enough young men to fill Shea Stadium twice. I was determined not to become one of them.

The entire country was tuned into the war. Every night, millions of people, coast to coast, actually watched it on the six o'clock news. In the comfort of their living rooms, they watched actual film footage of the jungle carnage. From their easy chairs, the smell of home-cooked suppers working on their appetites, they listened to the gory statistics as the daily death tolls from both sides were reported. Hearing them day after day, people eventually began accepting these numbers as if they were half-time scores of inconsequential high school basketball games. Americans had come to see so much horror that the horror was gone. Unless, of course, it affected you, or somebody you loved, or worse yet someone you *had* loved.

Naturally, my family's relief was immense when my brother, Sylvester, completed his twelve months at DaNang that September. He had come out of there unscathed and was now finishing up his hitch at Homestead Air Force Base in sunny south Florida.

With Sylvester finally safe, it was now time to worry about myself. And isn't that the worst? Isn't self-worry the most intense, most devastating form of that cruel emotion? Of course Theresa was by my side, always sharing this worry, but she was sharp.She tried to play down its potency by not talking about it. And, as alienated as my parents and I were, they too were worried to death. We constantly heard on network TV, or read in The Daily News, about places previously unknown to us. Dangerous, faraway places with death-rings to their names like Keh San, Phan Rang, Ple Coup, Cameran Bay and many other places we had no business being in.

I didn't want any part of such a fiasco, but ideals didn't count for anything unless you happened to be rich or famous. Unfortunately for someone like myself, there weren't many options, only blue-collar choices; the draft, Canada or jail. Every day was shrouded with fear – fear that my draft notice might arrive in the mail.

When summer ended I left my part-time job at the rectory for a full-time gig on Wall Street. Every day I'd ride the subway into Manhattan to this nothing job at a brokerage house. For eight hours a day I sat at a long table, inside a windowless room, hand-counting giant blocks of other people's stock certificates. Other than Fridays at five o'clock, the only highlight of this arduous, mind-numbing sentence was going on the coffee runs. As you can imagine, the days were very long, especially when you factor in the twenty minute walk to the subway and an hour and a half train ride – both ways. That's almost twelve hours! On top of that (thanks to Theresa's coaxing), three nights a week after dragging heels out of the subway I had to grab a bus out to Queens College. I'd screwed around so much in high school that my four-year average was a dismal 69%. You needed an 85 average to go full-time, free, to the city colleges. The only other way for flunkies like me was to go nights, get fifteen credits with a B average or better, and then you could matriculate and go during the day for free.

It was a pain in the neck but I was carrying nine credits and doing well. When the first term ended in December, I had a B+ average. Just two more courses and I'd be going full-time, days, which would make me eligible for a coveted college student deferment. But time was working against me.

profile, a literal picture of youth. But the one I liked best was the first one, the one of us cheek to cheek, both of us enjoying vivacious, unencumbered, heartfelt smiles. It was a picture of happiness in its purest form, a happiness that can only be felt in the morning of our lives, a happiness that can never be recaptured or duplicated afterwards. Our eyes were radiant with this youthful brightness, and naive hope.

A few minutes later, a wet strip of tiny black and whites slid magically into the holder outside the booth. Theresa's head leaning against my shoulder, we studied the pictures in earnest. "This first one is like poetry," I said. "You can have all the others, Theresa, if you want, but I'd love to keep this one in my wallet."

"Ahhhhh! Aren't we the romantic ones, Dean Cassidy, talking about poetry and such things. Never would have known it twenty minutes ago when you wanted to beat up that man on the train."

"Awright, awright, stoooppp. It's just that I think it's a great picture."

"I'm just kidding," she said. "Sure! You can have it ... my favorite is on my dresser mirror at home. The one Regina took of us at the Copacabana."

We left Woolie's and headed for Gertz Department Store where the Q-12 bus stopped. It was only about a half block down but, before we got there, we passed the Hurdy Gurdy, a new old-fashioned hot dog and hamburger joint. I noticed four dopers standing just inside a plate glass window. They were looking out at the passers-by expectantly, their noses so close to the cold glass they each produced their own little fog spot. Their nervous eyes clicked side to side, checking out everybody out on the wide sidewalk. I could see they were getting testy, jumpy for their next fix, wondering where it would come from, looking for Mister Tambourine Man.

A minute or so later, we got on the bus line, and I fished a single from my wallet. That old cowhide wallet still felt alien in my hands, lighter and thinner, even though months had passed since I cleared out all the pictures of other girls. That same night, also to prove my allegiance to Theresa, I made the supreme sacrifice by dumping my 'little black book'. It was a hard-to-find tiny job, so small that it actually fit inside a compartment in the wallet. It had been chock full of numbers and addresses too, so many that, to help my recall, I had to jot where I met each girl next to her name. There was also a rating system consisting of one to four check marks, but, I won't go into that right now.

While waiting on the bus stop, I slipped the now dry new picture of Theresa and me inside a plastic holder. It was cracked but you could still see us pretty good. Then I realigned an existing snapshot of myself. "I'm sure not crazy about this picture," I mused aloud.

"Which one?" Theresa asked, resting her head on my shoulder while looking into the wallet.

"This one," I said, pulling the tattered billfold closer to her. It was a wallet size of my senior picture, the one they took for the school yearbook. I had on my only sport jacket. The green and white madras Sylvester had handed down to me along with his Jade East when he was getting ready to report to basic training

"I got a haircut at the 75-cent joint down in the subway the day before it was taken," I said, "and the bargain-basement barber butchered me up real good."

"Is that supposed to be a tongue twister, Dean?"

"Whaaat?"

"The bargain-basement barber butchered me up real good. It's almost like the blue bug ... "

"How'd you like a punch in the nose, young lady?"

"What picture? Lemme see," Theresa said, leaning closer, pressing a breast to my elbow, holding my wrist now. "Ohhh...you look so cute."

"Yeah, sure. It was raining like hell that day, and I had to walk six blocks from school to the photographer's studio in that shit. It was the worst bad-hair day imaginable. Not only was it cut too short to begin with, but it looked even shorter when it crinkled up in the rain."

"It looks fine ... handsome," Theresa said, clinging to my arm with two hands now, looking up at me with exaggerated goo-goo eyes. "And, anyway, it's a lot longer now," she said, flipping it in back where it laid a few inches over the collar of my varsity jacket. "You're starting to look like a certified hippy."

And, it was true. My hair now obscured my ears, which was just fine by me since I'd always thought they were a bit too big and too high up on the side of my head. I liked the way I looked. And there was that statement my appearance made. My hair told the world *I'm a nonconformist, anti-establishment-against the Viet Nam War, excuse me, the Viet Nam conflict. Against any rules or laws enacted to stymie one's individual rights and all forms of public manipulation by the profiticians.*

I'd become old enough to vote the previous spring but had no plans to exercise this right, responsibility, privilege, or whatever else the media was calling it at that time. I couldn't devalue my convictions by voting for one of two phonies. The old 'lesser of two evils' is in reality the 'evil of two lessers'.

One of the few differences Theresa and I had was that she was apolitical. Maybe she, like so many other Americans, preferred not to think about what was happening to them. They trusted 'their' government would protect them, wouldn't let them lose their dream. Sure! By 1967 rumors were already circulating that within ten years there would no longer be a middle class, but Americans still believed justice and fairness would prevail, the good guys would always win, just like in the John Wayne movies. But this over-optimistic belief that the good guys would always prevail was slowly dying, along with 'the Duke'.

Just as the bus pulled up, a raw-boned, middle-aged man, a burn-out, started ringing jingle bells in front of the entrance to Gertz's. You could see in his expressionless eyes, his creased face and slack body that he'd been to hell and now was trying to find his way back. Sitting behind a tripod with a metal kettle hanging in the center, he looked so pitiful in his baggy Salvation Army uniform. With my perpetual heartfelt pity for lost causes, now magnified by the holiday season, I told Theresa to stay on line, and I went and dropped a buck in his kettle. The guy didn't say thanks, but I understood. As I walked back across the sidewalk, I noticed a guy in a different kind of army uniform, The U.S. Army's. He was a young soldier, home on leave, striding by with two friends in civvies. The kid wore a Vietnam Campaign Ribbon on his chest and, on his face, a look that was much too solemn for his years. Theresa glanced at him and then back at me. She could see how bummed out I was. I feared that things were going to change. For the past nine months since we'd been dating, everything had been going all too well in my life. Good things never seemed to last for me. I had these bad vibes that I too would be in a uniform before I could matriculate full time at school.

I said to Theresa, "I got a feelin' my hair's not going be this long for much longer."

"Let's not talk about that now, Dean," she said looking down at her shoes. With the toe of her little suede chukka boot she meditatively rolled a discarded cigarette filter on the sidewalk a few times. Then she mashed at it.

I would be nineteen in May, but wouldn't complete the rest of my required courses until June. They'd been drafting guys as young as eighteen. Although neither of us would admit it, deep down Theresa and I both knew they'd probably get me. This gloomy knowledge had been tearing at me more and more frequently lately, and accepting such a dismal fate grew more difficult rather than easier. I'd be losing everything - my freedom, my hair, friends and family, a college education and, most of all, the love of my life, my Theresa. The chance that I might get killed, never see her again, was genuine. And we had so many dreams yet to fulfil: marriage, kids, a house with a green lawn and white picket fence out on the island. But now, despite still being just a teenager, all of this was in jeopardy.

All along Theresa had acted as if avoiding talking about the draft might prevent it from happening. Intelligent as she was, she preferred to lock such negative thoughts out of her mind just like she did the cruel injustices of self-serving politics. But, lately I'd noticed her eyes going off to faraway places with increasing regularity. More and more often she was getting lost in her troubling thoughts.

As the Q-12 labored away from its stop, I caught her again. Taken hostage by those thoughts, peering out the window into the Queens night, she desperately searched for solutions to an unsolvable problem.

Chapter 12

After getting off the bus a block early on Bowne Street, Theresa and I picked up some snacks at the German deli. I bought a couple of 16-ounce bottles of Pepsi, a box of red pistachio nuts, two Devil Dogs and a big bag of cheese-covered popcorn.The store clerk unveiled her accent when she said, "A dollar and forty-nine, please." A buck forty-nine ... boy, those were the days.

When we got to 1B, I shifted the brown paper bag to my left hand and dug into the right-front pocket of my jeans for the key. I've always been that way, methodical. Change in the front left pocket, key in the front right, my wallet always in the right rear. Small habits never change.

Theresa stood by my side as I slid the key into the lock. She liked my mother and she felt very sorry for her, but each time I brought her home turned out to be a bigger fiasco than the last. She was apprehensive now. I could see it in her movements. Don't forget, we had been dating for nine months, so I'd learned to read her pretty well. And this night she was not her usual poised-beyond-her-years self. Now she was fidgety, unbuttoning her coat, tugging her sweater down around her waist, drumming her fingernails into her shoulder bag, all before I got the door unlocked. I'd never seen her so uneasy. It was uncanny, as if she knew something would go very wrong this visit. As I said earlier, I don't believe in such bunk, but it was as if she was having a foreboding premonition of what waited for us inside the apartment.

"It's OK," I said gently, "she'll be going to bed around eight. That's only a half hour from now."

I pushed the door open and stepped back to let her in first.

Instantaneously, Theresa spun back around at me. "Dean, there's no lights on!"

I looked over her shoulder. It was pitch dark in there. I flipped on the hall light and we stepped lightly to the living room. The lamp on the table next to Ma's chair was off and there were no candles burning on the tea-cart altar.

"Ma?" I said tentatively, my own voice sounding eerie in the silence. No answer.

Again I called out, louder this time, "MA, where are you?" My tone was a mix of agitation and concern, justifiable concern. This was scaring me. Mom had been threatening to kill herself for almost five years now. Countless times she'd said she was tired of it all, that she was someday going to jump in front of a subway train at the Main Street station. And lately she'd been making these nagging threats more frequently.

With this knowledge shrouding my nervous thoughts, I cried out again, "GOD DAMMIT MA, WHERE THE HELL ARE YOU?" With my concern quickly turning to fear, you could hear the transformation in my voice – twice, once when I said it, once when it bounced back off the walls. That dark demon, fear, had set up inside me and was expanding like a malignancy with every quickening breath. As I bent to turn on the lamp, all kinds of horrid scenarios raced in an out of my head.

My words were laced with panic and dread when I said, "Let me see if she's in the bedroom." It sounded to me like someone else had spoken the words, not registering until after I'd heard them. Then, as if I had injected it into my veins, a terrifying panic rushed through my body.

"C'mon," I said, rushing into the bedroom. "Shit ... she's not here, either!"

The window shade was still up. She must have left before dark. God knows why, but one of the few things she did around the house, other than praying and scrubbing her hands, was to draw our three shades when the sun went down. Maybe she thought she was closing out the devil or something. The glow of the street light penetrating our tissue-thin curtains cast a dusky rectangle on my parent's bed. It was empty and still made.

Theresa broke the unnerving silence. "Take it easy, Dean. Maybe she's out with your father somewhere."

"Nooo, Theresa. She's not out with my father," I snapped as I rushed for the phone in the hallway.

My hands shaking uncontrollably I looked up the number of the church hall in our battered address book. Hastily I dialed the black rotary phone, misdialing the first time, getting it right the second.

After a thousand unanswered rings, a familiar voice finally answered. "St. Leo's."

"Father, is this Father Bianchi?"

"Yes," he said, calmly.

"Father, this is Dean Cassidy. Is my Dad there?"

"Yes. Is something wrong, Dean?" He read it in my voice.

"It's my mother! She's not here! I just got home. She's not there with my father, is she?"

"Oh, good father in heaven, no, she's not," he said. Father Franco was my Dad's best friend and he knew all too well about my mother's problems. I heard a breath riddled with despair from the other end of the line, then Father said, "OK, Dean. Here's what I want you to do. Call the 109th Precinct. Tell them that your mother is missing. Tell them your mother's mentally ill and explain the situation, you know, the death threats and the fact that she never leaves the apartment. I'll get your Dad. We'll be there in ten minutes."

"OK, Father. Thanks." I hung up and called the police.

When the duty sergeant told me they couldn't file a missing person report unless someone had been missing for twenty-four hours, I had a shit-fit. I had explained the whole deal to the cop but, still, he told me, "We can't do the report yet, but I'll tell you what..." The guy seemed OK, for a cop. There was actually a hint of concern in his hardened voice when he went on, " ... see if you can find out what she's wearing. Ask your father when he gets there, maybe he knows. If he doesn't, check her closets and dresser drawers. If you can ascertain what she's wearing, I'll put a call out, have the units keep an eye out for her."

"Alright, thanks a lot. What's your name again?"

"Sgt. D'Amato. Just ask for me."

"C'mon, Theresa," I said, hanging the receiver in its cradle, "let's check the bedroom closet." When I said that, I realized exactly what we had to look for.

Stepping quickly to the bedroom, I told Theresa, "She's got this dress. It's a pale, pale blue. Kinda plain but kinda formal. A silky material." I pulled the string that turned on the bare 40 watt in the closet then I turned to Theresa, my voice breaking when I told her, "It's the dress she kept tellin' us she wanted to be laid out in, you know, like in a casket, when she dies of the cancer she thinks she has or ... or ... OHHH, Chrrrist ... or when she kills herself!"

Theresa laid a hand on my chest and said, "Take it easy, Dean. She might be OK." Then she really stretched it. "She's probably fine."

"Nooo ... ," I said jerking my head in quick little half rotations, "she'll never be fine!"

Abruptly, I began sliding hangers. One after the next, I shoved aside old skirts, dresses, sweaters and blouses, and my father's dress clothes which he only wore to church. Pushing everything to the right, I worked my way left, back to where the closet continued behind the wall for about five feet. It was like a cave back there. You could step inside the door, turn left, and go the five feet behind the thick plastered walls. But rather than step on the dozens of shoes strewn all over the floor, mostly my mother's, all second hand, I reached back in there and searched around.

"Is this it?" Theresa asked. She'd pulled a powder blue knit dress, one of ma's favorites, from the days when she liked to wear them tight and sexy. Ma had been a real looker before she'd gotten sick and begun her perpetual fasting.

"No," I said, looking way back inside the cave, finishing my search, carefully balancing preoccupation with dread and panic. With the elimination process now complete, I said, "She wore that funeral dress. It's not here ... anywhere. C'mon, let's call that cop back."

I yanked off the closet light without even thinking about the act, a reflex my father had conditioned in me with all his bitching about wasting electricity. Incredible how inconsequential things like turning off a light when your mother has probably just killed herself remain ingrained in your head. The subconscious is one hell of a mystery.

We'd just stepped back from the closet when Theresa held up a finger and said, "Wait ... listen."

I froze, tuned in my ears, there were distractions now--noises. I heard a jet decelerating high above the building, someone yelling outside in the darkness, and tired old footsteps from the apartment above.

"What is it?" I whispered impatiently. "We gotta call."

"Shhh, Dean! I'm telling you I hear something, in the closet." She grabbed my wrist with both hands and held it still. "It sounds like ... like faint breathing," she whispered

We froze. My chest felt constricted and tight. Then the noises faded and I too heard the breathing.

Desperately, I reached into the dark closet, frantically feeling for the damned light string again with my hands--like swatting flies in the dark. I found it, yanked it on again, dropped to my knees and started whacking away at the mountain of disarranged shoes.

Then I hit something, something solid. I swatted aside more shoes. Then I saw my mother's seemingly lifeless leg flat against the wooden floor.

Theresa and I were pulling her out of the closet just as Dad and Father Bianchi came rushing into the apartment. Father and I held Ma up, one of her arms around each of our shoulders, and we walked her. Her limp legs dragged along the living room rug as we walked in circles. Father kept talking to her, trying to break into her unconsciousness, while Dad called the hospital to get an ambulance dispatched. I looked at my father standing in the hallway next to Theresa. The phone in one hand, a Pall Mall in the other, I thought about how his damaged heart must be working triple time.

As Father Bianchi and I continued to walk Ma, Dad and Theresa went back to the closet to search for clues as to what my mother might have ingested. Amidst the shoes, they first found an empty pint bottle of Fleischmans, then Dad discovered that all his heart medication, about fifty pills, were gone. The prescription bottle was empty. Soon after that the ambulance arrived and raced Ma off to the hospital. The four of us followed in Father's Mercury.

Six hours later, in the morning's wee hours, after they'd pumped out Ma's stomach and stabilized her, the doctor at Booth Memorial Hospital told us her survival had been nothing short of a miracle. He said the amount of medication she ingested was enough to kill an elephant, let alone such a small woman. She was only an inch or two over five feet and had withered away to an emaciated eighty-three pounds.

And so Theresa and I had weathered another trauma. But once again, hard times, the truest test of love, had brought us yet closer.

Chapter 13

Those bleak cold months in the north-east always dragged on like prison sentences for me, sometimes like two consecutive terms. I think I had that winter phobia, whatever it's called, that brings on deep depression. But, elated as I was sharing my life with Theresa, the first two months of 1968 virtually flitted by. We were constantly on the go. We partied together, went to the movies and on double-dates. We even went to church together (yeah, I was going to mass once again). And, of course, we lay together. We made love in apartment building basements, stairway landings, meter rooms, wherever we could find warmth and privacy on those frigid New York nights. Sometimes while making out in my living room, our hormones whirring out of control, we'd do it right there on the floor. That was pretty risky business considering my parents were asleep in the doorless next room. That unhinged French door was still wide open, leaning uselessly against the bedroom wall.

We'd talk on the phone for hours when we couldn't be together, but we lived for the times that we could. And that's why I felt like a deserter when I asked Theresa if she minded if I went to Donny Scully's bachelor party.

You see, Donny had knocked up the super's daughter and they were going to have a shotgun wedding. Some chance that union had, with both of them still eighteen and marrying out of fear and nothing else. Their minuscule odds of a blissful marriage were diminished even more by Donny's irresponsible ways. Donny, just like the rest of us guys, had a penchant for boozy good times and an affinity for the sexy young ladies that seemed to be on every Queens' corner: blondes, brunettes, red heads, girls with long black hair that shined like coal.

Don't forget, these were the late sixties, when young women still knew how to dress, before the style-dictators put them into shorts that look like my Father's old wrinkled curtain-underwear, before those baggy-ass sweaters that hang to the knees like tents. Uhhhhh!

Back then, the sight of a pretty girl strutting the sidewalks was something to behold. They dressed in jeans tighter than their own skins and, in summer, cut them off so short that today they'd probably be

"I will come for you." Her lips pulled tight into that snarl-smile and she swerved around and strutted back to her game. Jimmy and I watched as this show-on-heels leaned over to bank one off the rail. When she did, the most perfect heart-shaped ass you've ever seen tilted way up and seemed to be pointing right at us. She took aim, blue-nailed fingers spread on the table before her, easing the cue back and forth seductively through a curled index finger. Her legs spread just right, stretching atop those spiked-heels, those solid silver cheeks looked like they were hoisted on stilts.

Damn!

"Shit man, I don't believe you!" Jimmy said, still gawking at that sequined behind. "You are one-lucky-sumbitch!"

After she sunk the three balls, Jimmy and I slipped back into the banquet room. By now a few women from the bar had found their way in and were flirting with some of the guys. In the far corner of the room, little Stevey Waters was puking a stomach full of yellow beer into a glass pitcher. Still shirtless, Donny was trying to put the make on one of the chicks, working on a sympathy lay, telling the homely thirty-something woman that she could be his last memory as a single man. Sunnyside Slim's addicted eyes were intent as he and the dope fiends he'd brought along talked about heading up to Harlem to cop some H. All the other guys were carrying on, their conversations and antics growing bawdier with every drink. As for me, I didn't have a clue where the rest of the night was taking me, nor did I have the slightest inkling of the tragic consequences I would pay for, both that night and the rest of my life, for making that ill-fated hedonistic trip. Needless to say, I know now that I should have left right then, gotten the hell out of that bar, ran all the way to Main Street and jumped the first bus to the Point. To my Theresa. But no! Instead, twenty minutes later, I walked out of Margo's Bar with a strange woman and misguided intentions.

All was wee hour-quiet on Lawrence Street when me and this 'Tina' (or whatever the hell her name was) tramped through the succession of somber-lit showers drifting down from the street lamps. Heading for her apartment, we walked quickly and said little. The only signs of life came from the all-night diner and an occasional passing delivery truck or weaving car. In the silent moments, the quick click of her heels spiking the cement sidewalk amplified as they bounced off dark storefronts. There really wasn't much to be said. Neither of us, for sure, was looking to build any lasting relationships. Our common purpose was solely to satisfy each of our own carnal appetites. But, dysfunctional as my mind was, guilt crept into it. Though I truly didn't realize what exactly I was doing wrong, for a fleeting moment I felt like I was about to commit a crime, a crime I'd be caught for, an underhanded infraction I'd have to pay, and pay big, for. But, unfortunately, this glimmer of foresight was just that, and it passed as quickly as it appeared.

Ten minutes after we left the bar, we came upon 'the projects'. That's where she lived, the Flushing Projects, a place any white-boy-outsider with even half his marbles (sex at stake or not) would have stayed clear of, particularly at such an hour, especially during the racially-charged sixties. But none of that bothered me because the beer had diluted any fear I should have had, plus, since I played basketball, I knew most of the black kids who lived there. Hell, they'd even given me a nickname, 'Dribbles'. Odds were pretty good that if anyone tried to jump me, I could prevent an ass-kicking simply by dropping a few names.

Like a protective, yet indifferent, mother she took my hand and guided me through the cluster of towering buildings. They were identical to those in every other city housing project, in every borough - cold, characterless piles of brick with cement promenades winding through them, potential danger at every curve, a veritable criminal breeding ground for disadvantaged human beings.

Inside her lobby, we didn't have to wait for an elevator - one was waiting for us - but the ride up seemed interminable. Instead of Muzak, this steel cubical was filled with the acrid stench of old piss. My temples throbbing, teetering on uncertain legs, the stink permeated my nostrils and I grimaced the whole way up. Rocking and swaying, I fought off the urge to vomit as the elevator ascended its shaft to God knows what floor. The shit backed up to my throat. I wondered what kind of animal could find peeing in an elevator to be a fascinating experience.

When finally the doors opened and my accomplice led me down the dusky hallway, she suddenly seemed even more alien, being in her own environment and all. As we padded along, I noticed that all the steel-caged overhead light bulbs were broken, except for the one nearest her door. When we entered its pitifully dim glow, she attacked me, spun to me, grabbed me, started kissing me, almost what I'd call violently! Then she tongued my ear with a fervor and went to work on my neck for awhile, before leaning away, looking into my eyes and muttering something, something in a rat-a-tat-tat, staccato Spanglish that I didn't quite pick up on. But, though I may not have deciphered the words, the universal overtones of passion in them were unmistakable. Next, she slipped her serpents tongue back inside my mouth and drew my tongue into hers. Once she captured it, she held it in her teeth for a hot moment, then started sucking on it and slipped her hand down the front of my jeans. She knew her shit alright. She'd gotten me ready, real quick, despite my first-degree drunkenness.

Still holding me firmly in her palm, she hastily unlocked the door with her free hand and led me inside like that.

It was dark in there. There were no lights on. But with the murky remnants of light that penetrated an old sheet, I could, albeit barely, discern shades and shapes. Dark as it was, I could see that it was just a one-room apartment--a living room, bedroom and kitchen all mashed into one. Still tethered to this woman, I shuffled my feet like a blind pervert as she guided me across the cramped room. After considerable bumping and stubbing on my part, we reached a bed. She bent over and switched on a night-light that had been jammed into a socket just off the bare floor, and straightened up. I could see her face once again. Only inches from mine, shaded like a cheap, grainy black and white, its hard features appeared even harder. "Juss relax now, honey," she whispered, squeezing my thing one last time before removing her hand from inside my pants. "Watch me ... and enjoy." Then, with her eyes still trained on mine, she took a slow half-step back, kicked off her heels and started squirming, teasingly, out of her brushed-on jumpsuit. Watching her shimmying, struggling to get it down past her half-bare hips, I knew she was enjoying this far more than I was. Once again, deep inside, I knew something was very wrong with this but still couldn't quite put my finger on it. But I couldn't back out now. What kind of man would I be? Her blouse came off next and then, lastly, her green bra. Somehow the loud color of it didn't shock me nearly as much as the fact that she bothered to wear one at all.

Face to face now, her totally nude, she took my hand and put it right there, straight to her most erogenous zone. Square on the triangle! I did what came natural as she stripped off my clothes, first my varsity jacket, then my shirt. After that, my Levis and Fruit of the Looms came down together. She slipped away from my right hand when she squatted down to work my pants legs over my ankles. Looking down at her now, her naked body folded up like a pocketknife, down on her haunches like a catcher giving his signals, her ass pointed down like she was taking a dump, she no longer looked anything close to sexy. Even with all that long-flowing platinum hair, she only looked dirty. It was at that precise moment, looking down at this nude whore at my feet that, out of the black, a beautiful vision strobed inside my head. It was my Theresa, so innocent, so pure, so good. Somehow she'd risen in all her splendor to the surface of my inebriated mind, but she didn't stay there. Like a split-second vision of a most lovely portrait, Theresa was gone again, disappearing when this other women, this meaningless stranger, got on her knees and took me.

What followed next was the first, and the only, sexual experience I've ever had where I felt like I was being used. This woman, this Tina, whoever, totally dominated the entire dark liaison. She got off her knees, rose to her full height, tilted me onto the rumpled bed, and proceeded to search every inch and orifice of my body. I felt like a sacrificial virgin forced into some sixth-rate porno movie as she methodically felt with her hands and tongue, from one place to the next, all the while moaning Spanish words of passion to herself. She devoured me like a half-starved predator tearing at its prey. And, I just laid there. I thought about how perverse this seemed. I thought about how grimy the sheets felt beneath my naked body, how they smelled of worse things than just old, cheap perfume

Finally, she stopped. I didn't know how much time had passed but knew it had been quite awhile because I'd heard several buses pass by down on the avenue and they didn't run all that frequent this late. She rolled onto her back and I mounted her like a roughrider. I rode her vengefully, working hard as I could to get even. I'd show her who the dominant one was. But the harder I tried, the more she liked it. And it went on and on, all the alcohol slushing inside my system prolonging the trauma. She was moaning and cursing beneath me, wiggling, rocking her hips, scratching my back violently, hurting me the whole time. She was so wild, so beastly that it scared me. But I had to be a man. Near the end of this bizarre tumultuous ride, I started having weird thoughts, scary thoughts. Who knows how someone like this gets her kicks. Maybe to her this bestial sex is just the beginning. Maybe she'll produce a razor and slit my throat. Maybe someone was behind or under the bed with a knife or a gun or something. Suddenly, I had a profound spooky feeling that we were not alone in this squalid room. Still bouncing on top of her, my wild eyes having adjusted to the semi-darkness by now, I scanned the room suspiciously for any movement.

And then I saw one!

Across the room, maybe ten feet away on the sofa, something or someone moved ever so slowly, ever so slightly, beneath a sheet. I thought, Jesus Christ, what the hell is that, a dog, a cat, nooo ... it's too big.

Then I heard my voice. It was dripping with doom. It said, "What's that ... moving on the couch?"

Not stopping, still pumping away, she buried all her fingernails deep inside my behind, snuggling me yet tighter against her burning Latin flesh.

"What the hell is that?" I asked again, still going through the motions.

"It eez only my grandmother ... Do not worry ... " She was murmuring the words, urgently, expelling a few with every frenetic breath she released, " ... she ees blind ... and deaf ... come on now... " she demanded, "do not stop ... harder, harder ... yesss ... I am almost there!"

I couldn't believe my ears. Here we are, humping away like two mongrels, and her grandmother is right there on the sofa.

Then the whole room tilted. It wasn't spinning yet, but it was maybe ten, twenty degrees out of plumb. The bed started moving too, rolling, surging up and down as if it were afloat on old waves. But to my relief, my titanic relief, there was another surge building too. It was within my loins. The end was now in sight. I wanted to finish this thing and get the hell out of there before I got sick. I buried my face next to hers in that filthy pillow and clamped my eyes shut. I gritted and ground my teeth. Tightening my grip on this crazed woman, I concentrated the best I could as we bucked on. Just for a couple of moments more, for then my body began to tremor and twitch spasmatically, my eyes rolled frantically beneath their hoods, and I moaned with the sensation.

In just seven seconds it was over, seven misspent seconds that prevented me from ever again looking at Theresa Wayman the same way, seven seconds that would, for the next thirty years of my life, taint every waking hour and so many of my dreams. Don't believe for a moment that time heals all wounds. Time may dull the pain but the deepest wounds never heal.

Chapter 14

The next day was hell. Forget my four-star hangover - I'd weathered those before - this was much worse than physical trauma. From the moment I opened my bleary eyes that Sunday morning (and vomited in the aluminum trash can alongside the bed), I was overwhelmed by guilt in its darkest form. I suppose that's one of my few commendable traits; I don't carry guilt well. I suffer hard for my misdeeds. Some people can simply write off all their dishonourable behaviour, just dismiss it, forget about it, but not me. I can only handle it for so long, and then I weaken. Once the burden of my deceitfulness becomes too heavy, I can't handle it. I have to shed it. And now, keeping the truth from Theresa, seeing her suffer was beyond torturous. She kept looking at me with such sad, sad eyes. So concerned, she kept asking, "You sure you're OK, Dean? Did I do something wrong? Are you getting tired of me?" Hearing these innocent questions from my best friend, my lover, my soul mate, ate at me like a malignancy. My guilt was only compounded by each of her questions, her pleas, and each one brought me closer to a confession. After just a few days I was on the brink.

By the time Friday lumbered around, I'd admitted to myself the inevitable, that I could no longer handle it, that I couldn't contain this immense burden. I had to tell Theresa everything. It's funny, but just coming to this decision allowed me a small feeling of consolation, like a bit of my black soul had lightened-up again. You know the feeling. You've had it! We all have, albeit some more than others. Coming clean can be damn hard, but be that as it may, as early as the planning stages, just thinking about fessing-up always rejuvenates one's hope in themself.

Anyway, getting back to my story, the small relief I'd enjoyed quickly disappeared when I got home from work Friday. When I came upon the entrance to my building and saw Ma's extra sad face waiting for me in the kitchen window, I knew something was up. Normally she'd be in 'the chair' or on her knees so this had to be something real serious. Two steps later, when I pulled open the heavy steel and glass entrance door, I realized what it must be. Instantly my stomach felt like it had stretched and dropped to my knees, like someone had dropped a ten-pound mushroom anchor in it. Next, before I could even put my key to the lock, Ma opened the door to 1B. She began to sob as she lifted an official looking envelope to me. Inside that envelope was a subway token and a letter that began with the word "Greetings".

My suspicions had been correct. I had been drafted.

At seven-thirty, I met Theresa under the clock. My plans had been to tell her all the bad news after we took in a flick at the Prospect. But as soon as we started toward the theater, I knew there was no way I could sit through a two-hour movie. We looked at each other in silence as we crossed Main street with a herd of other people. We hung a left and, as we passed in front of Triple Nickel Pizza where you could still get a slice and a Coke for a quarter, a tear rolled down my cheek and I said, "Theresa ... we need to talk ... "

I remember the smell of cheese and sauce wafting from the parlor's street-front counter when I asked Theresa, "Do ya mind if we go to Jahn's for awhile ... before the movie ... have coffee or somethin' ... We have to talk."

"Of course," she said. "Sure ... whatever's bothering you ... we can work it out, honey." She, too, was tremendously relieved that this thing was finally coming to a head. But when she smiled up at me from beneath my arm I also saw that apprehension had shoved the brightness from her eyes. Her face lost its glow like the sun does when a dark cloud drifts over it. She too had been frazzled for almost a week, and by now she just had to find out what was wrong.

Two blocks later, when we stepped inside Jahn's Ice Cream Parlor, she tightened her grip on my waist even more, stretched her lips, though they didn't part, and looked at me with as much assurance as her big chocolate eyes could muster. We took a booth at the back of the rustic establishment where a much better Tiffany lamp than the one at Theresa's house provided a subtle glow on a lacquered, mahogany table. The place was almost empty, unlike it used to be after one of our school basketball games or it would be after the movies let out later on. The waitress was upon us almost instantly and she didn't do much to hide her disappointment when all we ordered was coffee. Nevertheless, by the time I pulled out my cigarettes, offered Theresa one, and just lit only one for myself, the waitress was back with two steaming cups. When she left, I took a long hit and prepared to spill my guts. "There's two things I have to tell you, Theresa." With hopes of softening her up, maybe getting a little sympathy on my side, I figured I'd tell her about the lesser of the evils first, that I had been drafted and might get myself killed. I paused, took another hit from my Kool, wearily exhaled the smoke with my words. "The first is that I got my draft notice today. I've gotta go down for my physical next week. I'll be going to Fort Dix in a few weeks ... for basic training."

At first she took this news as if she'd expected it, because she did. As much as she'd tried to block it out of her mind, she knew deep down that since I was pushing nineteen, I'd probably be drafted before I could get enough credits to go to school full-time and qualify for a student deferment. We'd both known it was all but inevitable. But her resignation quickly turned to shock just like mine had a couple of hours earlier when I had read the notice for the first time. Now the inside of her eyebrows arched high and the tears I'd expected welled. Mixed with mascara, they fell in dark rivulets down her cheeks.

"Oh shit! Oh no, Dean! Tell me you're kidding. Tell me this is just a bad joke."

I punched out my KOOL, took her hands in mine, and held them on the wooden tabletop. "I wish to hell it was. But it's true. I've gotta' go. It's ... " I paused and looked at our hands piled together, and tried to be brave. " ... It's just two years. It'll go fast," I lied. I knew this was complete bullshit. We were still at the age when a summer lasted forever. To us, twenty-four months was no different than twenty-four years. Anyway, it wasn't just the time thing that was on our minds. We both knew there was a damn good possibility I might wind up in combat, or worse.

"I'll write every day and call when I can ... " I said, trying to force a reassuring smile. It didn't work. It was too much of an effort. I couldn't prevent my face from drooping when I said, "Ahhh shit, Theresa, I don't want to go."

We just sat there for awhile holding hands on the table, saying nothing, just taking in, no, adoring, each other's teary face. Then I glanced around, making sure no one was close enough to hear, sucked in a long breath, let it out real slow and said, "I've gotta' tell you the other thing too, Theresa. But, I want you to know ... this isn't gonna be easy for me ... matter of fact it's gonna be even harder than what I just told you."

"What? What?" she pleaded, trying to coax the words out of me as fast as possible. "What could possibly be worse than you getting draaaf...?"

It had dawned on her!

Her eyes widened like I'd never seen them. Her jaw fell. She looked at me as if I'd just slid a honed steel blade into her chest and turned the handle. Her face blanched. "Ohhh no! Nooo! Don't tell me, Dean."

"Yeah, Theresa, I did," I said in a defeated tone. "I had sex with another girl ... I mean a woman. Last weekend ... the night of the bachelor party. But Theresa, honey, I was drun ..." She jerked her hands from mine now. Like they were suddenly in a fire, she yanked them away. She dragged them across her eyes, then her cheeks and put them around her neck like she was fighting off a strangler. She froze like that, staring at me, no, through me, seeing who I really was. Shock, disbelief, hurt, and then disdain flashed over her face in that precise order. I saw these emotions evolve in her eyes and in the configurations her lips took on.

In a weary voice, like someone drawing their final breath, angry tears spilling from her eyes, she asked weakly, "Why ... Dean ... why?"

I almost upended my coffee as I desperately reached my hands across the table, palms up, hoping she would take them. But she didn't. She pulled way back into her seat, putting as much distance as possible between us.

"Theresa, honey, please, I told you ... I was drunk. I would never, never in a million years ... "

"Never mind, Dean," she snapped. "Save it." Her voice had gone icy, icier than I'd ever heard it. Her tone was more hateful now than it had been to her mother the night she introduced me to her, more than during the misplaced camera episode on our prom night. I knew then there was no turning this mess around.

She jammed her cigarette pack into her purse and she stood to leave. "Don't even tell me why. I don't want to know all the details. I know enough already. Myyy God, after all we've been through together, after all the plans we had ... and ... everything we shared. The special feelings, I, like a sucker, thought we shared." She paused briefly, sniffled once, then raised her voice and summed it all up, "My friends were right about you, once a run-around always a run-around. You turned out to be some bastard, Dean Cassidy!"

But then, as quickly as she'd shot out of her seat she plopped back into it again.

A glimmer of hope - maybe the worst was over, maybe she'd stay with me, eventually accept and forget the horrible mess I'd made. Well, not really. She'd never forget. But maybe the memory of my despicable infraction of our love and trust would eventually grow dusty and fuzzy, fade with time.

But that wasn't why she sat back down at all. Though my view was obscured by the table top when she lifted her left ankle over her knee and began fumbling with it, I knew exactly what she was doing. She was undoing her ankle bracelet, the one I'd bought for her, the one she'd admired in the jewellery store window the night we met almost a year ago, a symbol she'd worn on her left ankle to let all of Queens know that she had a special guy.

"No, Theresa, please no."

"Sorry Dean ... If you only knew how sorry I am that you did this to us," she said, placing the impossibly-delicate, gold chain next to my coffee cup. "Hmph! And to think I believed you were the real thing. You've broken my heart."

Standing up again she noticed that a pair of old ladies, bingo types two booths away, had been eavesdropping. She fixed her eyes back on me and placed her palms on the table top. Leaning toward me, she lowered her voice to a whisper, a cutting whisper that dug deeper into me than if she would have screamed it. "Dean, don't come after me. Don't call me. I-don't-ever-want-to see-you-again!" She pivoted her head back and forth slowly and said, "This is not just talk ... I-am-dead-serious!"

Had she screamed those words at me, I might have been able to attribute them to momentary anger, but she looked me square in the eyes and, though there were tears in her own, her tone had been even and deliberate. She meant what she said!

She walked out of Jahn's, and out of my life. I didn't chase after her. I knew her too well. She wouldn't have spoken to me if I had. My breach of her trust was unforgivable. As much as she had loved me, maybe still did, she was too ethical to overlook my loathsome deed. She would

98

never have done such a thing to me and couldn't fathom how I could. I owed it to her to at least let her walk away now, without making it any more difficult.

I called Theresa the next morning, a Sunday, but she hung up on me. The following week I called her every day in the evening, right after work, including Thursday, the day I passed my physical down on Whitehall Street. Soon as I stepped into the apartment, even before saying hello to my mother, and my father if he was there, I'd stop in the foyer and dial her number. I prayed that she'd come around, reconsider. But no, each time Theresa or her mother answered they'd hang up as soon as they heard my voice. I'd call right back but the phone would ring and ring and ring, each ring another unanswered plea for forgiveness.

Chapter 15

That first week without Theresa was hell in its purest form. Every waking hour I dwelled on what a mess I had made of my life. At night I got plenty of rest but little sleep. I went to bed around ten like I always did during the week, but it took hours to escape into sleep. Lying in that open door bedroom, my pillow over my sorry head trying to muffle my father's goddamned TV shows and the steady rhythm of the avenue outside, I wondered what Theresa might be doing. How was she taking it? How bad was she hurting? I had premonitions of how horrible it would be in a steamy-hot jungle full of enemies, snipers obscured in trees, lining me up in the sights of their rifles. Tried to imagine the smell of death but couldn't. Would Theresa and I ever get back together again? Would I come back in one piece, minus a piece, or in a body bag? Surely Theresa would have another guy by that time even if I did make it home safely. Jesus, I'd fucked up! If only I could relive that night.

Then all I'd have to worry about was keeping my ass alive.

Of course, lying in bed those long nights, I prayed that Theresa would call. Whenever the phone rang I'd jump out of bed, make a mad dash through the living room into the foyer and snatch it from its cradle. But every time, it was somebody else, usually Dad's lady friend from Saint Leo's or one of the guys. With each call, my hopes died a little more. And each morning when I woke, nothing had changed. Those mornings were rough too. I'd lay there thinking how, had I been faithful, she would have gone with me to Viet Nam. She would have been my strength over there, stood by me forever if I made it back. We would have someday gotten a Cape Cod with a white picket fence, I'd have finished off the attic, we would have had kids, a dog, maybe a collie. But no, I thought, none of that would ever happen. I had trashed all those lovely dreams.

One evening, a week and a half after Theresa walked out of my life, less than two weeks before I was to be inducted, I did get an unexpected phone call. But it wasn't from Theresa. It was from someone I'd never met, a call that would bring me to my knees, literally, alongside my mother, in front of her tea cart altar.

100

Almost all hope of hearing Theresa's voice gone by then, I picked up the receiver and said, "Hello."

"Hello! May I speak to ... er, Mister ... Cassidy ... " I could tell the guy was reading our name, "Mister Dean Cassidy, please?"

Who the hell is this, I wondered. The man's voice was rigid, wooden and emotionless. Was it the cops? I hadn't done anything illegal lately.

"Yeaahhhh, this is Dean Cassidy."

"Mister Cassidy, my name is Herbert Filmore ... "I thought he had a black guy's voice, now I was sure. " ... I'm with the Board of Health in Jamaica." He paused, letting that sink in, then went on. "The purpose of this call, Mister Cassidy, is to advise you that someone you've had sexual contact with has been diagnosed as having a venereal disease, and that, in the state of New York, it is mandatory that any person who contracts such a disease provides us with the names of every individual that they have come in sexual contact with."

"Whooah, whooah," I interrupted, the blood pounding in my temples, my voice breaking now. Could this be legit? Goddammit, I can't take anymore. "Is this ... is this some kinda joke or somethin'?"

He'd obviously been asked that same question before. His answer poured through the receiver like it had been rehearsed. "I'm afraid not, Mister Cassidy," he said. "This is not a prank call. Somebody has provided us with your name and we need to have you tested."

"Who is it? What's their name?" As if I didn't know.

"We aren't permitted to divulge that information, Mister Cassidy. I'm afraid I can't even tell you the sex of the person."

"Well don't worry about that, I can answer that one, I ain't no homo." By this time, my demeanor was a brew of mad and scared. I was thinking, *Oh man, I can't drag Theresa into this mess.* "I don't have to give you no names, do I?" I asked.

"If you prove negative, no; if positive you would be required to."

"Shhhit," I heaved a deep sigh into the receiver. "Where in Jamaica are you? When can I get this over with?"

First thing the next morning, I took a bus to the Board of Health on 168th street. I thought it ironic that the bus I had always taken to Theresa's, the Q-65, was the same one I was taking now to the opposite end of its route, in Jamaica. During that troubling ride, I envisioned every possible scenario. What if I had contracted syphilis or gonorrhea, or something, and passed it on to Theresa that one last time we had sex, three nights after I'd been with that tramp?

After they drew my blood, Filmore told me it would take three days to get the results. Needless to say, I was scared to death the test would come back positive, and I had lots of time to worry about it. I just couldn't handle this additional burden--not alone--like I had everything else. With nowhere else to turn, I actually told my parents that night. My father said he'd pray for me at church, and I prayed side-by-side with my sick mother by candlelight for four consecutive nights. I did a lot of soul-searching. I thought back to my last confession a year earlier just before I'd met Theresa when, in a dark booth, that priest told me after hearing my sins, "Son, you have been living the life of a pagan."

Maybe I had, but I knew people living much worse existences. And, anyhow, wasn't I just a product of my environment? Freak that priest! That was the last time I ever confessed my sins to any man.

Mom and I prayed and prayed. Totally consumed by my black concerns, not once did I leave the apartment during those days. What would it do to Theresa if the blood test results came back positive? Hadn't I already done enough to her? I swore that if the results came back OK I'd never bother her again. I swore to myself. I swore to Christ. And I kept on praying.

Of course, the day that they were supposed to have the test results, they didn't. Filmore told me, "Sorry. We've been so overburdened, so backlogged, that your results won't be available until tomorrow, after three PM." The horror would have to be prolonged.

The next day I called him at one o'clock, two, and three. Still no results. I made Filmore promise he'd call me the minute he heard. I told him I'd be sitting by the phone, waiting. I had talked to him enough times by now that we had established a relationship of sorts. He was a nice enough guy, all differences considered, but still, this was one relationship I would rather have lived without.

Four, four-thirty, still no call. They closed at five. "This is bullshit," I said aloud, then dialed Filmore's number again.

"Yes, Mister Cassidy, hold on. They just this minute put them on my desk," he said, sounding preoccupied, thumbing through his paper stack of potential VD candidates. "Here you are, DEAN Cassidy!"

"C'mon Herbert, tell me something good." That was the first time I'd called him by his first name. Somehow, this small nicety, this sign of familiarity, made me feel as if I were increasing the odds of a favorable report.

"Just a second ..." he said, then started mumbling under his breath, an indiscernible flow of fractured words, just syllables I could get no meaning out of. As I waited, I bit off part of a thumbnail too low. When I peeled it off, a tiny piece of stubborn flesh tore with it. Dark blood rose instantly. I sucked at it, looked at the thumb and watched the blood reappear. I repeated this process a few times.

"Negative, Mister Cassidy! Your results have come back negative."

Thank Christ! Thank you, Jesus!

"You sure, Herbert? I don't want anybody callin' me back saying it was a mistake."

"Your social security number is 094-42-2237, right?"

"Yeah that's it. Look ... thanks a lot Mister Filmore ... Herbert. Take care."

At last something had turned out well. A few flames of my personal hell had been extinguished. I'd been on such a bum streak I thought it would never turn around. At least now I wouldn't have to drag Theresa into some VD network. You can't imagine how relieved I was. But true to my own form (my emotions always coming in pairs), I suddenly felt foolish as well as relieved. Now that this dilemma turned out OK, I felt ridiculous about all the hours I'd spent on my knees alongside my mentally-damaged mother. Now that the heat was off, I felt a little cracked myself. Now that my spirits had brightened a few watts, the whole four-day ordeal seemed way too melodramatic.

I've never prayed on my knees since. Not once. Matter of fact, it wasn't long after that that I stopped praying altogether.

Chapter 16

The week before my induction, I made two last-ditch attempts to get Theresa back. It had been only two weeks since our breakup so, of course, I hadn't even begun to get over her. Hell, here it is now thirty years later and I'm still damaged. But I was in the beginning stages of accepting my loss. It was like I had, due to my own neglect, lost an arm or a leg and woke each morning to great pain but was growing accustom to that limb not being there. The gash in my heart was still fresh also, but I was learning to live, I mean exist, with that too. But I still cried. In my bed, each morning and every night, I bawled like an abandoned infant. Big tough city kid! RIIIGHT!

Time was running out. I was leaving for Dix the following Monday. By Thursday I was certifiably crazy. I couldn't take it anymore. I had to see her. The desperation festering inside me came to a head and burst, bringing me to a state of unrestrainable recklessness. All this time I had abided by Theresa's wishes, I'd left her alone. But by now I had to talk to her, no matter what.

By the time I got off the bus at the Point, I thought I'd surely implode from all the anxiety raging beneath my skin. I quickened my pace. Tramping up Broadway, my heels pounding the cement so hard I could feel the shockwaves traversing my spine, fragments of desperate thoughts raced through my head, none of them staying long enough to make any sense. Running on pure adrenaline now, not having an inkling as to what I would say to Theresa, or rather how I would say it, I did notice something. Changes. Everything that had been so familiar now seemed very different. Bogart's Bar looked seedier and more hostile. The streets were narrower. The clear winter sky didn't seem as blue and it no longer held promise. The snow that had fallen white a few days before was now depressing old city-snow, brown hard ice-piles lying like miniature mountain ranges alongside storefronts where it had been shoveled aside days before. Hoofing along, my hands clenched tight in the front pockets of my Levi's, I felt like I no longer belonged in College Point, like I was an intruder in a foreign country or an unwanted guest at a party.

When I reached the bookstore, I stood outside with my back to it.

God, I thought, I hope Theresa's alone in there. I drew a long cold breath, held it a moment, then spewed a misty stream from my nostrils. Here goes. This is it! I spun around and peered into the glass. Theresa wasn't there! Some other girl was, a girl I'd never seen before stood behind the counter. Theresa always worked weekday afternoons, two to six, since she graduated from Saint Agnes's. Could she have quit? No. That wouldn't be like her. Since she'd been moved around so many times she'd developed this strong sense of stick-with-it-ness. She wouldn't just quit. Her job here had enabled her to save enough tuition money to take a few classes at Saint John's University. She'd planned all along to continue working there.

"DAMMM!" I said, stomping a Converse All-Star on the sidewalk. A passing couple, two little moribunds, arm-in-arm, hunched within their somber black coats, gave me a short, skittish peek then sped up a little. It had been one of those deals where you build yourself up to face some monumental hurdle, put yourself through holy hell preparing for it, and then it's got to be postponed. Talk about a bummer! Totally discombobulated now, completely out of options, I went straight to Theresa's house.

When Mrs. Wayman answered the doorbell, she soon negated whatever hopes I'd had, no matter how remote, that Theresa and I might get back together again. The stench of cheap-ass whiskey on her breath, she wedged herself between the door and the jamb and started reaming me out. She told me I had some ass coming around after what I had done to her daughter. Suddenly she'd become such a concerned mother. Toward the end of her verbal assault, yelling for the whole neighborhood to hear that I'd better quit calling on the phone too, after scaring off a flock of sparrows, she suddenly shut off, mid-spiel, as if someone had lifted a hi-fi arm from a loud, grating record. She smeared a nasty, contented smirk across her mush and with great satisfaction, and bared teeth, snarled, "On second thought, go on, knock yourself out. Call all you want!" She extended her neck now, high as she could, and began bouncing her head from side to side cockily. Continuing to have a jolly good time devastating me she said, "It don't matter, 'cause next week, this time, the phone'll be disconnected."

Then she lurched backwards into the hall and with both hands heaved the door closed, right in my face. As I back-stepped from the

main thoroughfare, we knew from experience that the side streets here were quiet, that they were buffered by high-crowned trees and well-maintained, true middle-class homes, with driveways. To us lowly apartment dwellers, Bayside was high class.

We found a liquor store and each of us bought a pint of Boone's Farm for eighty-nine cents. With Ungy's only a block away now, we turned the first corner, bagged bottles in hand, and ducked into an alley behind a Greek restaurant. Under the cover of darkness, blocked on one side by a dumpster big as an elephant, we started guzzling. Hell of a mixture, whiskey, chased with apple wine. Back then we'd drink anything. If you were there, you remember the motto, "If it feels good, do it!"

Soon my body had gone limp and the top of my head went numb. Not the ideal condition to be in when hoping to reconcile with a loved one. But I was tight. What if she and her friends changed plans? What if they decided to go somewhere else? "Come on, guys, let's go," I said, exhaling the last hit off my cigarette, flicking it at the dumpster. "We can finish drinkin' this on the way over there."

It was getting late and I wanted to get on with this.

Before we went inside Ungy's, I almost tossed my cookies out front when I forced down the last of my Boone's Farm. My stomach was filled and stretched with the whiskey-wine brew, and it was backed-up to my throat. My head pounded in sync with the music that boomed from the bar out onto the street. All three of us were painted green by the neon 'Ungy's' above the entrance, and I felt green on the inside too. I bent between two parked cars to stand my emptied bottle next to the curb and started retching and gagging over the gutter. I thought for sure I'd get sick. I hoped I would. I knew from experience I'd feel better if I did. I shoved a finger down my throat but still no luck, only a long green string of bile that stuck to my finger.

Since there was no live band at Ungy's, there was no cover charge, no bouncer at the door checking proof, collecting money, stamping hands. We slithered and slid through a wall-to-wall assemblage of humanity before settling next to a half-wall that separated the bar from the dozen or so tables and the dance floor beyond them. The place was like thousands of others on any New York Saturday night. Young people were everywhere. Beneath a looming, blue, smoke-cloud, they engaged in loud conversations, competing with all the merriment and the 'Rascals' belting one out on the juke about 'Good Lovin''. These were party-animals in their late teens to late twenties, playing hard after a grinding week of school or work, guys and girls wearing bells, polka dots, paisley, army fatigue shirts, headbands and bracelets. Hundreds of them, standing cheek-to-jowl, drinks in hand, rapping away, all squished tight inside this club. Out on the wooden dance floor, that couldn't have been any bigger than our living room at home, there must have been fifty people grinding away to a slow one that just came on, a single, huge, solid mass of human cells swaying this way and that beneath the slo-mo strobe lights. It was obvious that Ungy's owner, or owners, believed in 'supporting' their local fire inspector.

Striking a match, a new Marlboro bouncing in his lips, Jimmy asked, "Ya see 'er?"

"No, not yet," I said, as if I were only thinking the words while intently scanning the crowd.

Then, his voice energized like it had been zapped with a thousand volts Donny blurted, "DEE CEE, LOOK!" He threw a finger toward a table fronting the dance floor where couples were mauling each other now to the Stones' 'As Tears Go By'. "Isn't that one of her friends?"

It is the evening of the dayyyayyyayyy,
I sit and watch the children playyyayyyayyy...

"Yeah! That's Regina! Her friend from school! The one we went to the prom with!" My heart was racing, pounding uncontrollably inside its ribbed cage. "She's here, man! She's gotta be!" There were more chairs around the table than it was designed to accommodate, all of them occupied, except two, side-by-side. Was Theresa sitting there with another guy?

Then Donny jerked his head in the direction of the dancers. "Over dere. I see 'er. She's dancing wit' some dude."

This was it! The alcohol, the blaring music, all the loud background conversations, Theresa there somewhere dancing with another guy, I was frantic. My voice gushing with urgency, I yelled."Where, where is she?"

"Right behind that asshole wit' the plaid pants and the short hair.

Man ... you're fucked up ... here," Donny said, palming the back of my head, pivoting it in the right direction.

Sure as hell, there was Theresa cheek-to-cheek, belly-to-belly with another guy.

Without a word, I started toward them, but Jimmy grabbed my shoulder from behind and said, "Hold on. Where you goin', man? Wait till the songs over, then go talk to her."

"FFFUCK THAT!" I said, yanking away from my friend's grip, taking off, pronto, through the labyrinth of tables and people. No stopping me now. Instinctively, like any self-respecting, dominant male in the animal kingdom, I was going after what was mine. Amen! Simple as that. I saw and I reacted, pure instinct, forget the thinking process. There was nothing to evaluate. That sonofabitch had his arms around my girl.

Some short-haired dude and his squeeze were dancing in my path. I stepped left, they swayed left, I went right, they swayed that way, I shoved them out of the way. Clenching each other tighter, for stability now, they struggled to remain upright.

The chick let out a yell. "WHAT DO YOU THINK YOU'RE DOING, ASSHOLE!"

The music played on.

I sit and watch as tears go by-yy-yy ....

Theresa and her partner unglued themselves and spun around to see what all the ruckus was about. When she saw it was me, shock flashed across her lovely face, then, just as quickly, those exotic eyes became enraged. She knew there was going to be trouble.

"DEAN! NO!" she shouted, throwing my name like a warning and a reprimand both, sort of like when you catch your puppy pissing the carpet.

Then her new friend turned his pretty-boy mug in my direction. He was another short-hair, must have been Mister plaid pants' fraternity bro. He'd turned just in time to see my balled up, boney fist coming with his name on it. I connected, his legs jellied, and he went down. Just that fast.

I thought it served him right. I didn't trust anyone who was still dressing collegiate. My own wardrobe had metamorphosed to the

110

revolutionary clothes of the late 60s, plain clothes that made a statement, told the world who you were, what you thought of the 'establishment' that kept the little man down. This guy was obviously a part of that select group, or his daddy was anyway. Besides being with my girl, I saw in him everything I hated, the type of college boy who had no idea what it was like to sweat tuition, or the draft. Someone who'd never had a toothache in his life. A silver-spooner who never once saw the inside of a mid-week, empty refrigerator, never had to fill his empty belly with triple-decker mayonnaise sandwiches on white. A dandy who probably had a new Vette parked outside and lived out in Port Washington too. But the bottom line was he was dancing with my girl. And no matter how he was dressed, what he had or didn't have, I would have cold-cocked him just the same. Nevertheless, his appearance made my drunken assault that much easier.

Girls screamed, and the dance floor crowd dilated instantly. Theresa was pushing on my shirt with both hands as I tap-danced on the guy a couple of times with my size elevens.

"STOP IT, DEAN, STOP IT!" she screamed.

That's when I felt this beefy arm hook me from behind. Some bear had locked it around my neck and was dragging my sorry ass backwards, on my heels, through a carpet of peanut shells.

Though I hollered, "LEMME GO MUTHAAAFUCKA!", with my neck constricted as it was, half the volume stayed inside my chest, sort of like Marlon Brando in the 'Godfather'. My eyes were bulging in their sockets and my breath was hard coming.

Then, two more goons grabbed my arms, helping the force behind me. Amazing how much strength you can muster when you're really, really pissed. Six feet tall and only a hundred and forty-five pounds, I was giving the three of them all they could handle. Jimmy and Donny watched closely. These guys were BIG so they knew to lay low, unless they got too aggressive. If the bouncers would have started hitting, they would have gotten beer bottles or glass mugs over their heads, no matter how big they were.

Looking back at Theresa as they dragged me to the door, I hollered, "C'MON OUTSIDE, THERESA! GODDDAMMIT, C'MON!"

But she didn't. She just stood there, hands on her hips, in a scolding pose, watching me get thrown out. But, I could swear that, along with

We didn't have a prayer. Even if this had been even-up, these men were TOO BIG! Even the two short ones had shoulders wider than most doorways, chests thick as sides of beef.

"OK, you hippy pieces of shit," growled the biggest one, the one who first grabbed me inside Ungy's. He was right in my face, reeking of salami or garlic or something. In his tough guy, staccato style of cutting words, he made his point reasonably clear, "Weeah gonna beat yaw asses!" With that out of the way, he shoved me in the chest, hard. Back-peddling a few stutter steps on the sidewalk, I fought to keep my balance until I slammed, and I mean slammed, back-first, into a parked car. Shit, that really hurt. *This bastard's gonna kill me.* My hands on the small of my back, quick dashes of biting pain shooting through a network of nerves, I lost it. I blurted, "Big fuckin' man! You got a hundred pounds on me. Gonna make you feel good to beat my ass? Bring it on, tough guy." As I said all that, I was thinking, '*Go head man, put me out of my misery.*' I didn't give two shits about anything at this point.

Then like a lion about to finish off his prey, the guy moved in on me, his impossibly powerful fists balled like two rocks at his sides. The wise guy was waddling toward me, very slowly, for affect. He and I both knew what he was doing. Taking his time, giving my fear a chance to regroup, drag out the experience as long as possible, adding another dimension to my fear, allowing me plenty of time to contemplate the worst before it actually came.

By now the other three tough guys were shoving Donny and Jimmy around too.Out on the boulevard headlights were flying by like high-speed white fireflies. You know that dream you have where you're trapped in some horrible predicament and there's no way out? Well this was it.

But an idea came to me. I thought, '*Freak it man, I'm dead anyway. Might as well go for it!*' and, in one single motion, I lunged for the car's antenna and ripped it off the fender. I had the steel rod cocked when the sound of skidding rubber grabbed my attention. A passing car had stopped short, fishtailing in the street, right behind me.

Who the hell is THIS? I asked myself without moving my lips, if you don't count the tremble in them.

When an arm jutted from an open window of the stripped-down

Plymouth and plunked a flashing red light on the roof, we all knew who it was.

"Awright, break it up. Wuss goin' on heah?"

Shit man, there is a god!

I couldn't believe it, here I was seconds from the beating of my life, and out of nowhere comes these plain-clothes cops. I would have surely been dead meat once this monster wrestled the antenna away from me, especially since I had every intention of swiping him with it a few times first. But all that wouldn't be necessary now and, as you can imagine, I was relieved as hell.

As the cops piled out of the Plymouth, I dropped the antenna, kicked it underneath the car that was holding me up.

After the wise guys told the cops what I'd done and it was my turn to speak, I of course lied.

"I did not. Some other guys did it. We saw 'em. When they split and we were standin' out there, we knew these guys would blame me 'cause I just had a fight in their place, so we took off."

It was obvious the cops didn't like the odds, four grown men against us kids. The cop who seemed to be in charge asked them if they saw me do it.

The Sicilians, Neapolitans, whatever they were, admitted they hadn't actually seen me do it. The top-cop then told them they could press charges against us but that it would be pretty much a waste of time since they didn't see me do it. He said that even if they did, it would be their word against mine. In his next breath, he told us we could file assault charges against them. Well, these guys sure as hell didn't want any police reports bringing attention to themselves or their money-cranking club, and we just wanted the hell out of there, so it was a trade-off, so long as they never laid eyes on us again.

When it was just about settled, I coaxed one of the plain clothesmen aside, told him we didn't have a ride out of there. If we had to wait for a bus, these guys would surely do a number on us. I copped a plea, whispering urgently to the balding cop with the sympathetic face, "Please, man, you gotta give us a lift outta here!" And, they did.

That, thank God, was the last we'd ever see of those hoods. And, I thought, surely it would be the last I'd ever see of Theresa Wayman also, though countless times over the next twenty-nine years I would wonder if it was she who had saved my skin that night. Had she called the police from Ungy's after the bouncers took after us. I'd always wonder if, despite all her anger and resentment, she still cared at the end. And, had I remained in her heart, like she had in mine?

Chapter 17

Just like that moldy old cliché threatens, life did go on. I went into the army on Monday, April 2nd, 1968. I did basic at Fort Dix, New Jersey, where I endured my fair share of harassment and more. For, you see, the drill instructors right away picked up on my New York accent. My speech, devoid of any rolling r's, was a dead giveaway. Every time I answered a question or spoke for any reason, I'd be stereotyped as one of those trouble-making New Yorkers. Rubber-stamped by mindless redneck sergeants from provincial-thinking little podunk towns where the only way out is through the doors of the military recruitment offices.

It seemed like every time I opened my mouth, the same tired Southernese dialogue always followed. "Where you from, boy?"

"New Yawk, suh. New Yawk CITY, suh!"

I soon learned that that response invited harassment. I found out right away that everybody west, south, and north of the G.W. Bridge hates New Yorkers. But, by emphasizing the CITY at the end of my hometown's name, I was giving the instructors a little zinger they could do nothing about. A perpetually pissed-off lot, my reminder to the DIs that 'the city' was still part of these 'United States' always seemed to further darken their foul demeanors. And I loved it. Whether their constant state of anger was a charade or for real, didn't matter to me. Every time I said "New Yawk CITY, suh!" it was like saying, "up yours, sarge" and getting away with it. It got to the point where I welcomed any such confrontations. What could they do? Put me in a trash can, slam the lid, beat on it for hours with a stick, drive me insane? I don't think so.

All in all, for a New Yorker, even with my little zingers, I managed to keep my nose reasonably clean throughout basic training. Smart enough to realize that was the way to go; I did whatever I was told and did my best to (as they say in the military) "get my shit together".

Believe it or not, it turned out that basic training was the best thing that could have happened to me so soon after losing Theresa. Up at 0500, back to bed at 2100 hours, every minute of every day filled with military nonsense, war games that required almost constant

not to, I want you to know that you'll always stay in my heart and thoughts forever.

Loving you always,
Dean

Every afternoon at mail call my heart pounded a desperate cadence and my stomach tied itself into a tight, double-overhand. The other guys got letters from wives and sweethearts, but not me. Every time Sergeant Killian called out my name, I'd try to appear calm and casual; totally incongruent with my feelings. I'd almost implode from the anticipation each time I stepped forward for my letter. But the envelopes with my name were almost always lilac colored, Ma's stationery. The stuff she'd mail ordered from a Franciscan monastery somewhere in upstate New York. Each time I got close enough to recognize the envelope, my heart would plummet like a blood-red brick. Then my hopes would sink deeper as the pile of mail shrunk in the lifer's black hands.

One day, about two weeks after I'd mailed the letter to Theresa, Sergeant Killian said "Cassidy!" for the second time that mail call. I had already gotten the letter from Ma. So, when sarge scaled the letter over all the shaved heads to where I was crouched in the back of our group, I about jumped out of my skin.The projectile coming my way was white. Hope, fear, shock, excitement crowded into my psych. But when I scrambled after the letter and picked it up from the barrack's spotless floor, devastation soon replaced all those emotions--pure, uncut, total devastation. For it was the letter I'd mailed to Theresa, returned, unopened, "MLNA" coldly stamped over her old address.

They had moved. Just like her mother threatened and I'd figured. To where, I was clueless. Mrs. Wayman had taken good care of keeping me in the dark by not leaving a forwarding address. Surely I was at least the biggest part of the reason why she hadn't. She'd successfully severed the final tie between Theresa and I. I was now certain that as long as I lived, I'd never rest my eyes on Theresa again, never find out if she still loved me. Such a cruel fate seemed incredibly inhumane. Knowing there was a chance she might still love me, but that I'd never know one way or the other, was agonizing and would be for a long, long time. The day I got that letter back was the first time in my life (but not the last) that suicide--that most permanent of all solutions--lurked inside my brain.

But somehow, I'm sure it had to do with youthful resilience, I pushed on and completed my basic training. Next stop was Quantico Virginia, for more training. Infantry training! That nagging fear of going to South-East Asia had, by now, evolved into a dreadful inevitability. 'Sam' was whipping me into shape, teaching me how to use his war tools, as well as my own hands, to kill people, human beings just like myself, people I'd never even met but was supposed to hate enough to kill. The way I saw it, we had absolutely no right even being in Nam, let alone killing its people. Whether they wanted to be, or not to be, communist, was their business. This was a century-old civil war going on in those jungles clear on the other side of the planet. I didn't want to fight anyone, communist or otherwise, unless they came marching up Sanford Avenue. But, what I thought or wanted meant squat. Corporate America and the politicians they owned had all the say. And they were at that point in time pushing hard once again to escalate their "conflict", designing the grim fate of one heartbroken kid from Queens and hundreds of thousands of others they neither knew or gave a shit about. The profiticians were trying to do to Viet Nam the very same thing they do to every third-world they muscle in on today, make it safe for capitalism in the guise of democracy.

Nevertheless, on an absolutely-flawless Virginia spring morning at the rifle range in Quantico, something happened that would redirect my imposed destiny. While I finished firing my M-16 from the cross-legged position, about to go prone, an instructor tapped my shoulder and gestured for me to go with him. I pulled out of the line of soldiers who were blasting away at targets as if their lives depended on it, because they soon would.

Leading me to a waiting jeep, the smell of burnt gunpowder still pervading my nostrils, the instructor told me I was wanted at the first sergeant's office. When I asked him why, all he did was shrug and point at a waiting GI jeep. I climbed into it and asked the driver the same thing. As he threw it into gear, he said he didn't know and that he only had orders to pick me up and deliver me to numero uno's office. The conversation ended there. I slouched back in the passenger's seat, fired up a Kool, and pondered what the hell could be going on.I knew it had to be something pretty serious, some kind of emergency for sure.

As we bounced away from the rifle range along a lumpy dirt road, despite the brilliant sunshine and balmy temperature, I had this cold hollow feeling and felt the goose bumps rise on my arms. Could it have something to do with Theresa, I speculated. Nooo. It had to be Ma. She must have tried for an early exit again. Christ, could she really be dead? I was beginning to well understand how after forty years of unhappiness, a human being just might resort to such desperate measures. Hell, I'd only recently turned nineteen and already I'd entertained such thoughts. Rocking and rolling along on that spine-jarring jeep ride, I thought about how my whole world was caving in, and wondered if I myself would ever make it to forty like my mother had.

But the awful news that day wasn't about my mother, or Theresa, or my brother, Sylvester. It was my father. A few hours earlier his damaged heart had stuttered to a stop at Saint Vincent's Hospital in New York City. He'd been driving his cab in Greenwich Village when, out of the blue, his left arm started aching like hell. In just minutes the pain became so intense, so unbearable that he rushed himself to the emergency room. Forty-five minutes after they admitted him, he was gone. Ma had gotten two phone calls, the first when she was resting in 'the chair' between rosaries at home, drinking that disgusting concoction of apple cider vinegar and honey she hoped would cure the cancer she didn't have. The nurse had advised her that my father had been admitted. By the time she'd gotten out of her dingy, stained robe, showered and dressed for the subway ride into Manhattan, the second call came. Dad was dead. He was only forty-one years old.

I changed out of my fatigues, threw a few things into my old peeling cardboard suitcase, and caught the first flight to Kennedy Airport. I'd never been on a plane before and, to be straight about it, I didn't much like it. Not being in control and all. I had already learned that some people are lucky and others are not, and knowing damn well what category I fell into, being twenty-nine thousand feet in the air seemed like no small risk. Even before we left the ground, my palms got all sweaty, staying that way the whole trip. But, once we were up there awhile, I did settle down somewhat. My allotted two free screwdrivers warming my insides, smoking heavily, I watched the gridded countryside drift beneath the zooming jet. My concentration all consumed by my thoughts, I watched the farmland down there, not really seeing it, just having a green daydream. Christ, what a year, what a life, I lamented as I recollected the recent unfortunate events in my life: Ma losing her sanity, me losing Theresa, now Dad losing his life. It was amidst this airborne-funk that I, for the first time, questioned my mortality. Jesus, I thought, his dad - my grandfather - died early too, when I was a baby. He was something like forty-eight. Terrific! Some freakin' wonderful gene pool I surfaced from.

Struggling with this dark revelation, peering over a fiercely-vibrating (sure to break off) starboard wing, something emerged from the colossal vegetable patch below, telling me we were over New Jersey. It was a group of round holding tanks huddled together alongside a gray string of a highway, oil refineries committing their ecological carnage beneath a self-imposed noxious yellow atmosphere. A yellow gloom-cloud of toxic air had spread for miles. I'd seen this mess before from the ground when my father and I drove through it (holding our breaths the best we could) on the only over-night trip we'd ever taken together.

It was early in the spring, three years before, when I was sixteen. Somehow I'd convinced Dad that a fishing trip together might be kind of neat. The news had reported that due to a stalled cold front, the spring migration of striped bass was holed up off Seaside Heights New Jersey. Local surf fishermen were making phenomenal catches. I'd worked and worked on Dad until finally, to my amazement, he actually agreed to go. That's when we drove through that poisonous fog. I remember how shocked I was to see obscure little homes scattered here and there, engulfed in this environmental holocaust. To think that any living thing, human or not, could survive in that contaminated air was brain-boggling. Looking down at it from the air, I wondered once again what the cancer rate must be for the poor souls destined to live there. I couldn't imagine how big business got away with such immorality. But then it all became crystal clear when I brought my eyes back inside the plane and looked at the very uniform I was wearing. I shook my head pensively and let out a long, troubled sigh.

A few minutes later, a dwarfed New York skyline rose from the horizon. As I watched it lift higher and higher from the edge of the earth, my thoughts returned to that fishing trip, to when we were leaving our house for Seaside Heights that morning. I remembered Ma telling Dad to be sure to get a nice motel room, Frank, and Dad promising we would. But that night, as darkness fell on Island Beach State Park, I had my doubts. After a long afternoon and early evening of fruitless fishing, hearing over and over from the fishermen, "You should have been here yesterday", we trudged across the sand, father and son, side-by-side back to our fifty-seven Fairlane. Standing in the darkness, we silently broke down our two-piece rods. In order to engineer the poles inside our jam-packed trunk, Dad had to rearrange everything inside - a thermos, a foam cooler, half-empty bait containers, fishing rags, the two sand spikes he'd sprung for that very morning, a tackle box and the same battered suitcase that was riding with me now in the belly of the jet. He was quiet the whole time. I knew his mind was working on something and I was pretty sure what it was. "You know what," he finally said, slamming the trunk closed, "Whadda ya say we sleep right here in the car?" I just knew he'd been carrying that idea in the back of his mind all day. Early that morning two red flags had gone up inside my head when he'd promised Ma we'd get a room. Like most working stiffs in society's cellar, he always tried to figure a way to save a buck. Though I can't say I blamed him, I had to be honest when we ducked inside the Ford, and I told him it was getting pretty nippy out and that sleeping in the car might not be such a good idea. Scrunching prone in the front seat, wrestling his thick legs under the steering wheel, he just let my comment hang in the air until it dissipated and I laid down in back.

For about ten minutes I tried to tough it out. I shook and shivered from the cold and inactivity. Soon it became too much and I had to say, "Dad ... I think we better get a room. I'm freezin' my ass off."

"Nahhh. Don't worry about it, you'll get warm."

Then, in a teasing tone, I threatened him, "I'd-hate-to-have-to-tell-Maaa."

A few more wordless moments passed as I laid there waiting for his response, shaking harder, hearing only the call of a lone night bird and the breaking waves on the beach. Then, finally, some grunts and groans came from the front seat. Its springs started squeaking as Dad wrestled himself up. After considerable effort he sat up, slid behind the wheel, and cranked the engine over. He was as relieved as I was. I know because when I climbed up front, although it was dark, I could see him unsuccessfully fighting back that sly smile of his, a smile I didn't see very often, a smile pulled so wide it exposed his missing eyetooth on that one side. This was one of those rare, brief moments when he seemed more like a pal than a father, one of those memorable times when, for just awhile, he transcended that wall that so all too often separates father and son.

Per the captain's orders, I punched out my cigarette as the jet circled over the heavy clouds shrouding Kennedy Airport. Closer to it now, I thought of my father's lifeless body laying somewhere down there, so alone, inside a cold morgue. Tears came to my eyes and then another isolated instance when he had gone out of his way for me played out in my mind's screen, the time he took Donny and me to Yankee Stadium when we were about twelve. At that time you could sit in the bleachers for only eighty cents. I remember the price because all through batting practice, and the first inning too, Dad pitched and bitched about how expensive it was. But despite all his bellyaching that warm sunny day, we still had a super time. In the flesh, we saw Mickey, Yogi, Roger and company wearing their pinstripes out there on that impossibly green Bronx pasture. From our vantage point, the batters appeared as nothing more than white specks but, being so close to 'the Mick' each time he trotted out to centerfield, made me feel as though I had a cheap seat in heaven.

But the real highlight of the game was even bigger than seeing all that. It came late in the game when the Tiger's Jake Wood bounced a ground-rule double into the bleachers. I shagged after that ball as if my life depended on it. When I got close, I dove past three empty seats, just beating about a dozen black kids to it. Sprawled out on the concrete, feeling that ball in my hands, was like a dream come true. I was holding solid gold. But it wasn't mine yet!

The gang of kids must have figured since I was such a skinny little kid they could easily tear my prize away. Before I could get up from the cement, every one of them was on top of me, kids of all shapes and sizes reaching, yanking at my arms and the ball. But I squeezed that stitched-leather-sphere so tight that a grown man, heck even number 7 'The Mick' himself (if he wasn't such a nice guy), couldn't have wrestled it away. When finally Dad and a couple of other men, also in white undershirts, cleared the pile on top of me, I still had the ball. In my small world, at that point in time, getting that ball was bigger than anything imaginable. I wouldn't have traded it for a year of free egg creams.

For the next three years I fought off a nagging urge to play with that ball. It wasn't easy. A few times I came real close. But I didn't use it. The ball remained on my dresser, perched atop the cardboard 'Yankees' megaphone that held the popcorn Dad had bought me at the Stadium that afternoon in 1961. But eventually, just before my fifteenth birthday, I weakened. It was on a bright Easter Sunday afternoon, across the avenue in the schoolyard, that I put a bat to that once sacred ball. It only took about fifteen minutes of me and the guys whacking it around on the asphalt to trash it. In that time, most of the seams had split and the leather had gotten all chewed up. The scuffed cover was literally hanging off. I put the wood to it one last time and knocked it off completely. As the ball of string rolled down the painted left field line, we turned to split. Jimmy or Donny, I'm not sure, had spotted Susan Dibenedetto and a few of her girlfriends strolling the sidewalk licking ice cream cones on the other side of the chain-link fence. As we took off after them, a little Puerto Rican kid called out to me. He wanted to know if I wanted what was left of the ball, he'd probably wrap it up in friction tape, give it a new life. We were on the other side of the fence when I hollered to him, "Go `head! It's yours!" Then me and the guys turned our eyes back to the girls up ahead, to their swaying, bouncing behinds. Somehow they didn't look the same as they had the summer before. There was now something strangely different about them, something very fascinating.

Though the turnout at Dad's wake was small, anybody who meant anything to my family was there, except the one I loved most in the world. My father's friends from The Holy Name Society showed up, my friends, and the few relatives from Mom's side that still talked to her, the very few she hadn't estranged since her first breakdown. The only two remaining family members on Dad's side of the family - Grandma Cassidy and his sister, Aunt Delores - had flown up from Florida, too.

Of course, Father Bianchi came every evening, staying until the funeral home closed. As always, he was there for my family to lean on, there for Ma, me, Sylvester, and Dad. I still remember Father's exact words as we knelt together alongside the open casket. He said, "Dee Cee, look how relaxed your father's face is. He's at peace. He's in a better place now." Though I wasn't so sure about the last part of what Father had said Dad's face was relaxed, like I'd never seen it before. When he was alive, it was always stressed, troubled by my mother's illness, by money problems, often by both. I remember how terribly upset he became every month when the car insurance came due, how every time he worried about "where the dough is coming from" to pay it.

Like most working beasts, then and now, my father had no estate. He'd worked hard, sold cheap the best years of his adult life, just so his family could subsist. All he had at the time of his death was the Falcon and its payments. His only other possessions were his wedding band, which he took to his grave, a Timex watch (water resistant but not waterproof) with a badly-scratched face, and a fourth-rate stamp collection that was the closest thing to a hobby he'd ever had.

But although he didn't have many 'things', he did leave me something priceless, a way out of the U.S. Army, a way to derail my inevitable jungle tour in South-East Asia. At the wake I found out from Father Bianchi that I just might qualify for what the military calls a 'hardship discharge'. He told me to call my mother's shrink and ask for a letter explaining her mental condition. I had that letter folded in my wallet along with a photostat of Dad's death certificate when I flew back to Quantico. The day I returned, I brought this documentation to the base commander's office. They advised me that, yes, I was a candidate for a hardship discharge. But after a week had passed with no further word, I got antsy. Never being good at waiting, I decided my best course of action was to go the crazy route, just to increase my odds.

It was a gamble. They could have thrown me into the brig when I told them I could no longer go on with my infantry training, that my only thoughts were of my sick mother and my dead father, that concentrating on the training was no longer possible. To really convince them that I was emotionally distraught, and this was the riskiest part, I told the commander on my follow-up visit, "Sir, you obviously can do whatever you feel is necessary with me, the brig, whatever. But ... but I can't do this anymore." I figured this to be the ultimate bluff. Just the mention of jail surely would convince him that my desperation was heartfelt. After I made my pitch, I did like any good salesman or hustler would, I shut up. I waited for him to say something next.

Lucky for me, this brigadier-general turned out to be a pretty cool head, for a lifer. He told me he'd recommend discharge proceedings and that he'd personally expedite them also. The only negative thing about the meeting was at the end when he told me to get a haircut.

Damn, I thought, my hair is just starting to cheat over my ears a little. I wanted a head start on growing it before I got discharged. I told him I was sorry but, really, I was tapped out, spent every last dime on the emergency trip home. I couldn't believe my eyes when that general pulled out his own wallet and handed me a buck. At that moment, despite the fact I'd have to get a haircut and my inherent disdain for the military and all authority figures, I could have kissed that general right on his rising forehead.

Six days later I was out of the army, an honorably discharged veteran after only four months of active duty. Of course, my release was bitter-sweet since it came as a result of my father's death. At the same time, I was thrilled beyond words, and devastated. Well, maybe not exactly devastated because it still felt as if he was alive; out of town maybe, on a trip, or in some hospital, but not dead. The reality of his death took months, no, a couple of years to truly sink in. And the deeper it did, the more I realized how precarious my own existence was. No longer did I enjoy that false sense of security, that luxury, that sense of immortality one enjoys while both your parents are alive.

After mustering out of Quantico, I returned to Flushing and immediately began questioning anyone and everyone who knew Theresa. Nobody had a clue as to where she might have gone.

As much as I hated to do it, I even telephoned her closest girlfriends. I knew it was pretty much a waste of time, that had they known Theresa's whereabouts they probably wouldn't have told me anyway. Nevertheless, each time one of them told me they didn't know anything, I was fairly certain it was the truth. Though I pretty much figured this before I began my fruitless inquest, futile as it seemed, the phone calls were necessary for my piece of mind.

All of Theresa's friends, including Regina, had been cold, standoffish at best. Except for one, a good-looking Irish blonde named Deirdre Collonics. A friend of Theresa's, I'd always had suspicions about. You guys know the type, the one who suddenly becomes much friendlier every time your sweetheart is out of sight or earshot, always smiling at you at parties, sitting next to you far too often for it to be coincidence, moving extra close, a hip or a thigh pressing tight against yours every time your girl goes to powder her nose or whatever. Well, that was Deirdre. But her come-on was much more direct when I talked to her on the phone this time. I turned her down gently, giving her some kind of vague maybe-down-the-road comeback.

After exhausting every lead, I was certain that Mrs. Wayman must have again gotten some ill-perceived bad vibes from a black person or persons, that she didn't want anyone to know, friends or not, where her and Theresa were headed. Maybe she didn't even tell Theresa where they were going. Maybe she did tell her. Possibly Theresa was starting to buy her ridiculous theory. Maybe that's why she had never contacted any of her New York friends. Maybe! Maybe! Maybe! The bottom line was that I had come up with zippo, zero – zilch, that I'd have to go on traipsing through life with only half a heart.

Chapter 18

The next five-year chunk of my life is the haziest of my adult memories. All that remains are some random fragmental recollections, mostly places and incidents. That and a handful of blurry visions of a few of the many nameless women I spent time with. I really freaked out, grew my hair to my shoulders along with a rather sinister-looking Fu Manchu. I partied hard and slept around plenty. With lots of help from Anheiser Busch and more than a few pot-pushers I met along the way, I was sometimes able to anesthetize my pain. Sometimes I even managed to have a reasonably good time, but they never lasted. Any such relationship was always short-lived. To be straight about it, none of those wild nights did a thing for the emptiness I felt inside. Not come sun-up anyway. Not over the long haul.

That what you might call 'semi-time warp' began right after my discharge when, on a lark, Jimmy Curten and I split to Colorado for the summer. We drove out there in a hundred-and-thirty-five dollar Plymouth I'd picked up. We quickly found a small place to rent in Aurora, just one block east of the Denver city line. With the help of the state employment office, we found work just as easily. They placed Jimmy and me with Burlington Northern Railroad. Both of us were issued a yellow hard hat and before we knew it we were gandy dancers. Along with about fifty other young dudes from all over the country, we laid tracks through the foothills of the Rocky Mountains.

Denver was a swinging town and we had one wild time out there. From day one until we split in September, it was a non-stop beer-drinking, pot and hash smoking, sexed-up marathon. Although most of my remembrances of 'The Mile High City' are shattered and scattered, two remain clear as crystal.

One is of the first night we went partying out there. A preview of what was in store for Jimmy and I that entire summer.

It was a Monday night, not a good night for finding ladies. But after three nights on the road, we were ready to pound down more than a few brews. Early in the evening at an empty little nothing bar in downtown Denver, we'd gotten a tip about a place called Mister Lucky's. The place was a huge three-story disco with a band on each floor - rock, country, whatever you like. It wasn't even nine o'clock when we motored into its sprawling parking lot and already it was two-thirds full. We couldn't believe that on a Monday night any place would be jumping like this one was. Anyway, Jimmy and I were leaning against the first floor bar maybe ten minutes, hadn't even finished our first beers yet, when we met two chicks, stewardesses on a layover from Detroit who, two drinks later, were more than willing to check out our room at a sleazy no-tell motel called the Tumble Inn.

The next day we found, and moved into, the apartment in Aurora. It was a nicely furnished one-bedroom job in a brand new building just off East Colfax. They'd had two vacancies to choose from, one on the first floor, one on the third. There was no deliberating. Jimmy and I both preferred the one on the first floor, and it turned out to be a wise decision because it wasn't long before we had new acquaintances, females of course, knocking on our bedroom window at all hours of the night. Needless to say, we were always happy to accommodate them, unless of course we already had company. What a town!

But as ridiculous as it sounds, even out in Denver I always kept an eye open, bloodshot or otherwise, for Theresa. Every time I saw a black-haired girl of her stature, my heart would flip and gallop until I made a negative identification. Probably two hundred and thirty million people in America back then, yet I still had small, ridiculous hopes of someday running into her. I kept up this vigil for nearly thirty years.

Despite the good time we were having out west by summer's end, we were beginning to miss home. Then, one early September Saturday afternoon, right after a golf-ball hailstorm subsided, we made a spur-of-the-moment decision to load up the car and head back to New York. I well remember that first night on the road, partly because I was sober, and partly because it got very hairy.

It was about an hour before midnight. We'd been driving along a desolate blue-highway running arrow-straight through an endless sea of Kansas wheat fields when, out of nowhere, an intense electrical storm came up on us. In the snap of a finger, this God-awful wind developed, bringing with it thick walls of driving, horizontal rain. Bold cloud-to-ground lightning strikes lit in flashes the sky and the landscape from one horizon to the other. The thunder was impossibly loud. Every time it rumbled we could feel the road shaking beneath my balding tires.

Then, right in the middle of all this natural fury, what do you think happens next? The windshield wiper motor crapped out.

As much as we wanted to drive out of this mess, find a motel, we had no choice but to pull onto the road's shoulder and wait. After a while, exhausted from all the driving, Jimmy climbed into the back seat, I killed the engine, and we both tried to get some sleep. But it wasn't going to happen. Suddenly the wind got cooler and stronger yet, so strong that the Plymouth started swaying on its tired old springs. One time, I swear, the driver's side wheels actually rose an inch or two off the grassy shoulder. As unnerving as this was, it didn't happen again. Soon fatigue overcame concern and we managed to fall asleep for awhile. The last thing I remember before falling off was what sounded like a train roaring close by. I thought this awfully strange since we'd seen no tracks, nothing but those wheat fields, for the last hundred and fifty miles.

When we awoke an hour or so later, the rain and winds had eased up some so we resumed our search for a motel. For sixty long miles I drove, chin jutted over the wheel, my soaked left arm out the window, wiping rain off the windshield with one of my old army fatigue shirts. Eventually, in the middle of that statewide wheat field where another two-lane highway intersected ours, we came upon a small motel. Unlike the trip to Denver, when a Holiday Inn along I-10 in Columbia Missouri wouldn't give us a room because our hair was too long for their liking, this little mom-and-pop place did take our money. When we got inside that room, both of us far beyond exhaustion, our eyes hanging out of our heads, it took one titanic effort for me to stumble across the room to the closest bed. Still fully clothed and plenty wet, I lost consciousness mid-fall as I toppled into it.

The next morning, when we rose with a bright, promising sun, we felt reasonably refreshed though not exactly new. Kind of like a hangover that had been dulled by plenty of sleep. Right after showering and dressing, Jimmy and I were drinking free coffee and smoking in the motel's lobby when we overheard a conversation between a bread delivery man and the desk clerk. They were talking about a tornado that had touched down the night before. About fifty miles west, the delivery man said. I knew then that the roar I'd heard alongside the highway, when the car was rocking and rolling, hadn't been from any train.

When we got back to Queens, Jimmy and I got another apartment. Neither of us wanted to go back home. Once you leave, it's awfully tough going back. Even if my mother had shaken her demons I wouldn't have. Considering her condition, she was getting by OK without me anyway. Sylvester had been home with her since his discharge from the Air Force. Between her social security survivor's benefits and what Sylvester earned as a clerk down on Wall Street, they had no problem paying the bills. With 1B being rent-controlled and inflation still a new word in most people's vocabularies, living was still affordable. With the help of the GI Bill, Sylvester had no problem paying for his night courses also. Hell-bent on getting his degree, being the brainiest in the family, though maybe not the smartest, he went to Queens College four nights a week after work.

Getting a college education may have been an all-consuming goal for Sylvester, but I no longer cared about it. As far as I was concerned, any future I might have had ended seven months earlier when I lost Theresa. Hurt and bitter, I felt I was getting educated just fine. I thought I was kind of like Louis Lamour, getting my smarts outside the classroom from real-life experiences. I was majoring in sex education, and minoring in adventure and good times. Like that old Grass Roots' song, I wanted to only 'Live for Today'.

For the next three years in Flushing, that's exactly what I did, partied hardy at clubs in Queens, Manhattan and out on the Island. Then I became antsy again. I needed a change of scenery. Like my father had most of his life, Jimmy and I had nothing jobs as cab drivers so we wouldn't be leaving any big careers behind. We weren't locked into anything, and when I suggested splitting again, Jimmy was more than game. This time so was Donny Scully. Yup, his hollow wedding vows to Susan Dibenedetto had long since lost what little meaning they had to begin with. That charade only lasted eight months, until Jimmy and I returned from Colorado. Shortly after Susan gave birth to their baby boy, Donny lost what little ability and desire he had to continue the charade. Stevey Waters did not come with us. He was upstate and out of the picture. In his third year at Syracuse University, after screwing off the first two, he was buckling down, thinking about med-school. So the three of us headed south this time, to Florida.

Needless to say, like it had everywhere else, Theresa's ghost followed me down I-95. And after we got there, that big red tropical sun never set on a day that I didn't think of her. I was still haunted by all those hurt-filled replays of happy, innocent times from a period in my life when I still had a viable reason for living. But despite this burden, this unshakable loss that would torment me no matter where I went, I adapted reasonably well to life in Fort Lauderdale. How could I not? The town was an Eden for us single guys, its sugar grain beaches eternally basking, blanching, beneath that warm southern sun, the unique fragrance that every day hung over the thousand spread blankets, the sultry scent of Mother Ocean blended with gallons of Coppertone rubbed on so many bikini-clad bodies., and all those 'Fort Liquordale' night spots, all filled with golden-tanned women, all there for the taking.

Though summertime in 'The Sunshine State' is, to put it mildly, hot and oppressive, the winters are magical. We found the trade-off well worth it. At least Jimmy and I did. Less than six months after we arrived, Donny went back to New York with a topless dancer he'd hooked up with. But Jimmy and I stayed. For three years, we shared a two-bedroom apartment off Commercial Boulevard. During that time, Jimmy had a succession of nowhere jobs with plenty of down time in between. A lot of months I had to carry him. But, Jimmy was my friend, had been for a lot of years, so I kept my bitching to a minimum.

My first job in Lauderdale was as a groundskeeper at Holiday Park on Sunrise Boulevard. It was a sprawling city park with several baseball diamonds, tennis and basketball courts and an auditorium on the grounds. The acres of grass in between these facilities kept me atop a rider mower, alone with my thoughts, for countless hours.

The gig was a no-brainer which was fine by me. To me, working was, and still is, merely a necessary evil. The less stress I had to endure for a paycheck, the easier I could tolerate it. I didn't much care about having 'things', never had many anyway. And what you don't have, you don't miss. You might yearn a little if you let yourself get caught up in that mindset, but you never miss them. As long as I had reliable wheels, a roof over my butt, two squares a day, and enough scratch to party on weekends, that was fine. I was in my twenties and had no idea what I wanted to be when I grew up. I didn't know in my thirties either. It wasn't until just a few years ago, after leaving forty behind, that I finally realized I wanted to be a writer, but more on that later.

When I wasn't cutting grass, or reapplying baselines on the ball fields at Holiday Park, I whiled away a lot of time fishing. Mostly on Anglin's Pier at Lauderdale by the Sea. It was a convenient spot since Commercial Boulevard dead-ends where the pier stands out of the ocean on its spindly wooden legs. I went there often. Sometimes, on a Saturday or Sunday morning, if I got out there before sun-up (I learned early on, that was the magic time to have your line in the water), I'd spring for breakfast at the tiny restaurant at the foot of the pier. Anyway, the first time I got into a school of Spanish Mackerel out there (sorry, I should pass this one up but somehow I just can't), I was 'hooked' on fishing. Because I enjoyed it so much, I quickly learned a lot about the sport and was soon making some pretty respectable catches.

But my attraction to angling wasn't just about how many fish I could yank onto the pier's planking. It transcended that. The truest reward, although I did love the anticipation and the excitement of catching fish, was the sport's cerebral benefits, the calming, almost spiritual beauty of the ocean at daybreak, the sometimes total concentration of the act that leaves no room in the mind for other burdens. Then there was the often impossible challenge of outwitting a piscatorial creature that had a brain the size of a BB. The rush I'd get when some mysterious, unseen powerful force frantically bent and bounced a rod in my trembling hands. The alarming scream of my reel's drag, as a fish hightailed for the Bahamas, reminding me that the last remaining yards of line were melting off the spool. Yes, I had finally fallen in love again, with fishing, a passion that would remain in my heart, right beside my other love, for the rest of my life. Every time I connected with a good fish, the whole rest of this crazy, troubled world ceased to exist. Just like it had the year I danced with Theresa Wayman.

Two or three times a week, after work, I'd drive down A1A to Bahia Mar Yacht Basin where I'd stroll leisurely along the very docks where John D. McDonald's fictional character, Travis McGee, docked his 'Busted Flush'. In the beginning I enjoyed watching the charter boats come in with their catches after a day at sea. How I longed to myself troll the Gulf Stream's indigo waters. To go out on a sport fishing boat and hook up with such gallant battlers as the dolphin, wahoo, sailfish and, maybe just once, the majestic blue marlin. During those walks along the sun-blanched docks, I fantasized about catching direct descendants of the same game fish Ernest Hemingway had done battle with forty years earlier down in the lower Keys.

But such a thrill was much too expensive for my budget. The catches displayed on the dock's racks in those early evenings had been cranked in by people of a different class; sunburnt tourists with more money than should be legal. Write-off conscious corporate types, people who didn't know a reel's drag from its free-spool. It seemed sacrilegious that these people could buy an encounter with such noble game fish. After a while it enraged me to think that the fish brought in each day, drained of their life and color, were so often used as mere bait to land bigger catches such as mergers, multi-million dollar accounts and leverage buyouts.

Despite all my ill feelings, when I befriended a skipper named Fred Wrinkle at Bahia Mar and he offered me a job as mate on his 36 footer, I jumped at the opportunity.

Each morning, as we headed out to the blue water, I'd do my best to hide my resentment toward the day's party. Grudgingly, like most of the rest of the world's workers, I masked my true feelings.

Nevertheless, I loved being out on the ocean. The smell of warm sea air always seemed to heal my spirits. I loved the boundless gifts Mother Ocean offered when her mood was benevolent. Gifts like the unexpected appearance of a huge manta ray rising to the water's surface like a half-ton butterfly, its broad wings sweeping ever so gracefully, so daintily. And the sudden sight of skyrocketing kingfish, surface feeding, lifting off from schools of baitfish, looking like so many electrified silver rockets as the sun reflects off their sides. Then there's the pastel-colored dolphins that always surprise you even though you're looking for them near the floating lines of sargassum weed. The swinging bill of a lit-up sailfish is a magnificent sight as it rises to a flat line behind the boat. But, the thrill of all thrills was when a rare blue marlin, big as a full-size Cessna, literally flies out of the water after feeling the hook's sting.

Silently I always rooted for these majestic fish every time a customer put the hook to one. Always I'd savor the relief I felt when a sail, a dolphin, or even a lucky barracuda, would jump clear of the water and throw the hook, free once again to roam the ink-blue waters of the Stream. At such times I'd be so very thankful there were still a few things in this upside-down world that big bucks could not buy, still a handful of people, things, emotions and experiences that have no price tag. But what I didn't know was that one night after two years of mollycoddling Captain Fred's charters, fate was going to bestow one such priceless gift on me.

Chapter 19

November 8th, 1974 was a Friday. Though it has nothing to do with why I remember that date, we made a banner catch that day. An early cool front had pushed a huge school of kingfish down to Fort Lauderdale and all that day, out over the second reef, we loaded the fish box with these oversized members of the mackerel family. The seas were heavy, the bite did not stop and neither did the four carpet salesmen who'd won the charter in a company contest. The trip was fun but chaotic. Eight continuous hours of beer guzzling (them, not me), joyous yelping, tomfoolery and tangled lines. Rough as it was outside, and with all the beer they drank, it was no small miracle none of these guys got sick. Soused as they were by the time we tied up, I didn't think they'd be able to find their car, let alone remember to tip yours truly. But they did. After I'd cleaned and iced down their catch, which was no small task, they came through big-time. Fifty smackers.

Watching the four of them do a wobbly crab-walk across busy A1A, making their way to the Yankee Clipper's bar, I wondered what had screwed up their mobility more, the beer or all those hours of pitching and rolling in five foot seas. They somehow made it across the street alive and I merrily began my ritualistic duties of cleaning the boat and all the expensive tackle. Finishing up as the red Florida sun set behind a forest of sailboat masts, I locked the cabin, double-checked it and was out of there. I hadn't had a beer since the previous weekend and by now I was ready! I planned on having one hell of a night, even if I was going out alone.

Full of Friday anticipation, I drove to my apartment and showered away all the salt and kingfish scales. I got into some clean faded Levis and a laundered yellow button-down shirt that enhanced my fisherman's tan nicely. I slipped my bare feet into my deck shoes, slapped on some Brut, grabbed two bananas from the top of the fridge and was out the door. I was winging it alone because Jimmy had gone off with a Dunkin' Donut's waitress on a three-day trip to the 'Mousetrap' up in Orlando.

Scarfing down the bananas, I cruised back down A1A in the darkness. Radio semi-loud, some geek DJ pitching 'deals' on new

Oldsmobiles, I flowed toward the beach with the Friday night traffic. Man, I thought, am I ready! I had that urge to get snockered that's always irreversible once my mind's made up. I hoped to get to the Elbo Room early enough to get a stool at the bar. Yeah, the 'Elbo Room', that notorious hangout of spring breaks past, and 'Where the Boys Are' fame.

It was still early when I arrived. About a dozen people were at the bar, mostly leftovers from happy hour; a couple of early-birds like myself. I plopped on a stool near the front window and ordered a brew, and another, and another. I watched the tourists and characters parading by outside on the sidewalk as I pounded them down.

About an hour went by before a couple of other mates I knew from the marina came in. We talked about tides, winds, tackle and recent catches. They'd had a few before they left their boat and were now downing straight shots of Jack, getting pretty loose real quick. And I wasn't far behind. They were going to a party up in Pompano and, although I turned down their invite, I jumped when they asked if I wanted to do a couple of doobies. Though the place was starting to get crowded, I gladly relinquished my barstool and went outside with them.

When I floated back into the barroom, roughly twenty minutes later, the music seemed much louder and more intense. But I'm sure it wasn't. The place had become more crowded and livelier. I went to the bar, bought my umpteenth bottle of Miller Lite. With nowhere to sit, I shuffled tentatively around and through pods of bodies over to the Wurlitzer. I leaned a hip on it. The floor rolled beneath my feet like old waves. The heavy bass blasting from the juke sent exaggerated vibrations up and down my rubberized skeleton. I tried to appear straighter than I was but it wasn't easy with my brain beer-sopped and my reflexes decelerated from the marijuana. Methodically I checked out all the fluff in the crowd, half-focusing on a couple of good-lookers with black hair. But my eyes kept pulling back to a girl with hair of different color. She was sitting very erect, like a model, with two girlfriends at a table near the bar.

Fairly certain I'd caught her stealing a few glances in my direction, my interest piqued even more. But with all the people roaming around, coming, going, dancing, horsing around, I could only catch short, intermittent glimpses of her. Her chestnut hair was long, thick, brushed back like a lion's mane. In the bar's dim light, during my next blurry glimpse, I was able to focus on her a bit longer. I noticed she had an extraordinarily pleasant face. As I was taking it in, two guys approached her table. Then some people blocked my line of vision again.

'Shit,' I thought out loud 'I can't see her now.' Damn, she looks interesting. Get the hell out of the way. Craning my benumbed neck just a bit, I tried to find her again.

There was another break in the crowd. I slowly straightened my neck, a delayed reflex. Can't let her think I'm easy. Don't want to look like I'm gawking at her. But, then I saw her nod her head at the guy rapping to her, and a small smile lit her face beautifully.

I thought for sure it was too late now. The guy probably said the right things, pressed the right buttons, connected with her. Surely that's why she smiled. But then she pivoted her head quickly, directly at me this time. Our eyes locked for just a moment before a biker and his mama started grinding away, blocking our line of vision again. I still remember the song that came on the jukebox at that exact moment, 'To Love Somebody', by the Bee Gees.

I saw her making her way through the crowd, heading in my direction.

She came up to the juke and started perusing the selections. With considerable effort, I lifted my eyelids. Trying to be inconspicuous, I took in this girl as she fed a couple of quarters into the machine. Very pretty, I thought, in a 'milk and honey' sort of way. That long, long hair, whooshed back the way it was, added just the slightest hint of recklessness, making her quite provocative. Sort of like the Breck Girl in a risqué mood. She had generous curves in all the right places and a tiny waist that accentuated them. I was struck by her waist. I'd never seen one so trim on a women whose eyes (with her heels on) were almost even with my own.

Her long legs stilted real high, she leaned over the front of the jukebox which allowed her a better look at the selections and me a better look at her solid, half-moon hips and up-tilted behind. Her denim jeans, stretched to the limit, looked like they'd been tattooed on her. Up top she was a little bigger than average, which never hurts. As she leaned a little farther forward to hit the selection buttons, her back flexed, her tube top rode up just a bit further. I found this to be quite sensual and tantalizing.

I took a swallow of beer then, with my tongue all loose and clumsy, I turned to her and managed a line, the weakest of all lame lines. "Heyyyahhh, you come here often? .... I don't think I've seen you before." I followed up those profound words with a lopsided goofy smile.

Despite my lackluster performance, she lifted her head and turned to me, our eyes meeting up close for the first time. She made a quick assessment of my face with these kind looking, outsized eyes that sparkled like green jewels. Remaining poker-faced, except for those eyes that seemed incapable of deception, she answered my stupid question with, "Maybe I've come here once too often."

Instantly I took offense. I'm always quick to take offense because most of the time I go out of my way not to give any. I tried to conjure something nasty to say to parry her snotty remark. But before I could, her lips spread into this magnificent warm smile, an infectious smile like that of a loving mother's, an inviting smile that spoke without words, just like Theresa's used to. It said, I've been looking for you ... waiting for you ... for a long, long time.

Completely disarmed, my emotions skidded to a stop just short of revenge then pulled back towards civility. Though half-bagged, I still had enough sense to realize some be-bop snappy line just wouldn't cut it this time. I had a strange feeling this wasn't going to be just another one night stand. I sensed she was different, maybe even special.

That quick, I warmed up to this young woman. I didn't even know her name yet. Hell, we'd only exchanged a few words. But still, it was almost like six years earlier, when for the first time in the hallway at Saint Agnes', I saw Theresa. There had been many women since Theresa, but none of them quite like this one standing next to me now. I felt a tinge of hope, a feeling long gone from my repertoire of emotions. I remember thinking, maybe this is the one, the one who can bring me back to life.

Without stumbling on my words, I managed to ask, "Can I buy you a drink?"

"Thanks, but no thanks."

She punched in her last selection. Neither of us said a thing. She turned back to me again, looked right through my eyes, giving me an opportunity. I wanted to say something but I was at a loss for words. Meaningful words, anyway. The condition I was in sure as hell wasn't helping any. Our brief intimate connection was weakening. I could feel it. She felt it.

Damn! What's the matter with me? Why can't I open my big mouth? I think she's gonna just walk off now? What about that smile she just gave me? Maybe she always smiles that way to everybody. Maybe it wasn't custom made for me.

The smooth continuity of our brief encounter seemed to have run its course when suddenly her face lit again. I thought she was going back to her friends but she didn't. She looked back into my baby-blues and said, "I don't feel like another drink. But ... I wouldn't mind taking a walk on the beach, get a little fresh air maybe. You look like you could use a little."

Bingo! Wowwwee! Shazam! She wants to take a walk! Even if she's not Miss Right, who knows, maybe we'll at least get it on, down on the beach somewhere.

There it was again, that irrepressible, primitive male libido at work, always willing, always ready to engage in the act that propagates the species.

But this wouldn't be a one-night-fling. Just like when I first met Theresa, I didn't even think of trying any funny stuff. All we did was walk and walk and walk in the cool night air for several miles on the sand, clear past Hugh Taylor Birch State Park where the beach changes from public to private, all the way to where Lauderdale's condo canyon intrudes the coastline, where so many characterless concrete towers barricade the ocean view and defiantly scrape at the stars. Just before we came up to them, we turned around and headed back toward the Elbo Room.

Though the two day nor'easter had by now lessened to a comfortable breeze, there were still some leftover waves energizing the surf. Large but half-hearted rollers broke lazily along the surf line, intermittently drowning out the man-made clamor along route A1A and the motel row adjacent to it. On the way back we took our shoes off and sloshed through ankle-deep seawater as it washed foam onto the sand.

Just as so many women in my past had told me I was, Maddy

Frances Rownan was very easy to talk to. A bit shy when we first left the Elbo Room, she soon loosened up after feeling our good karma strengthening. Without effort, we eased comfortably inside each other's heads. Soon we were hand in hand, talking effortlessly, learning about one another. The only pause in our conversation occurred when we peered out together at a solitary white light drifting imperceptibly in the offshore blackness giving away the horizon on this moon-less night. Then our bare feet still spanking the surf's wash, we resumed our conversation, speaking of the usual things with unusual interest. We were like two strangers who'd seen each other's pictures, liked them, and were now meeting for the first time. We had so many questions, and were so full of anticipation.

It had been a long time since I had this kind of interest in a female.

Chapter 20

During the weeks that followed, Maddy Frances and I came on strong and fast, seeing one another most evenings and every weekend. As always, money was tight but she didn't much care about going out. Our being together was all that mattered to her. Hanging around my place, or her's, was just fine. So was taking a walk, a drive in the car, or fishing from the pier together on a Saturday morning. She'd always ask me what I wanted to do, what I wanted to watch on TV, what would I like her to fix for a Saturday night dinner, should we see this movie or that one? On Sunday afternoons she'd even iron my clothes. Everything she did was for me. For the first time in my life I had the notion that some people actually got satisfaction, even happiness, by doing for others. Of course, I'd heard about such people but had never known any of them, not intimately anyway. As tough as it was for a hedonist such as myself to understand such selfless behavior, I was beginning to.

But, as much as I had come to appreciate Maddy's many sacrifices, they were continually overshadowed by the ghost of Theresa. Yeah, I'd think, *Maddy's great*, but then cerebral visions of my first sweetheart would appear and quickly diminish her loving gestures.

I cared for Maddy Frances, cared for her a lot, yet my heart still ached for my lost Theresa. Back and forth I went like that, over and over, my feelings jumbled, confused, knotted. Although six years had stolen away since that last night I'd seen Theresa, I still kept the vigil alive. Just like I had in Colorado and back in New York, I continued to look for her every day, everywhere. At clubs, the marina, the beach, while grocery shopping. And yes, now even while out on dates with Maddy Frances. Once again, I know it sounds pretty crazy, the minuscule odds of finding Theresa, but hadn't she lived in Florida for awhile when she was a kid? Before I met her? She might have told me once what town she had lived in but, if she did, I didn't remember. It just may have been Fort Lauderdale. Hell, I thought, with all the New Yorkers that transplant down here, it very well could have been. Maybe her mother had dragged her back here. Though I knew it was a long shot at best, the thought that she could be living in Lauderdale, no matter how remote the odds, gave me hope.

When I used to go to pick-up joints, I always bird-dogged black haired women. I had a thing for them. Italian, Jewish, oriental, Greek, it didn't matter, the longer their hair, the better. As long as they were decent looking, they'd be my first target for a one night stand. Heads of other shades were mere consolations. It was a fetish I didn't need any shrink's help to diagnose.

But none of those raven-haired ladies did much for me, not in the long run anyway. Neither did the redheads, blondes or brunettes. Maddy Frances was the one. By far the best substitute for Theresa I'd come across. The only one! For a long time before I met Maddy, I'd been like a little boy who'd lost his mother sizing up every potential replacement his father brought home. Despite her losing out in most of my unfair comparisons, Maddy was damn good looking, and intelligent to boot. And though she had the kindest eyes you'd ever seen, they didn't fairly represent how beautiful she was inside. To this day, I've never encountered anybody as selfless. Those are the reasons why, despite my confusion and uncertainness, I responded to her startling question the way I did the night of January 15, 1975, only sixty-eight nights after we'd taken that first walk on the beach.

It was a Sunday evening, around 8 o'clock. I had given Maddy a full body message on my sofa which of course led to other things. After making love, still naked beneath the afghan she had crocheted for me, we laid quietly on our sides, clinging to each other in the darkness. Her breath still hot and heavy on my neck, I buried my face in her flowing hair. The scent of lilac enhanced in the dark quiet room, I caressed the small of her back. A moment later, as I slid my hand down to her soft, velvety cheeks and started kneading them, she whispered my name as if it was a question.

"Dean?"

"Yes?"

"Do you realize ... how much I care for you?"

My hand froze with one of her cheeks in it. There was a momentary pause before I said, also like a question, "I know you love me." She'd been telling me that for about three weeks.

She lifted her head, brought her face flush to mine. Dark as it was, we could just see each other now.

"I love you more than anything," she said. "I care more ... much,

145

much more for you than I do for myself."

Stunned into silence, I wondered what could be so heavy. What was this leading to? I said, "I love you too, Maddy." And, I meant it. I only wished my love was unobstructed.

"Enough to marry me, Dean?"

My hold on her went limp. I was mummified. This was something I was nowhere near prepared for. A real shocker. Still face to face, I lifted a wisp of hair from her eye, gently cupped the nape of her neck and let out a long sigh. We had grown very close in just a couple of months, but this proposal, despite my impulsive nature, I was not ready for.

"Would I marry you? You mean like ... in six months ... a year? I'm not sure of your question."

She lifted her hand to my cheek, smoothed it. "Let me rephrase that, Dean." Then she made herself shockingly clear. "If I ask you to marry me ... tomorrow ... will you say yes?"

"Whooooshhhh, you are serious, aren't you?"

"I love you. I've never said that to anyone. Even when I dated Len for those two years, I could never say that. But with you it's different. You're very sensitive, Dean. Maybe overly-sensitive sometimes, and that's a big part of what I love about you. And ... and I've never known anyone as honest. And you're a darn good kisser too," she added, playfully tapping the tip of my nose with her finger, lightening the moment a tad.

Then a warm smile formed on her lips. She brushed my face with her eyes and went on, "I want you all for myself, Dean Cassidy. Let's do something crazy, let's get married tomorrow."

"Tomorrow, but, Maddy ... "

"You said you love me!"

"You know I do."

"How old are you, Dean?"

"Twenty-four, almost twenty-five, you know that ... quit toying with me."

"I'm twenty-three, and as nuts as it may sound, I've never been surer about anything in my life. You said tomorrow is an off day, no charter. What do you say?" Her eyes still holding mine, she straightened up on the couch and switched on a lamp. I also sat up, took a smoke from the pack on the end table, lit it up.

"Where we gonna get married?" I asked dubiously, more than a trace of annoyance in my tone. *Man*, I thought, *I don't believe this is happening.*

"Key West. I've got it all figured out. I'll spend the night here, that way we can get up real early tomorrow, leave while it's still dark out. I'd just have to make a quick stop at my place ... pick up a few things. Oh Dean, wouldn't that be exciting?"

"What about your job?"

"I can call Frieda. Darwin's going to be out of town all week. Things'll be real slow. They can get by without me. They won't mind. They'll be happy for me ... you know I work for great people. We can drive down to the Keys and get married by a justice of the peace. Fred'll give you a few days off if you call him. Just tell him, you're ... we're ... getting married. Look, Dean, you know I never push you for anything. That's not my way. Just say no and I'll drop it. I won't pressure you. I won't be mad. We can go on like we have been."

She paused a moment, picked up my hand. Then, while intently watching my face for a reaction, she went on, "I want to spend the rest of my life with you, Dean. If you don't want the same, or if you're not sure, just say so. I'm only asking because I know I'm ready."

Pensively, I stubbed out my cigarette then looked back at her. When I did, out of nowhere, that booth picture Theresa and I took at Woolworth's, the night we discovered my mother in the closet, flashed crystal clear on my mind's screen. I saw it in black and white but with perfect resolution. I saw every detail. Hell, I should have been able to, I'd looked at it a thousand times. A day never passed that I didn't take it out from beneath the Levis in my bottom dresser drawer. At least once a day I'd look at it, usually at bedtime, if only for a moment, and return to the best of times. What with all the moving around I'd done, that photograph was one the few things that had followed me. But who was kidding who? I'd probably never see Theresa Wayman again. My continuing romance with her had been like a novel with no last chapter. Would I squander the rest of my life in limbo or had the time come to move ahead, to at least try to live again?

Sounding surer than I actually was, I said, "What the hell, Maddy ... hell yes. Let's do it."

And, we did. The next morning we got our blood tested at

Fisherman's Hospital down in Marathon. This was 1975, before the Keys became so commercialized and congested, the year before America's bicentennial birthday, which was when the southernmost opportunists launched their big-time tourism push down there. It was the height of the season when Maddy Frances and I walked into the tiny hospital's waiting room, yet it was all but empty. The only people there were the two nurses on duty. Both in bare feet. Both super-friendly. We opened up to them instantly, admitted that we'd only been dating for sixty-nine days. They thought it was really neat that we were getting married so spontaneously. All smiles, one of them got up to shoo a stray cat that had wandered in the front door, the other went into an adjoining room to tell the doctor what we needed.

A moment or two later we overheard him telling the nurse, "They're getting married! Why, send them right in. And don't charge them anything. The tests are on me." We were both baffled and grateful that a complete stranger could be so thoughtful. That was the beginning of our enduring (yet bitter-sweet) love affair with the Florida Keys.

Later that afternoon, at the Monroe County Courthouse Annex down in Key West, the justice of the peace was every bit as accommodating as the doc and the nurses had been. "Sure," she said, "I'm not busy. Let's do it right now. Have a seat." She extended her hand toward two empty chairs opposite her desk.

As we lowered our butts onto the wooden seats, a worker from another office popped her head in the open doorway and told the justice she's going out for an ice cream cone, did she want one? "Sure," she said, "chocolate."

Then she looked across the desk at us. "How 'bout you kids, would you like one?"

We thanked her, but nervous about the monumental step we were about to take, we passed.

Five minutes later the co-worker returned with two dripping cones wisely encircled in paper napkins and we were Mister and Mrs. Dean Cassidy.

Chapter 21

In the beginning there were many times I had doubts. Had I done the right thing? But doubts are not misgivings, and I was never, ever, sorry for marrying Maddy Frances. She was the proverbial one in a million and I had been blessed to have found her. I would not have lasted with an ordinary girl, nor would an ordinary girl have lasted with me. With us I mean, me and Theresa Wayman. For Theresa would just not leave.

But, as so often is the case in this peculiar life thing, though most days crawled by, the months and years piled up quickly. And things changed. Eighteen months after our Key West wedding, Trevor was born and a year later Dawn came along. They were both still babies, only a few months old, when Maddy had to return to work. Each morning, when she dropped them off at day care, her soft heart would tear a little more. Handing them over was the worst. Every time she surrendered Dawn or Trevor to a member of the ever-changing day care staff, they would wail. And Maddy would cry too as soon as she turned her back to their tearful pleas and flailing little outstretched arms. Rushing back up that walkway to her car, followed by those screams and visions of those tiny red faces and kicking feet, she'd fight the tears. But always she lost. Her make-up always ran as she drove to work. And often, later on at her work desk, when she looked at the pictures of her two babies, her eyes would well.

Just like it had become for so many other American mothers, it was mandatory for Maddy to supplement her husband's degenerating income. Though not at gunpoint, she was nevertheless forced to abandon her children for a job. Corporate America was shaving labor's income and benefits while pushing the already gouged prices of goods and services through the roof. Most men could no longer support their families, and why? So that instead of making just a handsome profit, corporate stocks would skyrocket. Greed ran rampant. Wealthy shareholders became disgustingly richer at the expense of the family unit. They literally smashed that unit. The higher the Dow went, the lower the quality of life became for working families. The way I saw it, Corporate America was responsible for the breakdown of the family and for two generations labeled X and Y. And one day, down the road, I would write about just that

Not many working women had any energy left for their children during the few remaining waking-hours left at day's end. But somehow, at the end of each and every exhausting day, Maddy always managed to squeeze in some quality time with the kids. Though they did not survive unscathed - I could sometimes see in them the scars of their neglected generation - Maddy's super-human efforts did make a lasting, positive impression on them both. After work, she'd come home, put on dinner, turn on the washer and dryer, do dishes and make lunches for the next day. She went non-stop from sun-up until nine at night. And after all that she'd push even more to give Trevor and Dawn a bit of the matriarchal attention they deserved and so badly needed. Maddy Frances was, and still is, one class mother.

I'll be the first to admit I wasn't half the parent she was. Maybe I can blame it on my own haphazard upbringing, the lack of time and interest my father had for me as a child, the frequent debilitating depressions passed on to me by my sick mother. Hell, I simply wasn't happy with my own life, the endless string of meaningless, low-paying jobs, the ever-present financial struggle and, of course, Theresa's ghost. Whatever the reasons, I often wallowed in self pity. Of course I was never abusive to the kids or anything like that, but I certainly was no little league dad either. It's a crying shame I didn't realize just how much I loved my kids when they were growing up. But, hell, I'm not alone. After all, don't most folks make much better grandparents than they were parents?

Like I said, I had a heck of a time holding onto a job during those years. I really went through them. It would take all my fingers, and yours, to count the payrolls I'd been on during those twenty years. Rarely did I keep a job for a year or more. Paid vacations were a rarity for me. I sure did it all: sold furniture, doors, time-shares and kitchen cabinets. I painted houses, drove a hack, and did some wood butchering on a couple of occasions. One time, for a few months, I planted new water pipes beneath the Florida sand and I fixed the old ones when they burst. Those are just some of the jobs I'd had but did not hold. Always having a low tolerance for boredom, I found it in quantity everywhere I worked. I wouldn't find out what I truly wanted to do until I hit my forties. But, despite all the earlier job-jumping,

Maddy Frances still hung in with me. She looked past this deficiency and all my other quirks. All she saw was the complete package and she loved it deeply.

The longest I ever lasted on a gig was the four years I carried mail at the Fort Lauderdale Post Office. I might have actually kept that job, even handled the monotony, had it not been for all the harassment. Somehow I managed to eat whatever crow the postal supervisors laid on me during the ninety-day probationary period but after that charade ended, I went right back to my old ways. Like I said before, I never gave anybody grief without reason, so I sure as heck wouldn't take any. Not when I'm right. Never. Justice would always prevail, the good guys would always win, or so I thought. Unfortunately, all that went out the window along with the last John Wayne movie. Ahhh, The Duke! If he was still around today, he'd be enraged by the lack of integrity that has devoured the spirit of his country.

A prime example of this lack of integrity is the U.S. Postal Service. If you're like me, and can't put up with constant, unprovoked, unwarranted abuse, you'll never cut it working for the P.O. Don't even bother taking the exam. It's not worth all the anguish. Believe me, I know!

Management constantly broke my shoes because I openly expressed my opinions. Rat-a-tat-tat – disciplinary letters-of-warning poured into my personnel file. I fought every single one of these bogus reprimands through the grievance procedure or by claiming discrimination to E.E.O. And I won every time. But still, the letters kept coming. Even after I was awarded an accommodation letter for being the only carrier to show up when a tropical storm ripped through south Florida, they still harped on me. The award meant nothing. What mattered to them was that I kept on fighting for my rights, and nothing more. They were hell bent on making an example out of me for rocking their leaky boat. Boy, did I make that old tub pitch and roll, but nobody else would.

Most of the carriers I worked with, male and female, were afraid to fight. Gutless is the way I saw them, constantly backing down from management. Always doing more than the union contract required for fear of being suspended without pay. But they loved to see me lose it, because when I fought for myself, I was also doing battle for them.

Eventually I got sick and tired of all the fighting, stress, anger and hate. And one morning, after four years of martyrdom, I took what would be my last stand, out on the loading dock.

It was mid-January and, as always, the snowbirds had flocked to their South Florida enclaves for the season. My route was part of that row of towering upscale condos that block the ocean view as well as beach access for everybody else along 'Lauderdale by the Sea'. The mail volume on my route, City Route #19, quadrupled in season. All the winter people had their mail forwarded from wherever they had come from. Well, talk about mail! Every last one of these beautiful people amassed half a forest worth of paper by season's end. If they had saved all the mail they received during the four months, they roosted in Florida, each snowbird could have cram-filled a Dempsey Dumpster. Home town newspapers, Wall Street Journal's, Barron's, magazines, letters, junk mail, packages, annual reports and, of course, their endless streams of misbegotten dividend checks. I had it all on that ill-fated Monday morning.

It wasn't the first time that Sinko, a 204-B (supervisor in training), his ever-present Masonite clipboard in hand, counted my mail as I humped it from the loading dock to my jeep. No little guy, Sinko was about six-two and two-sixty. Loose flesh sagged from his chins, as well as the gut that obscured his belt, but still, he was a powerful man. His sleeves, always rolled above his elbows for effect, exposed two beefy forearms and impossibly thick wrists. His chest was thick also and he had shoulders wide as a door. One of those naturally large-muscled men who their entire lives like to throw their size around, that coarse, obnoxious type that, because of their size, never see any need for diplomacy or politeness.

Once again he tried it with me that Monday. As if I was dirt, he snarled, "Cassidy, you need to be back by four o'clock. Don't want no overtime today."

"Whooooah, hold on. You better check your arithmetic. I've got about twenty-seven feet of mail here, that works out to somewhere around ten and a half hours."

"Sorry, pal," he said in his taunting, merry way. "We gotta cut down on OT. Just be back by four or you know what'll happen." He pulled his disproportionately small mouth into a curly belligerent smile and leaned his ruddy mug right back into my face. It wasn't the first time that he'd gotten close enough with his corn-kernel teeth so that I could smell his foul rhino-breath.

I stepped back, for a breath of fresh air, not because he intimidated me. That was when it dawned on me that I'd better check him out. "How many feet of mail you got me down for, there, boss?" I asked, drenching the last word with cynicism as I leaned toward his clipboard. His handwriting was as ugly as his face, illegible as a doctor's scribble.

"Hey, don't strain your eyes. Let me help you here, Sparky," he said, jamming his fraudulent documentation to my face so close I could barely read it. It was blurry but I just could make out what it said next to route 19 and my name. Just as I suspected, he had falsified my mail count. He'd written down nineteen feet, shorting me credit for eight, disallowing a full third of the delivery time I was entitled to. Seeing this now, right in my face, my demeanor swung from perturbed to livid in a nanosecond.

I smacked his goddam clipboard away from my face, sending it airborne. All his papers dispersed mid-flight, floating to the ground like so many 8 1/2 x 11 yellow autumn leaves.

Now, I hadn't locked asses with anyone since I was twenty-two years old, but I knew that was exactly where this was heading. For four years I'd taken their bullshit, fought paper with paper. Now I'd had it. I was sick of it all. I felt my hands take on an adrenaline tremble. My voice betrayed me too. It strained and cracked when I spoke, just like it had when I was a kid back on the block, during the heated exchange of words before a fight. My fists balled at my sides, trying hard to squeeze the shake out of them, I leaned into Sinko's big face.

"Look, m-mutha f-f-fucka ... " I was so hot that my diction (splintered as it was) returned from the streets of Queens. You can take the boy out of the city, but ... blah, blah, blah. Although I'll never completely shake my accent, it had diluted somewhat over the years. I'd been making a concentrated effort to roll my r's. Freak that shit now! " ... YOU DINK THIS IS SOME KIND A FFFUCKIN' GAME AW WHAT, SINKO? I GOT A WIFE AND KIDS TO SSSUPPAUGHT. WHO DA FUCK YOU DINK YAW SETTIN' UP HEAH?"

My furious bellows bounced back and forth off the loading dock's three surrounding block walls like jai alai balls at a fronton.

"Keep your voice down, Cassidy," Sinko snarled, "or I'll drag your ass into the old man's office right now."

"YOU AIN'T DRAGGIN' NOBODY, ASSHOLE!"

I'd had it. Thirty-three years old or not, there's some crap that can be settled only one way. I shoved the bastard hard as I could with the heels of my hands. More like two synchronized snappy jabs than a push.

Sinko stumbled back a few feet, regaining his balance just as one of the big steel doors nudged open a bit. It was Anton Ford, another suck-up 204B. He stuck just his head out to see what all the commotion was about.

I spun back at Sinko just in time to see him telegraph a right roundhouse at my head. Powerful maybe, but slow as hell. I parried the punch with my left and quickly rotated my torso, putting all I could muster, shoulder and all, behind a damned good right cross. That punch was propelled by four years of abuse, frustration and anger. I nailed him hard on the left temple, so hard there was a sickening thump like a ball bat smashing a gourd.

The fat man went down, like right now, as if somebody on horseback had lassoed his ankles mid-gallop.

Then, Ford came running over, screeching and hollering like his usual bad-assed self. But, as quick as he started, he shit-canned his designs to brow-beat me. When he got close enough to see the rage still screaming from my eyes, he realized he'd really pushed his luck. And this time his luck had run out.

I went completely nutso on him, slamming him time and again with a flurry of quicker-than-the-eye rights and lefts. A blur of jabs and hooks that, had he had the time to think about it, he never would have dreamed some honky was capable of. Swear to God, when he went down, he landed right on top of Sinko who was still out cold. It was then that I realized the severity of my actions. Right or wrong, I knew I was in deep shit. I panicked, leapt off the dock and beat heels across the parking lot to my van.

But there was no running from this. As each minute ticked by, I grew more panicky. I knew I was a lot of things but a fugitive was not one of them. An hour and twenty minutes later, I turned myself in to the Broward County Sheriff's Department.

For the next six weeks, I sweated the repercussions the postal

154

service might take. I'd committed a genuine, certifiable federal offense. They could have put me away for a long, long time. But they elected not to. They didn't prosecute. And I knew exactly why they didn't. Because of the unwanted publicity such a decision would surely generate. Publicity, plus the fact that if I had to fight this thing, they knew I'd come back with both barrels blasting. Shoot, I had plenty of ammunition. They knew I'd kept notes, documentation, on scraps of paper. Dates, times, names and particulars of all the innumerable harassment episodes they had put me through. To this day I resent not going after them legally before I'd reached my breaking point. Not that I'm in any way sorry for decking those antagonists, that was very satisfying, but had I sought legal revenge, I just might have collected some serious compensation for all they had put me through. But there's no use in thinking about that now. Besides, if it happened all over again, even though I'm now forty-seven, I'd probably handle it the same way.

Ultimately, the postal service fired me. That was all they did. But, for all those weeks, I sure sweated. Only one thing, no, two things, that happened during this period made me feel I had any chance of getting off the hook. The two post office shootings. Yup, twice during those six weeks, there were post office killings in two different states - Arizona and New Jersey, I think. Regardless, in both cases, a distraught postal worker opened fire on his supervisors. When the smoke cleared, three people were dead. Though I didn't condone what they did, I knew firsthand what had driven those workers to such desperate measures.

Of course Maddy stood by me through the whole ordeal, constantly reassuring me (though she really didn't know) that everything would turn out OK. That time in a federal pen was highly unlikely. She backed me on everything I did, always cushioning the predicaments I got myself into with her indefatigable optimism. She helped soften all my problems except my hidden dark secret. Oh, she knew about Theresa, of course. When we were dating, I told Maddy all about our relationship. But, in the ensuing years, she had no idea just how strong my feelings remained for that phantom girl, how often I thought of her, how I still yearned for her. I felt awfully guilty about that, but awfully incomplete without Theresa also. She just wouldn't go away. Sure, as the years passed, I got caught up in the demands of everyday life and thought of Theresa Wayman maybe a tad less often. But that heavy sense of loss, and the intensity of my longings for her, never diminished. I felt like an adulterer even though over all those years I'd managed to never once cheat on Maddy Frances. I fought off more than a few opportunities for what some might view as recreational sex, non-committal flings where the participants rationalize that none of the unknowing parties will be hurt by what they don't know.

Over the years, I met my fair-share of flirtatious women, acquaintances as well as co-workers. During those periods when I was in sales, I even had some customers come on to me. Several ladies actually followed up the sale we'd consummated with a card, or a note of thanks, for helping them. Riiiiight! Although they had surely noticed my wedding band, those thank yous always included the sender's phone number. A few of them went so far as to call me at work. One told me, "I just wanted to tell you the bed I bought from you last month is well broken-in now and verrry comfortable. As a matter of fact, I'm in it right now!" And then there were the passes made by female co-workers, most of the time subtle invites to lunch or for happy hour drinks. But I always refrained. Each time I backed away, gently. Who knows, maybe I actually learned something that ill-fated night back in 1968. Maybe when I walked out that squalid room in the Flushing Projects something positive actually came with me.

That doesn't mean remaining monogamous was always easy. I know! I don't want to start any gender wars here, but a man is a different animal than a woman. Mother Nature must be one staunch feminist because she's damned men with a ceaseless desire to screw everything that walks. The urge may quell somewhat with age, but if you keep yourself in reasonably good shape that instinctive drive never completely dies. Some people feel it's outright unnatural to fight off such urges but our society trains males, from their crib days on, that one partner is all you get. And, difficult as it was, my conscience remained congruent with that ingrained belief. For more than two decades my record remained unblemished.

But the biggest test imaginable was yet to come.

Chapter 22

"What do you want to be when you grow up?" is a question usually posed to children. But until I crossed, ever so warily, that gloomy entrance to middle-agedness, that threshold with no welcome mat, I hadn't a clue as to what I wanted to do with my directionless life. Nothing I was qualified for interested me. My favorite aphorism was 'I'm too serious about living to be too serious about work'. I thought I'd always feel that way. But about the time I began reading at arm's length, and needed to spring for my first pair of reading glasses (four bucks at a Pompano flea market), it became crystal clear what I wanted to do with my life, whatever was left of it anyway. I wanted to write.

I finally realized that the creative well within me, no matter how shallow it might be, was the reason I never held a job for long. As necessary as the act is, soulless work ruins the best part of a man. It's an unconscionable waste of time. And that's why I never stuck with anything that my heart wasn't into. Always I was looking for something with substance. I needed everything or nothing at all. I had now come to realize that selling furniture, laying water mains, and everything else I'd sold the best part of my life for, had done nothing to satisfy my romantic or creative side.

I don't recall exactly when, but somewhere along the way, my intellect (limited as it may be) matured somewhat. My reading interests finally transcended the sports pages. I got into books; the real stuff, writings that brought to light the big picture. I started reading fiction, non-fiction, bios, whatever. It was on the pages of novels, supposed fiction, that I found the most truth about what is most important: the human condition. The older I got, the more I read. The more I read, the harder it became to find another good book, one that would hold my attention for more than just a few pages. I started thinking, *hey, I can do this, I can do better than this. What could be so difficult?*

Then I found out.

For two years I stared at the same blank page of a Spiral notebook. Two years! I couldn't come up with word one. But I did read a lot about writing. Anything and everything I could get my hands on about the trade, I consumed with a passion. Passion? Me? Hrmmph! That was one long-lost emotion. This writing thing was something I thought I might really get into if only I could get started. But month after depressing month, I sat in my recliner, red notebook in lap, writing nothing. For the life of me, I couldn't understand why nothing would come. I know now. I simply wasn't ready. And deep inside my agonizing brain, just beyond my consciousness, something told me that. There were still basics to be learned before I could begin putting meaningful, interesting ideas on paper. Eventually, after feeling I had reasonably educated myself, I did put my well-chewed Bic to that curled and coffee-stained first page.

Just three chapters into the first draft, I decided on a title for my novel - 'Look What They've Done to Our Dream'.

As I continued to transfer the story from my head onto paper, I'd sometimes fantasized about the book becoming a tremendous success. Sure, I knew how minute my odds were in an industry as hyper-competitive as publishing. I knew my dreams were probably mental-masturbation. But still, I couldn't help musing that 'Look What They've Done To Our Dream' might actually sell, that my story might wake the sleeping masses, enlighten them, wake up the ninety-seven percent of Americans who were still asleep. Maybe even kick-start an eleventh-hour movement to save an America that had been all but trashed by the insatiable greed of the privileged few, the despicable ones, the handful that control big-business and politics, those 'profiticians'. I wanted everyday people to realize that 'The Dream' had become just that, and to see how close to the end of the 'Freedom Trail' we actually were.

I would tell readers how my protagonist, Billy Soles, a forty-nine-year-old power company lineman, had been beat up by an increasingly corrupt and uncivil American system. On the first line of the very first page, Billy would grab readers by saying, "I might still live in the same house on the same street as I did twenty-five years ago, but I sure as hell don't live in the same country." That would get their attention right off the starting block. Then Billy would go on to tell how, " A rich man's heaven is a working man's hell." He'd point out how, beginning around 1970, he watched the American culture and lifestyle decline. How the price of milk had risen from twenty-three cents a quart for the first time in his memory. How the cost of a cheap car quintupled from three grand to fifteen thou in just twenty short years. How a half-empty box of breakfast cereal skyrocketed from thirty nine cents to as much as four and five bucks during the same period. Bobby Soles was going to tell all about synthetic corporate inflation and how Wall Street cashed in on it while he watched his buying power and benefits steadily dwindle. I hoped that 'Look What They've Done to Our Dream' would ever so graphically illustrate how big government and big business have ravaged the souls and lives of the entire working class, how millions and millions of women, children and men like Bobby Soles had been financially and, in turn, spiritually assassinated.

Once I got the story going, my emotions and convictions spilled with the ink onto all those empty pages. For thirteen months, word by word, chapter after chapter, I plowed ahead. I wrote whenever I could, before and after work, on weekends, during lunch breaks. While driving in my van or scarfing down a meal, I'd compose scenes, watching them play out on my mind's screen. The story was coming effortlessly now because I was writing about the increasingly hard times Maddy Frances and I, along with all the other working beasts, had lived through for the past twenty years. Of course Billy Soles, my story's hero, was my own alter-ego.

There were times when I thought the story was no less than great. Other times I'd figure, *who the hell am I kidding, this is shit.* But Maddy's unrelenting enthusiasm and encouragement always kept me moving ahead. Well, almost always.

When I was about two-thirds finished with the first draft, I hit a wall. I didn't nudge it, I flat slammed into it. As if the jolt had knocked me unconscious, I just shut down. Literally overnight, my creative juices dried up. I already knew the ending but didn't know how to get to it. Nothing could help me advance it. I tried everything I could think of to get over, under, or around that wall. The harder I tried, the more confused I became. I was helpless. For a full two weeks, I failed to produce a thing. Another of my life's few passions had deserted me. I felt myself slipping deeper and deeper into a spirit-zapping black depression. My moods grew more and more foul. I actually became afraid, afraid of myself, and with good reason. Then, one ill-fated day, I hit bottom.

Maddy Frances had already gone off to work, and the kids to

school, when I decided I'd dial-a-day. Hoping that a freebie day off might help my creative slump and my funk, I called in sick to Searcy's Furniture World where I was under-employed at the time. But two cups of coffee and two cigarettes later, I could see nothing was going to change. Slouched in the recliner with my pen and notebook, and a bad case of the black ass once again, all I could do was stare out the glass sliders and daydream.

After a while I started tracking a band of mean storm clouds that were quickly eating up the blue sky as they billowed high and ominous toward the house. Soon the dark clouds fused into one, and the entire sky was shrouded in a deep-purple blanket. It grew impossibly dark outside. The grumbling thunder grew louder. A fierce wind came up and began assaulting the big Poinciana in our little backyard. Birds fled as the tree's hulking limbs rocked and groaned. Smaller branches danced to a more frantic beat and the tiny leaves of the Poinciana shimmered in the sudden gale-force wind.

I became mesmerized by this apocalyptical scene. Kind of like the way you get when you're in the dentist's waiting room. With nowhere to run, nowhere to hide, you just sit there resignedly, trying to concentrate on the calm, fifty-gallon world of aquarium fish.

I sat like that in the living room for a long time, sulking. Just like the weather, my state of mind grew gloomier and gloomier. I began reflecting on my past life again. Since my fortieth birthday a few years prior, I'd been catching myself looking back more frequently. It seemed every time I got down I looked back for solace. But all I ever found there was that same old, heart-wrenching sense of loss. I also questioned everything in my life - my relationship with Maddy and the kids, the daily mundane and hopeless struggle for dollars, my own seemingly senseless, bland existence. Then I started playing that mortality numbers game again.

Damn, I thought, I can't believe I'm older now than Dad was when he died. My life is more than half over unless, God forbid, I live to eighty-four. Could I really have been with Maddy almost nineteen years now? Jesus, where did they go?

Each new dismal thought crowded out the last, two thoughts inside my head concurrently, till one eventually overshadowed and outlived the other. Fragments of unhealthy contemplation slipped in and out of my consciousness.

What happened, I asked myself, to those sweet simple days of youth? Lord, how I ached for that period of my life when in every sense I was closest to being alive. I missed like a lover, like Theresa, how it was before entering this spirit-strangling state they call adulthood. I missed how it was before spontaneity seceded to villains such as judiciousness and responsibility, before the sweet, sweet music that Theresa and I had danced to died. How long had it been now? Twenty-something years? Nooo, it couldn't be!

But it was.

Christ, why is everything so complicated now? Nothing is easy. Everything is so burdened by that R-word, responsibility. I was beginning to understand how menopausal men sometimes just chuck it all and take off, leave everything behind, cross that proverbial fence, test those different grasses on the other side while they're still able to, go for the adventure before it's too late. And maybe, just possibly, recapture a glimmer of youth past.

From my easy chair, I fought this cerebral battle for about three hours. Then I was worn. My mind drained, tainted now with sorrow, I admitted to myself this once again would be no day for writing. I'd squandered the whole morning, shot it in the ass, come up with nothing, nothing positive anyway, just debilitating sentiments about the glory days and a dreadful perception of what lay ahead for me. This depression had smothered me. It was more than just another of my bad moods. I'm talking wicked, vile, ain't now escapin' it, panic-inducing depression. I really needed help with this one. So I dragged myself into my van and headed for the Circle K. It was horrendous out but I absolutely needed a six pack. For the full six blocks, nose to the wheel, headlights beaming high, I pushed through the blinding, driving rain. Mean-assed zillion-volt bolts of lightning snapped all around me, lighting up this otherwise impossibly-dark daytime world.

Wanting to make the trip worthwhile, I bought a sixer of 'tall boys'. For sure that would anesthetize my hurting spirit.

By the time I got back from the convenience store, the blinding rainstorm had moved on, the lightening had quit, and the thunder had reduced to a benign, distant rumble. I eased the van into the garage like I'd done countless times before when I was alone. You see, the only

161

cassette player we owned was in the van's dash. All we had in the house was the old stereo Maddy and I bought when we were first married. Just a turntable. It only played records. That's why I had to sit in the van every time I wanted to reminisce with my Supreme's tape.

Those old songs always brought Theresa back more vividly. They helped excavate memories buried in my psyche, forgotten places, happenings, and visions of Theresa Wayman. The sixer of 'Old Millwater' helped too. It helped me recapture her image by clearing all the shit from my mind.

From inside the garage I closed the overhead door so we could be alone. This was mine and Theresa's time together, and I didn't want any neighbors detracting from it. Anyway, if they saw me, they'd think I was crazy sitting in a van inside a god-awful hot garage for a couple of hours. Even if they knew what I was doing, they'd never understand. For nobody, no matter how empathetic, can truly feel someone else's hurt. And that's just as well.

I went into the house, put four beers in the refrigerator, turned the A/C setting down real low, and opened the kitchen-to-garage door. I stood our plastic floor fan in the threshold, carefully aiming it into the garage so it would send a cool breeze into the van's open door a few feet away.

I mounted the worn, torn driver's seat, turned the key to accessory, switched on the tape player and filled the Caravan with music. I lowered the volume a hair, popped open the first half-quart and fired up a Carlton. I took a good long hit, let my tight shoulders fall against the seat's backrest, then exhaled the smoke with a sigh. I tried to relax, let my mind do its work. The lyrics of 'Someday We'll Be Together' stabbed at my soul and my eyes soon welled up. God, where can she be? I wondered for the thousandth time if I'd ever see her again. Lord, my heart felt so hollow.

I had long ago disciplined myself to wait till after my second beer before retrieving my keepsakes. Yyyyup! I'd held onto them for all those years. The tiny snapshot. The fragile ankle bracelet I'd given Theresa. The sterling silver ID she'd given me. Over the years I'd stashed them together in various places in the four different houses and apartments Maddy Frances and I had lived in. She never found them. I hid them well, always in spots that were easily accessible, places that could at

162

times be somewhat private, like a garage or our bedroom. Yeah, I know. You don't have to tell me. I'm not proud of it. But ever since we bought our third-hand van four years earlier, I'd been hiding them in it. It was safer than in the house. I'd buried them beneath the carpeting where it curled out from beneath the plastic molding by the driver's seat. Who'd ever look there?

Sliding my arm underneath the carpet now, way back there, past my elbow, I retrieved them. I laid them out gently, neatly, on the passenger seat. I straightened them a little more, then went inside to get my reading glasses and two more cold ones.

When I climbed back into the van, I popped one of the beers and took a long draw. Feeling like an adulterer once again, I put on my glasses. Lovingly I picked up the tiny black and white photo first. I could see us clearly now; Theresa and I, cheek-to-cheek, both of us wearing bubbly, youthful smiles, carefree loving smiles. I noticed my cracked front teeth that had long since been capped and the fresh gloss on Theresa's kissable young lips. Young ... we sure were that. Smooth foreheads, me with lots of hair, both of us with bright eyes, eyes lit with hope for a future together that would never materialize. Theresa's perfectly symmetrical small face appeared even smaller amidst her flowing black hair. My own face beamed like it never has since.

Diana and company's melodious lyrics filled the cement block, one-car garage, 'Some Dayyy ... we'll be tog-e, e-e-e-ther'.

As I looked at the picture, studying every detail, a tear splashed on the back of my hand. I watched it spread. With my glasses now on, I noticed the thousand hair-thin tiny creases on my skin. Shaking my head, I muttered to myself, "These sure as hell weren't there the night we took this picture!" Then my eyes returned to the picture. I saw many other changes, none of them good. My hair was much thicker then, and, of course, there was no gray around my temples. It swooped down over my forehead to my eyebrows where there was no sign of the two deep vertical frown lines embedded there now. Though my forehead was obscured in the picture, I knew the lines had not yet begun to set. I looked at them in the rearview mirror, three wide, horizontal fissures. Then I dropped my eyes and felt around the back of my head with my fingertips. All too easily I found that small, but malignant hairless spot.

Finally finished beating myself up, I looked at Theresa's image a second time, caressed it with my eyes. *She'd be forty-one now. Does she too have frown lines or crow's feet? Is she still beautiful or has she gotten sloppy and riddled with cellulite. Nah, not Theresa. She's gotta still be slim. She's not the type to let herself go. Too much pride for that. She's probably just like Maddy, in terrific shape if you don't count the few extra pounds on her hips and keister.* There I was, after all this time, still measuring Maddy against Theresa. I wondered if, despite how we ended, she still treasured memories of me, like I did of her. *I'm being an idiot*, I thought. The whole thing was probably just a year-long learning experience as far as she's concerned, a mistake and nothing more.

Ceremoniously, I laid the picture back on the seat then picked up the ID bracelet. It seemed much thicker and heavier when I was a skinny eighteen-year-old kid. I ran a finger pensively across the Florentine-finished face, then turned it over and read the inscription: *To Dean, all my love always, Theresa – 5/5/67.*

I put it back on the seat and picked up the ankle bracelet. Holding the fragile gold chain in my palms as though it were sacred, I studied it for a moment. Then I brought it to my face. I held it there awhile and it became wet with my tears. I rolled my eyes up to the drooping headliner above, squeezed them shut and let out a long, weary moan.

It was at this moment, that I made a long-overdue self-confession. I admitted that I could never again be truly happy, that all hope of even a semblance of a happy future was gone. All I had left was my memories, happy memories that now saddened me. I decided there was only one solution.

The afternoon sun had intensified, making it a hell of a lot hotter in the garage, almost unbearable. I was sweating beer almost as fast as I could swallow it. But the music played on, 'You just have to wait ... love don't come easy ... it's a game of give and take ... ' My lips quivered and I broke into a hard cry. Eyes glazed, shoulders lurching, I picked up my ID again. After fumbling with the clasps, I eventually managed to fasten the bracelet around my sweaty wrist. I held my hand out, fingers spread in the stop position, to assess it. Through my tears I saw even more gray hairs on my wrist than were there the last time I'd done this, maybe two months before. I gulped down what was left of my fourth beer. That was when the situation took a sinister turn.

I went back into the kitchen, grabbed the last two half-quarts, yanked the fan's plug from the outlet, moved it away from the threshold and slammed the door closed behind me. Back in the van, I wiped the sweat from my forehead, smeared the tears across my face and drew a deep breath. Then I started the engine.

It wasn't long before I became drowsy. I didn't know if it was the beer kicking in, or the carbon monoxide, or both. I kept on drinking.

In the past, even during my blackest depressions, when I'd had suicidal thoughts, I was usually able to shake them in their early stages. But a few times the thoughts lingered long enough for me to come to a conclusion if I ever did want to check out this would be the way I'd do it, fall asleep drunk and asphyxiate myself. And now I'd had it. I truly believed the best of my life was behind me, way behind me, with nothing worthwhile ahead. Yeah, I had Maddy, and she'd been wonderful, but our love had been sublime--deep and enduring, but slow and steady. I needed more. I needed rockets, fireworks, passion. But despite these voids, I was never able to up and leave her and the kids to search the country for someone I had loved before them. I might have been self-centered, hedonistic and over-impulsive, but I would never risk losing my family for somebody who, if I found her, would in all probability look at me like I was loony. Someone who, if she ever thought about it at all, most likely viewed our teenage romance as merely a crush, nothing more than puppy-love. Surely by now Theresa had a different last name, and a husband, and kids she loved deeply.

There was no going back in time and I no longer wanted to move ahead. So the only option that made any sense was to leave.

By the time I finished the sixth beer, my eyes were burning and their lids had grown incredibly heavy. The engine still running, everything had gone fuzzy and I began to feel like I was floating, like my soul had left its shell of a body, like it was drifting, levitating toward the sun. In my mind's eye I watched the roof of the house shrink along with the rest of the neighborhood as I rose skyward. The oppressive heat intensified as I soared higher and higher toward the stark-white, blazing subtropical sun. Then everything went black.

Chapter 23

By all rights I should have died. But, just like my mother's first suicide attempt in that closet and another one fourteen years later - and the vast majority of all attempted suicides - mine failed. It failed because I bungled it. Drunk as I was when I decided to end it all, I overlooked one small detail: there was only an eighth of a tank of gas in the van. My scheme had literally run out of gas. I don't know how many minutes, or seconds, or gallons I was from death, but I doubt it was many.

God only knows how long I'd been unconscious when my brain picked up a faint signal, a very weak sensation. Though my shoulder was being jostled vigorously, it only felt like a series of ever-so-slight nudges. Then I heard something, a frantic voice way off in the distance. Distant whispers. But gradually those whispers grew to screams. Fear-filled desperate screams. The Supremes returned too, singing louder and louder. The voice was familiar. Not Diana's, the first one I'd heard, Maddy Frances's voice. She was in a panic, shaking me, shrieking desperately, "OH MY GOD! NO! DEAN, DEEEEAAANNN! JESUS, NO! HONEY, COME BACK! CHRIST, NOOOOO!"

Slowly, ever so slowly, my eyelids parted, two light-blinded slashes above my cheeks. My throat was desert-dry but my clothes were drenched with perspiration. My tank top and shorts clung to my body like wet newspaper. So relieved that I had come back, Maddy, still in her work clothes, leapt on top of me and threw her arms around my soggy neck. She held my head tight against her chest.

"Ohhh, Dean, what's wrong honey? Are you alright? Why'd you do this?"

Before I could answer, her grip on me loosened, she leaned away and lovingly wiped the sweaty strings of hair back from my forehead. Then, holding my pitiful face in her hands, looking at me so adoringly, she asked in a calmer voice, "What's wrong honey? Why in God's name would you try something like this? Is it me, Dean?"

Of course she'd had no problem figuring out what I'd been up to. The garage wreaked of emissions, all the idiot lights on the dash were still lit red, my body was soaked, there were beer cans strewn all over the floorboard, I looked like I'd been on a round trip to hell, and the music was still blasting. Somewhat calmer now, yet still visibly disturbed, Maddy reached over me and the steering wheel and shut off the tape. Then she froze in that position, stretched across my slumped, limp, worthless body. Even in the condition I was in, I knew something was wrong. Then it dawned on me.

She'd seen the picture, face down, on the passenger seat. "What's this?" she asked quizzically, picking it up, turning it around. "What's ... who ... who's this?" Then it hit her., hard, square in the solar plexus. It knocked the wind right out of her. All the color left her face. She'd turned sheet-white. She was devastated. It was as if I, her, everything, the person she lived for, had thrust a hand inside her chest and yanked out her pumping heart. Her voice trailed off as she continued, "Ohhh, Deaann, don't tell me ... It's that girl ... that ... that Theresa, isn't it?"

Despite my grogginess, I realized the awful significance of this situation. I tried to make the first part of my explanation more convincing than was possible when I said, "Maddy ... that was a long time ago, before I met you...years before I met you. I told you how crushed I was back then. But that's not why I did this, honey." With that over, the rest was easier because it was true. "It's just that life was so much simpler back then. Wasn't it the same for you ... when you were a teenager, before all the hard times we've had to scratch, kick, and fight through? Hell, Maddy, if it weren't for the hard times, you and I wouldn't have had any times at all. You know what I mean. All the times I've been out of work, us always driving around in beat-up cars-- struggling to keep them on the road, the never-ending repairs, keeping the kids in clothes. Not even being able afford to get our fuckin' teeth fixed properly. I'm sorry. I shouldn't talk like that ... but look how long we've put off getting that cap you need."

I paused, took a deep breath, rubbed my temples, then looked this way and that evaluating the unpainted block walls surrounding us. "Even with both of us working, it's been a battle, busting ours month after month, for what? Just to make the mortgage payments on this old salt box is why. Shit! The American Dream! We're here, what, close to ten years? Ten years and the goddamn bank still owns three-fourths of it. Stay in it thirty years ... miss just the very last payment and guess what ... they can legally take it from you, doesn't matter that we would have paid twice the price of the house in interest alone. They could and would take it. Don't pay the sky-high taxes and big brother takes it away. On top of all that, now we need a new roof. Three thousand bucks! It might as well be a million. And how 'bout all those times we had to get cash advances on the credit cards, just to get by? That interest is eating us alive. All that and now I can't even write anymore. The one thing left in life that I really enjoy doing, can escape to, and now it seems like I've lost that too."

I took another long, deep breath, but again seemed to get little oxygen. Glancing into the rear-view, I noticed that Maddy had opened the garage door. I turned back to her hurt-filled green eyes, put my hands on hers, and went on, "I love you Maddy ... you know that. It's just that ... life ... for me, has become too difficult ... too demanding. I'm tired of getting beat up, honey."

With the white's of her eyes all pink and misty now, valiantly fighting back new tears, she said, "I can understand all that ... almost all of it, but what about this picture?" She leaned across me, put it back on the seat, face down. "I've tried so hard to make you happy, Dean."

My shameful eyes fell between my feet to the floorboard. Theresa's ankle bracelet laid there. I had dropped it when I blacked out. Stealthily, with my right foot, I brushed it beneath the seat. This sneaky act completed, I looked back up at Maddy. Seeing the painful disappointment, no, the heartbreak on her innocent face, I truly wished I had finished myself off. I wished it even more when she touched the bracelet on my wrist and said in a defeated tone, "And what is this, Dean?"

I felt like she'd just caught Theresa and me in bed.

"Nothing, it's stupid, just something she gave me. Maddy ... it was more than twenty years ago. Like I told you before, we were just kids. I love you, Maddy."

Then, though I hated myself for it, I lied a second time, "These things are just silly sentimental memories from another life!"

She was trying to believe all this but I knew deep inside she couldn't. Not totally, anyway. You don't live with someone for as long as she had, particularly with a lousy liar like myself, and not be able to discriminate the truth from bullshit. But still, as always, Maddy Frances let me off the hook. Though she was willing to endure this heavy heartache, I knew from that moment on she would have to live with another dead spot in her heart, a spot alongside the existing scar, the one she suffered when the kids were small, when she arbitrarily had to relinquish her God-given-right of motherhood for a lousy pay check.

Maddy helped me into the house still disoriented from the beer and toxic fumes. Once again she supported me, this time with her arms tight around my waist. I remember thinking, as we stepped onto the kitchen linoleum, what a lucky fluke it was that the kids hadn't been there for this horror show. Dawn had gone to a friend's birthday party after school and Trevor to baseball practice. Thank God they would never find out that their seemingly sturdy, philosophical father had been so weakened by life, that he'd sunk so deep into the black eerie depths of despair. Thankfully, I suppose, only Maddy and I would bear the weight of this dark secret.

After the ordeal, I began living life more tentatively, day by day, one step at a time, one depression at a time. I'd have to make a concentrated effort to handle whatever fate slung my way. No longer certain of my own emotions, how I would handle them, what they might lead me to, I forged ahead best I could.

The one and only time Maddy ever mentioned my suicide attempt again was the day after it occurred, when she made me promise never to try such a thing again. "Leave me if you have to, Dean," she pleaded. "I could almost handle that. Go away from me ... from our life together ... for a week or two, if it'll help. Find out what you want. Leave me for good if that's what you really want. But, please ... don't ever try to hurt yourself again. If anything ever happened to you, I wouldn't be able to go on. I wouldn't want to."

I swore up and down I'd never again try such a stupid thing, though deep down inside I wasn't all that sure. Now knowing that I had the capacity for such a thing scared the hell out of me when I thought about it. So I tried not to. Nothing is more frightening than fearing oneself. As for Maddy, she would remain true-to-form, always keeping her immense pain and dejection inside. But it had to be devastating to her, knowing that her husband, the man she lived for, had tried to end their life together, knowing there was always the possibility of a repeat performance and that she would probably always share his love with another woman. But I could only imagine how these things tore at her

169

because Maddy Frances exiled them all deep inside her heart.

As time went on, I'd sometimes try in some small way to make up for what I'd done to my wife. But each time Maddy would give me this look, a perturbed look. Like, *please don't patronize me, Dean. Let's get on with our life together. I'm trying to bury this thing.*

And I'd back off.

Chapter 24

In the weeks following the garage incident, I forged on, going to work at Searcy's, putting all my free time into my novel.

Yes, I was writing again. Just two days after I tried to (it's still hard to say) kill myself, the wall that had been blocking my writing simply collapsed. I wrote faster than a homesick stenographer on overtime. The words came so quickly my right hand could barely keep pace with my brain. In just two months, I finished the first draft of 'Look What They've Done To Our Dream'. With a year and change wrapped up in it, I was both relieved and sad to have finished. But, there was still work to be done. The next step was the long, arduous task of typing the story, almost three handwritten spiral notebooks, into my garage sale computer. Of course, after setting it up on cinder blocks and wooden planks in a corner of the living room, the printer wouldn't work right, so we had to go out and spring for a new one. The son of a gun set us back more than we'd paid for the whole damn shooting match. Maddy and I both hated like hell to put it on plastic, but knowing how important it was to me, she insisted.

With the system back in operation, I was hunting and pecking every chance I got. On weekends, when she had a little down time, Maddy would tap the keys for a couple of hours. As well as she could type, making headway was a slow, tedious process. Her and I both had an awful time deciphering my horrendous penmanship. Nevertheless, we eventually did get it all into the computer. And, when we printed out the draft, it almost looked professional. I said 'looked'. In a lot of places, as is expected, it sure didn't read that way. So I started all over again. From page one I began rearranging sentences, changing nouns and verbs, kicking out unneeded adverbs and adjectives, and correcting my spelling and punctuation. Then I did it a third time and, after that, one more before I was reasonably satisfied.

When I read some parts, I couldn't believe that I, Dean Cassidy, had written them. They were so eloquent, so convincing, so seemingly publishable. I remember Maddy remarking once, after I read her a passage, that it sounded like I'd read it from a real book. I told her, "I sure hope so," and we both had a well-deserved laugh. But, other parts of the story, no matter how many times and ways I revised them, remained, in my opinion, far from great. Again, I'm a pretty ruthless critic.

After polishing my work the best I could, I went about the business of trying to market it. First I sent query letters directly to publishers, three different batches at three different times. A few wanted to see the first three chapters, and one small press in Newark, New Jersey, actually asked to see the whole thing, but in the end they were all rejected. Then I sent a bunch of queries to literary agents. When their rejections started to pile up, I felt like chucking the whole thing. I didn't even want to check the mailbox anymore. But Maddy kept pushing me, insisting that 'Look What They've Done to Our Dream' was a terrific story. But with something like thirty-three rejections at that point, I lost all hope. Despite Maddy's encouragement, I knew what I'd read in more places than one was true, that a writer's spouse is almost always his or her kindest critic.

For four months those rejection letters came in as fast as the queries went out. Some were cold, impersonal form letters. Others didn't even waste paper on me. They just scribbled on top of the query I'd sent them (maybe not in these exact words but pretty damn close), "Thanks, but no thanks." I had all but given up, when that one positive response came from Jersey. They wanted to see the whole manuscript. But, after reading it, their interest waned and so did the last of my hopes. When I checked the mail one day and saw that big manila envelope stuffed inside the mailbox, I knew it was over. Although it was just another rejection, the editor was nice enough to include a polite personalized letter with the manuscript. It was kind of a consolation prize when in the letter he wrote, "Although you are obviously a very talented writer, Mr. Cassidy, we are afraid that your work isn't quite right for us at this time. I want to wish you the best of ..." Crushed as I was, his compliment made me feel a little better. But, it was too little too late, and I gave up on 'Look What They've Done To Our Dream'.

The only upside to the whole experience was that I handled all that bad news without putting another contract out on myself. Nevertheless, I was disgusted as all hell. I kept telling Maddy to forget it, it's no good. Fortunately, she didn't listen.

I was having a typically unremarkable Saturday afternoon at

Searcy's. It was maybe three o'clock when the office manager's blanched voice announced over the loudspeaker, "Mister Cassidy, line two ... Mister Cassidy, line two." When I picked up the phone and heard Maddy screaming, "Dean! Dean," it scared me to death. I thought I'd pop a rib or two the way my heart started bouncing, pounding, flipping around in there. Both my arms heated instantly with a flush of adrenaline, and the short hairs on the back of my neck stiffened like bristles. I thought, *oh shit, something's happened to one of the kids.* You see, Maddy was always, and I mean always, low key. That's her nature. I'm the excitable one. The way she was acting on the phone I thought for sure there had been some kind of family tragedy.

"What is it Maddy? What's wrong?" I pleaded, rushing the words out of my mouth so I'd get an answer faster.

Fighting to contain her excitement she said, "I just got a phone call from New York, from a publisher. She said she loved your story DEAN, SHE WANTS TO PUBLISH YOUR BOOK!"

I got instant chicken skin. Shit, this was better than Ed Mcmahon and his entire entourage, balloons and all, coming to the door with a giant check. Knocked for a loop, almost winded, I said,"No shit! What publisher? Nobody except that small house in Jersey even asked..."

"Yes they did, honey ... I'm sorry, but I didn't tell you. I was afraid you'd get more depressed if they shot it down. After that last rejection, I sent out a few more queries. I didn't tell you these people wanted to see the first three chapters because I didn't want you to get your hopes up. After they read them they wanted to see the rest. God, Dean, you have no idea how hard it was for me not to tell you. But, Dean, none of that matters anymore, this-lady-wants-you-to-call-her!"

"When? Right now?"

"Yes! Right now!" she said, her voice still hurried but suddenly choking with emotion. "She said she normally doesn't work Saturdays but that she had to do some things in her office today. She'll be there about another half hour."

My arms were still covered with those goose bumps and, hearing my wife now, this sure-to-be-canonized saint who had put up with my screwy antics for so long, crying with joy, brought tears to my own eyes. For a few moments we savored this positive news together. We basked together in the bright rays of happiness it brought, a level of happiness so pure (and alien) that I had to dilute it. Just a little, mind you. It's got to do with my pessimistic nature. I remember thinking *keep your guard up man. Good stuff like this just doesn't happen to people like you. This can't last, something's got to go wrong.* But the apprehension had a short life and I quickly got back into the moment with Maddy.

A few minutes later, after our feet were back on terra firma, we hung up and, with trembling fingers, I dialed the publisher's number. I'd been so excited when I scrawled it I could barely decipher it now. I wasn't sure if the twos were twos or sevens. Twice, mid-dial, I hit a wrong digit and had to hang up and try again. The third time, I got it right. The phone rang four times and, with each ring, my heart sunk a little deeper. Had she gone home already? God, I hoped not. The anticipation would kill me if I had to wait till Monday morning.

But I didn't. Someone picked up. "Olympus Books, Fran Danforth, may I help you?"

The words felt heavy and awkward coming from my mouth. "Hello ... er ... Ms. Danforth? This is Dean Cassidy returning your call."

"Yesss, Mister Cassidy, how do you do?"

"Fine, just fine, please ... call me Dean."

"Alright, Dean, if you'll call me Fran." Her voice was astute but not the least bit frosty, friendly in a kind of a semi-formal way. "As I explained to Mrs. Cassidy ... and, by the way ... she sounds like a lovely lady ..... "

"Oh thanks, she's got to be the best to put up with me."

Ms. Danforth chuckled once, then said, " ... well, as I told Mrs. Cassidy, we at Olympus would like to publish 'Look What They've Done To Our Dream'. Our selection committee feels the story is beautifully written, perfectly plotted and also timely. The characters are so convincing that they, as Mister Wainscot himself put it, 'leap off the pages and take you hostage.' We all feel that your voice is very, very strong, yet sensitive and intelligent. You've conveyed the theme meticulously, yet the narrative remains bipartisan. Your writing is terse and the dialogue is as good as any we've seen in some time. Dean, we would like to have you sign on with us. We would like to release your book early next spring, either March or April."

I said, "Everything sounds great so far." Purposely, I avoided saying too much, fearful that if I did, she might realize I'm not all that smart and possibly retract the offer. I knew this was a stupid thought and wondered why I did ignorant shit like that to myself. I was so excited I could see my heart pounding, no, dancing, beneath my shirt. I thought I might be having the big one right then and there.

"Terrific," Fran Danforth said, "because we are obviously very impressed with your work. So impressed that after reading your manuscript, we all wondered where a talent like yours has been hiding. You see, we are constantly on the lookout for promising new writers. It's a never-ending vigil in the publishing business. We scour the literary magazines, reading short stories, always hunting for new talent. And, every so often, we find a piece that we think is exceptional. When we do, we try to contact the writer to let him or her know we have an interest in their work. We encourage them to write a novel, and oftentimes they do and a marriage takes place. We have signed some of our top authors that way. But none of us recall ever have seeing any of your work or surely we would have contacted you."

"Well, to be honest with you Ms. Danforth ... I mean, Fran, 'Look What They've Done To Our Dream' is the first thing I've ever written. I've never done any short stories or anything. You see, when I got the idea for my story, I knew I wouldn't be able to tell it in just a few thousand words. I knew it had to be novel length."

"Well, no matter how many or how few your credentials, we at Olympus loved it, Dean, so much so that we would like to Fed Ex a contract to you first thing Monday morning." She paused a moment and I heard some papers being shuffled. Then she said, "I would like to give you a quick rundown, now, of what Olympus Books is willing to offer you ... if that's OK, if you have a minute or two."

"Sure ... sure, go ahead, Fran. I've got time." Like the rest of my life if that's what it takes ....

"OK. Good. First of all, Dean, we feel your story has better than mid-list potential, and we can assure you that if you opt to go with us, we will promote it. Now let me see here ... " There was another short pause and she hummed to fill it. "OK, here it is. I've been authorized to offer you fifteen percent of all royalties and ... ahhh ... an eight-thousand-dollar advance, which we would send to you as soon as we receive the signed contract back, if everything in it is to your liking of course. The stipulations are pretty standard but, if you'd like, by all means have an attorney look it over."

A minute later, after we'd hung up, I thought, *Myyy Goddd, an advance, too, e-i-g-h-t t-h-o-u-s-a-n-d d-o-l-l-a-r-s!*

Sure. I knew upfront money was often part of such deals, but this news all came so quickly. I had been so overwhelmed by the thought of getting published, that I hadn't had time during our conversation to even think about advances. All the good news had come so quickly. I was so happy, so authentically happy that for the second time in five minutes I was afraid something would go wrong and spoil it all. One of my father's pessimistic aphorisms passed through my head. If he ever taught me anything that turned out to be true it was "Don't ever, and I mean ever, count on anything until it's in your hand. Until you're holding it, you ain't got shit." All my life I'd calloused my most joyous occasions with this profound advice. And, luckily so, because many times over the years my father's way of negative thinking helped insulate me from major disappointments.

Despite my apprehension, this was one of my life's most exciting events, an experience that, for the first time in twenty-odd years, allowed me a few minutes of absolute happiness, that rarest strain of uncut bliss, a euphoria that I'd long before learned to revel in the few times fate happened to sprinkle it my way. God, I was ecstatic now. I couldn't wait to get home and see Maddy and the kids.

Of course, I called Maddy Frances back as soon as I'd hung up with Fran Danforth. I told her the contract was being sent out Monday, and that I'd be getting a fifteen percent royalty on every book sold. But I also attached a little white lie to this double-good news. Well, not really a lie, more like a sin of omission. Well, I guess it was both. I fibbed that I had customers waiting for me, that they were growing impatient, and I had to get off the phone when, in reality, I wanted to cut the conversation short so I could save the part about the advance until I got home. I felt a little greedy holding out on her, but I needed to experience firsthand Maddy's and the kids' reactions to this grand surprise. I just had to be there, had to see my wife's face light with joy. God knows, she deserved some genuine good news after putting up with my foul moods and depressions for so long.

Needless to say, the rest of the afternoon dragged. Every time I checked my Timex, I swore the hands had moved backwards. But eventually, six o'clock did lumber around, right on schedule, and I was out of there.

It was about twenty minutes later when I steered the van onto our oil and rust-mottled driveway. And, when I did, an alien expression commandeered my face. Uncontrollably, reflexively, my facial muscles pulled my mouth's corners in an unfamiliar direction, up, when I spotted the makeshift banner Maddy and the kids had tacked to our garage door. On an old sheet, yellowed by countless washings in our iron-ladened well-water, the big blue painted letters shouted: WAY TO GO DAD, WE KNEW YOU COULD DO IT! I was smiling alright, but at the same time I felt like bawling. It was a great feeling.

Just as I rolled to a stop, even before I could shift into park, Maddy came flying out the door. She dashed across our parched, weedy lawn and flung her arms around me. She bear-hugged me, tight as she had on that darkest of days, a year earlier, when she'd found me unconscious inside the garage.

With a cheek all mushed against my shoulder, she said, "Oh, Dean, I'm so thrilled for you."

My empty lunch box in hand, I hugged her back, just as tightly and lifted her off the driveway.

"What do you mean your thrilled for me? This is for US, honey. You never stopped encouraging me. You're the one kept sending out queries after I gave up. *We* did it, not just me."

"I love you, Dean. I'm sooo proud of you."

She took my lunch box, then my arm, and together we floated over the weeds and brown Bahia grass to the open front door.

Inside the house, I said, "Your gonna love me even more when I tell you something else."

Tugging at my arm like an impatient little girl, she asked, "What? Whaaat? More good news?"

"Yupper, but first, are the kids home?

She said, "They're in their rooms," then she called them out.

"Yeah, yeah, what is it?" Dawn asked trying to be cool. "Mom already told me you're story is gonna be made into a book."

"Way to go, dork." Trevor said affectionately, as he ambled out of his little bedroom with that terrific trademark smile on his boy-man face.

Both my kids stood there, hands on hips, thumbs out, the rest of their fingers pointing back, a stance they'd inherited from Maddy. Looking at the three of them now, all postured that same way, I could only shake my head. I had never felt more connected to my family than at that moment. Jesus, I thought, I'm lucky to have them.

"Wellll ... O KKKK," I said, alternating looks at the kids, "Mom told you guys the good news but there's a little more to it." I turned my eyes to Maddy and asked, "You ready for it?"

"C'mon, c'mon Dad," coaxed Dawn the Impatient. She might have been closer to her mother, but she was just like her old man.

"OK, here it is. Not only is the book going to be published, but I ... or I should say ... we ... are getting a cash advance on it also!"

"You mean like money? How much, Dad? How much?" Dawn asked.

I turned my eyes to Maddy's and I said, "Would you believe, eight, thousand, dollars!"

Maddy's face went pale. Her eyes got all froggy and her jaw fell. "Eight thousand dollars ... Dean, pinch me ... tell me you're not kidding."

"Yeah, honey, EIGHT LARGE!" I noticed her eyes had reddened. A solitary quiet tear dripped from her eyelash. The rogue cheek-roller traversed the side of her face. I stepped toward her and took her in my arms.

You have to understand what this money meant to Maddy Frances; she was the one who paid the bills. She wrote out all the checks. She was the one who mailed our sweat money off to opportunistic banks, utility companies, and all the rest. She was the one who for months had supplemented our shrinking incomes with plastic after Searcy's had cut my commission rate from six to five percent. Here we were, both of us working, living in an old house in a rapidly declining neighbourhood-- without any loans to pay--and we still had to use credit cards to pay for each month's unexpected bills. Then, on top of that, during Florida's summer months, the furniture business falls off fifty-percent. Forget incidentals! Just to subsist we had to use those instant-plastic-loans with their usurious interest rates.

Like most of the silent majority, Maddy and I were working harder and harder for much less. We couldn't even afford badly-needed dental attention for ourselves or our kids. I'd been chewing on the left side of my mouth for two years since a cracked porcelain cap on the right side kept coming off. Maddy and I each needed a couple of new crowns, and none of us had a physical exam in years. And to think they call such examinations 'routine'. For us, any dental care or medical attention, excepting emergencies, had become an unaffordable luxury. We'd never once owned a new car. Didn't want the payments. Instead we always drove around in two beaters. The van and the Skylark both ran like tired mules. Every mile we squeezed between repairs seemed like a gift. But now, these eight thousand dollars actually put us in the black.

We paid off the forty-four-hundred-dollar balance on those cards we'd used so judiciously and, despite Maddy's heavy resistance, I finally talked her into buying some much-needed clothes for herself. Not being much of a shopper, Maddy never was much for malls or mega-shopping centers. She only went to them when it was absolutely necessary. And she was as adamant about not buying designer clothes as I was. We both realized how foolish it is to actually pay for clothes with designers' names plastered all over them. For what, so we could pay ten times what they were worth rather than five, so we could make some mindless-status claim? Nope, I-don't-think-so! Neither of us could even begin to fathom how anyone would actually buy 'billboard-clothing', let alone pay exorbitant prices for that sweatshop junk.

Along with the few new things Maddy did buy, we got the kid's teeth fixed. And the van's A/C too. With the last eight hundred, we opened a savings account that paid a piddling four-percent interest. (Yeah, I know. Today they're paying even less). I swear I wanted to just keep the money in a dresser drawer, not participate in the bank's scam. But, at the time, there had been a rash of cat-burglaries in our neighborhood and Maddy felt better keeping our life savings, no matter how small, in a bank.

Despite all the negativity that shrouded our world, my family and I savored the good news I'd brought home that day. And that night, when we went to bed, Maddy Frances and I fell asleep, as we had thousands of times, in each other's arms. But something was very different. There were contented smiles on our faces. I distinctly remember that. I also remember waking up in the middle of that night, lifting my head from the pillow and looking oh so lovingly at my sleeping wife's peaceful face. Then I fell back to sleep and dreamed about Theresa Wayman.

Chapter 25

The next nine months absolutely doddered by. Each day felt like three. But, they did pass. And finally, in late March of '94, Olympus Books released the first copies of 'Look What They've Done To Our Dream'. The wait had been agonizing. For nine months the anticipation gestated inside me, each day growing weightier and harder to carry. But eventually, when I finally held a copy of the book in my hands, (though it's easy to say when it's all over), every punishing minute I had waited seemed well worth it. I was utterly euphoric that early spring day when it arrived by overnight mail. It was like all the Christmas mornings of my life jammed into one. I tore at that cardboard envelope like a kid does at the biggest gift under the tree.

"Easy," Maddy cautioned, her face alive with excitement, "you'll damage the book … Jees, Dean … look at you. Your hands are trembling."

"Yeah, yeah, yeah," I said as I wrestled the bubble-wrapped book from the cardboard Fed-Ex envelope. Then, standing side-by-side alone with my wife in the living room, we got our first glimpse of my novel.

"Dammm," I said, "look at this cover, Maddy. It's perfect."

As we studied it, she draped an arm around my waist, lodging a thumb in a belt loop of my Levis. The cover was a real grabber; star-spangled red, white, and blue. Beneath the title, in the center of a circle of white stars, was a graphic of a harried family standing in front of a small austere cement-block house. There was a husband, a wife and a baby. The adults were leaving for work, kissing goodbye next to two jalopies parked in the driveway, the infant whaling in the distraught mother's arms. A ball and chain was tethered to each parent's ankle. "Man," I said, "if that doesn't say it all. It-is-perfect."

Beneath this moving image, in bold blue print, was my name, DEAN CASSIDY. I read it to myself, three times. All I could say was, "Dammmm."

Rubbing my back by now in quick little circles, Maddy said, "It is perfect! Open it, Dean … to the back inside flap."

I was so excited, I fumbled the book, catching it mid-fall with a nervous stab of hands. "Real slick," I said as I opened the back cover.

And there it was. My picture! The grainy black and white bust shot of my good side that I had picked out. You see (against our normally-frugal judgments), Maddy and I had paid a moon-lighting photographer to come to the house and snap some shots. We wanted the jacket picture to be perfect. I was real glad now that we had sprung for the seventy-five smackers. The picture looked damn good, if I must say so myself.

"Honey, you look sooo handsome," Maddy Frances said.

I was posed in our backyard, in front of one of the tall Areca palms. Half smiling, I had on my favorite shirt, my old, blue-denim work shirt. The top three buttons were open, exposing my K-Mart, twenty-nine-dollar, silver neck chain. Still scrutinizing the picture, I told Maddy, "I have to admit, I do look kinda spiffy."

After that, we checked out the back cover. There were four blurbs, each giving praise to the book and author. The most impressive comments were made by best-selling author, Peter Hynchon. I read them to Maddy. "A beautifully written novel that masterfully illustrates what dark depths life has sunk to in these once United States, a true-to-life depiction, the likes of which you'll not read about in any newspaper nor see on the evening news, a perceptive, sensitive, passionate, heart-wrenching, utterly-beautiful debut novel. Brothers and sisters, meet Dean Cassidy, I expect he'll be around for a long, long time to come."

"I wonder if Peter Hynchon actually read it," I mused aloud.

"Of course, he did. Nobody's going to say all those nice things about a book they didn't even read."

"Often they do, Maddy."

"Maybe so, but all I know is it's one terrific story. People will love it."

"First they'll have to buy it," I said dubiously. There was that nagging inherent knack again, that talent I have for finding the darkest side of anything, no matter how good.

"They will buy it, Dean. That's why Fran arranged the tour next month. You'll sell books at those stores. People will read them, love them, and tell all their friends how good it is. Readers will identify with what you've written ... that's the most important ingredient. You said so yourself."

"Yeah, it is," I murmured as I opened to a random page. I read a few lines to Maddy and instantly our smiles returned. Then I closed the book gently and looked at my wife. An unfamiliar contented ring chimed in my voice when I said, "You know, Maddy ... no matter what happens next, this has been some thrill for both of us. Heck, we even got some money, and there'll be more. Not much, probably, but there will be more. I'm not going into this thing with stars in my eyes but, shoot, even if we just got three or four thousand more, it would be great. But, that's not what this is all about," I added, wiggling the book, "we've had the thrill of getting it published. That means far more than the money, no matter how badly we need it."

Maddy looked at me adoringly. She said, "That attitude, Mister Author, is exactly why people will enjoy reading what you have to say. There's nothing contrived in there, no phony sensationalism. It's all authentic. Your heart is on every page, Dean, and that's why people will love it."

Soon enough we would find out if she was right or wrong.

I knew all too well what the odds of success were. I knew how God-awfully tough it is to get readers to buy something by an unknown author. I'd read somewhere that only two percent of the American public can afford to buy hard covers on a regular basis. And that they usually buy books by those big-name, established writers, those authors who always seem to have a title, sometimes two at once, on the best seller lists. With thousands of writers and many more wannabees pumping out manuscripts every year, it's amazing how the same handful of mostly-mediocre writers always have something in the top ten.

Nevertheless, I can't begin to describe how thrilled I was that, out of the hundreds of thousands of unsolicited manuscripts stacked in publishing house slush piles throughout the industry, mine had been chosen from one such paper mountain. Just the fact it had made it 'over the transom', as they say, and into print, was truly remarkable, and damn lucky!

But, my struggle was nowhere near over. There would still be more obstacles. After all, for every goal we achieve in life, isn't there always another more important, more challenging one waiting right behind it-- sometimes more than one, waiting in the wings? Beyond my achievement of getting the book published and released, was the looming tour, and after that, the bottom line - sales.

For the next month, until the tour began, I remained true to form, agonizing about how it might go. Would 'Look What They've Done to Our Dream' be reasonably successful, or would it be a horrendous flop? You can imagine which way my mind leaned during those four weeks.

Chapter 26

Although Skip Frampton, the store manager at Searcy's, acted as if it was costing him blood, he finally gave me permission to take my vacation a month earlier than scheduled. How was I to know exactly when my tour would start? He pitched and bitched about how tough it would be to cover the sales floor with one less body. It didn't matter that he always flooded the floor with too many salespeople anyway. He loved to hire on more than we needed so that we'd all be good and hungry, so that when their few turns came to wait on customers, the salespeople would really work them over, try every trick and scheme imaginable, and some that weren't, so they could, as Frampton put it, "Get into their damn checkbooks." Then, as bad as conditions were, once Searcy's instituted that commission cut, even most of the honest associates began to lie, cheat and steal in an attempt to scrape together a half a living. It was a hell of an atmosphere, like working in a combat zone.

Every time Frampton broke my shoes about the vacation, I wanted in the worst way to tell him to kiss my ass. I wanted to quit, on the spot. But I managed to restrain myself, knowing I'd still need the soulless job when I returned from the tour. You would have thought he'd gladly have let me have time off, think it was pretty neat that I'd gotten a book published and all. But that shit didn't mean squat to ole Skip, a seventy-six-year-old man who'd never read anything other than business publications, the type of person who spends his entire life focused on only one thing, making money. Skip Frampton thought that since he was 'over' thirty-odd people, and he and his wife drove new twin BMWs every year, each with matching colors, appointments and cutesy vanity plates, that he had the answers to all of life's questions. But, like all such provincial-thinking know-it-alls, he'd never in his entire naïve life had clue one as to what the big picture is all about. Sometimes when I looked at this man, I'd think back to my childhood on the streets of Queens. I'd think how most of the underclass kids I had known knew more about life at thirteen than this mindless, pampered executive ever would.

Despite Frampton's opposition, on April 24th my vacation began and so did the book tour. Though I couldn't wait for this day to arrive, now that it was here and I stood in our driveway saying goodbye to Maddy Frances and the kids, I felt terrible. I had dreaded this moment. In all our years together, the only time Maddy and I had ever been apart was when the kids were born, when she had to spend a couple of nights in the hospital. Now, here we were, saying goodbye, not going to see each other for almost two full weeks, trying to act like it was a happy occasion. All four of us went through the motions, counterfeit motions, of a happy goodbye, kissing and hugging, feeling awkward, feeling like hell.

When I finally got into the van and slowly pulled away from the house, I turned, waved and snapped one last mental picture of my family. All of them stood the same stance – hands on hips, thumbs forward. Trevor, already three cow-licks taller than Maddy, stood next to her protectively, though I could see the strain on his face. Dawn, the toughest of our offspring, showing a rare bit of emotion, actually looked like she was going to cry. But Maddy, good old dependable Maddy Frances, waved, smiled dutifully and tried to look strong. But her smile was incongruent with the sadness in her eyes. She was smiling through tears, trying her damndest to hide them.

When I hung a left two houses up at the corner, I caught one last glimpse of Maddy Frances. Her back to me, she was stepping back inside the house. Her head was slung low, her shoulders hunched and lurching. Trevor had his arm around her. He was leaning over her, saying something, trying to console her. I turned my eyes to the road ahead then I broke down. I started bawling like a baby.

I thought about how I didn't want to leave my family and the comfort of our small private world for twelve full days. I got a bad, bad feeling. For some reason I was positive I would never see them again. This fear shrouded me like a thick morbid fog. I wanted to turn around and go back, but knew I couldn't.

Chapter 27

Twelve days, fifteen book signings – Borders, Barnes and Noble, and a few large independents. My itinerary took me from Boca Raton, up Florida's east coast to West Palm, Stuart, Vero Beach, and Daytona. After Daytona I was to pick up Interstate 4 across the state, then deadheaded south to Sarasota. After that, I'd proceed north again, on I-75, to Saint Pete, Tampa and a few other sizeable towns along the way to Atlanta, where the tour was to terminate on May fifth, Cinco De Mayo, and, purely coincidentally, my 43rd birthday. On the following day, a Wednesday, I planned to head home.

Olympus would be picking up all the expenses. Fran Danforth had reserved rooms for me all along my route, Holiday Inns and Ramadas. Sorry, Tom Bodett, don't bother 'leaving the light on' at the Motel 6 for me. I was stepping up a couple of notches this trip.

Since it had been late in the afternoon when I left that Friday, I decided to take the Florida Turnpike to my first stop in Boca. I-95 would be a mess and I'd get reimbursed for the tolls anyway. Cruising at sixty-five, I watched the western fringes of the so-called 'Gold Coast' blur by. New gated communities sprawled west, deeper into the Everglades while, to the east, older neighborhoods struggled unsuccessfully to maintain a semblance of dignity. Just north of Lauderdale, I passed one of Florida's few mountains, a man-made sod-covered mountain, a sanitary landfill so tall it appeared to rise smack into the gray storm clouds that were boiling just a few miles to the east over the Atlantic.

A short time later, I closed in on Boca Raton and my stomach began to tighten. For a month now, I'd played over and over in my mind a hundred different scenarios of how this trip would turn out. Usually I pictured myself sitting in an empty bookstore behind a folding table, looking pitifully foolish, with nobody approaching me. Still worse was when I pictured myself sitting like that in a crowded store. Either way, no matter how many eyes were or weren't there, they all carefully averted mine.

Man, I was really beating myself up again!

My only small consolation was that the previous Sunday's Fort Lauderdale News had noted in its Books section that, "Local author,

Dean Cassidy, will be signing his new book, 'Look What They've Done to Our Dream', at Borders in Boca Raton on Friday, April 24th, at eight PM." Though the paper didn't bother to review my book, at least they'd mentioned my appearance. Maybe that would help a little. At first I thought if they'd given me a full review, it would have drawn more people to my signing. A plug like that certainly wouldn't have hurt. But in my mind's very next perception, I thought, on second thought, scratch that idea, maybe a review actually would hurt.

As I rolled up to a tollbooth after exiting the turnpike, I thought, *Jesus, this is going to be embarrassing as hell.* Almost sick with dread, being so close to the first stop on my tour now, I continued to beat myself up. *What if my suspicions are right? What if nobody buys a single copy? I can just see the customers milling around, their faces. Their pitying eyes stealing glances at me sitting there like an idiot, thinking, 'Look at that poor bastard. Man ... he must feel weak. Glad I'm not in his shoes!'*

I also worried about how it might be in the parking lot at Borders – if somebody saw me in my old Dodge van. It would probably be around dusk, I figured, still light enough for anyone to see me get out of it. Quickly I became disgusted for allowing myself to fall victim to such a mindless concern. In my entire adult life, I'd never given a damn about what anybody thought, and here I was now, intimidated. Sure, the van had a hundred and sixty thousand miles on it, but I'd kept her in pretty good shape. Except for the small crease on the tailgate and the few dime-size spots I'd touched-up with slightly mismatched Discount Auto paint, it still looked fine. Well, it looked OK for its age anyway!

Then I slipped again. Shit. Who am I kidding? If anybody sees me driving this thing to any of these signings, I'll die.

Another cerebral tug-of-war began to mount. I started to lean the other way again.

You idiot! How the hell is anyone gonna' recognize you? The goddamned book just came out a few weeks ago. It's not like you're Papa freaking Hemingway, you jerk!

It was crowding five when I checked in at the Holiday. After I let myself into the room, all I could do was pace. And think. *Christ, this is horrible*, I thought aloud. Then to myself, *Will this thing get any easier as it progresses, or will it become even more unbearable?* After I exhausted that worry, I went to work on my clothes. *Am I dressed OK? I think I'm safe. Let's see, white jeans, my favorite belt with the embroidered school of bonefish swimming around it, powder-blue, button-down shirt, just the top two buttons open, too risky going with three tonight, and my Wal-Mart boat shoes. With socks! Now that's a first!*

Reasonably satisfied, I stubbed out my tenth cigarette of the day in a plastic ashtray atop the dresser. Already I was two above my daily quota. Should I call Maddy? *Naw, I'll be calling her when it's over, no sense depressing her too. Man, could I use a few beers. Hmmm! It's Friday! There's a bar downstairs! Happy hour! I'd love to down about four, just enough to take the edge off. If I pick up some Lifesavers, nobody would ever know. I HAVE enough time!*

I was actually considering hitting the bar when my conscience, that stern, unsympathetic voice, commanded me to, *FORGET IT!*

That was pretty much how things went till it was time to leave, when at seven-twenty I stepped out of the room into the motel's hallway and closed the door behind me. I can still remember hanging onto that knob, just standing there a moment. I let my head droop, drew a deep breath, listened to it as I let it out, then trudged slowly down the carpeted hallway to the elevator. It was like walking 'the last mile'.

Ten minutes later, I was driving along one of Boca Raton's busiest thoroughfares when suddenly a whole new fear took a hold of me, a logical concern about the affluence of this town. There were Benz's, Beamers, Lexus's and Lincolns everywhere you turned. I even saw two Rolls Royce's. That was on the boulevard. Alongside it, sitting back off the roadway in glitzy, manicured shopping plazas, were miles of chic, high-brow shops, extravagant stores and an inordinate number of (you guessed it) banks. There was a sprinkling of gated communities also, posh developments with armed guards and space-age, highest-tech security systems, bastions for the rich.

Feeling like a beggar on a mule, I steered the van amongst all these expensive people in their luxury chariots. I felt like I'd just touched down on a tenth planet. *Shoot,* I thought as I looked all around, *these people right here, parading in the lanes all around me, epitomize the very ones I'd bad-mouthed in my book, women with their face pulls, all those ostentatious hats, extra-wide brimmed straw hats that you felt like ripping off their perfect heads and scaling into oblivion. Then there were the men, with their pretentious grins and designer costumes, and their gaudy, pinky rings (strategically riding the tops of steering wheels), in-your-face garish displays of excess.* These were the four percent of our population that owns three-fourths of America. *Man ... I ought to go over real big in this town. REALLY BIG!*

True as every one of them was, I began ruminating over some of the aphorisms I had put in my protagonist, Billy Soles', mouth. One line in particular, when Billy says to his son, "Always remember that nobody, and I mean nobody, gets rich without in one way or another exploiting others along the way. Bankers, professional athletes, entertainers, doctors, business barons, they're all users." He then goes on to say, "Of course, son, if you really know your stuff and you could somehow corner them with factual accusations, they'd tell ya they don't see it that way. They'd vehemently deny that their being wealthy has anything to do with any working slob's losses ... I often wonder what such people might say if you told them that, as a result of their increasing fortunes, one in five kids in this country, the richest country in the world, go to bed hungry every night."

A few minutes later I was idling through Border's half-filled parking lot. Discreetly, I scoped out the situation before easing the van into a spot at the lot's remotest corner. After killing the engine, I checked all around one more time before getting out. It looked good, so I went for it. Feeling like a certifiable idiot, head down, I pushed myself across the asphalt toward the entrance. I felt at that moment just like I had that one day in the fourth grade at P.S. 20, back in Queens, when Ma made me wear to school, because it was all that was clean, one of my old, recently considered babyish Davy Crockett shirts. I wanted now, just like I had in that schoolyard, to turn around, run like hell, jump in the van, peel out of there and rush home to my family and the comfort of obscurity.

But, of course, I couldn't! I went inside, straight to the counter and asked for the manager.

When the clerk said, "Sure, one moment, Mister Cassidy," and paged her, it shocked the pants off of me. Somehow this small gesture of recognition, of familiarity, helped settle me down some. It was kind of like when, after days of dreading a root-canal, you finally sign in at the dentist's office and take a seat. As I waited for the manager, I turned to check out the store.

H-o-l-y M-o-b-l-y! I didn't see that when I came in!

Inside the entrance, facing it, but just to the left a bit, stood a marquis sign, done up real professional like, with MY picture on it, a big blowup of my book-jacket photo. Though, from where I stood, I could not make out all the smaller print alongside the picture, I could easily discern the bigger letters up top. My name and 'Look What They've Done To Our Dream' jumped right off the poster board. There were two pretty college-aged girls standing next to it. One of them whispered something to the other, then they both smiled at me. I smiled back sheepishly, then looked away, and that's when I noticed the desk. A cherrywood Queen Anne job, set back maybe fifteen feet past the sign. There was what I thought to be two highly over-optimistic stacks of my books on it, one on either side. *Ohhh shittt!* I thought. *There's three people standing over there, each of 'em fingering through my book.* Then another lady drifted next to them and picked up a copy. Not knowing what to do with my hands, my palms gone all clammy, I balled them up and shoved them in my pockets. Then the manager came up to me. We introduced ourselves and talked a few minutes then she led me to my fate.

Well, let me tell you, those books that were stacked so high, every one of them, and more, went! Boy, did they sell! The store's employees had to replenish each of the towering stacks three times. I talked non-stop with customers for the entire ninety minutes. I also autographed their books. I couldn't believe it was happening. This event was one of my life's all-time greatest. Not the greatest, but it was up there. Except for the fact that I wanted so badly to tell Maddy about its success, I hated to see it end. But, like all good things, it eventually did. I thanked the manager and staff then hung out a few minutes talking with them. I felt more than a little self-conscious when a few of them, aspiring writers, asked me all kinds of questions about technique and what not. With great humility, I gladly took the time to answer them the best I could. But, after that, after I stepped outside into the warm night air, all I could think about was getting my tail back to the motel, getting a phone in my hand. As I wide-strided across that parking lot, I felt a wide smile stretch on my face, an ironic smile. Eyeballing my van, I realized I hadn't even given thought to whether or not anybody would see me getting into it. Still not looking around as I unlocked the door, I slowly shook my head, chuckled, and said, "Son of a bitch Dean, you did it!"

Chapter 28

"Maddy, it's me!" I said into the phone, the words dancing from my lips like lyrics in a song. "How are you, honey?"

Hearing my voice, hers burst with relief, Oh, Dean! Thank God! I couldn't wait to hear from you." Then, in her next breath, her tone shrunk from relieved to tentative. "How did it go, honey?"

"Wellll ... OKKKK," I teased.

"C'mon! Please, Dean! Stop! Tell me!" she coaxed, beginning to sense the news might be good for a change.

"You wouldn't believe it, Maddy. It was fantastic. People actually came to see me ... to buy my book ... lots of `em. I talked and signed books for an hour-and-a-half straight. There were customers waiting in line to see me the whole time."

"Oh Dean," she said, her voice spilling with relief, "that's fantastic ... I told you everything would work out. Tell me all about it."

"It was unbelievable! I must've signed a hundred copies."

Hearing myself say these positive things seemed to substantiate the plausibility of the book's potential success.

"Jesus, Maddy, this thing could be big. I mean BIG! We stand to make some serious money." Then I got kind of choked up and my voice slowed. I said, "Maddy ... you know I don't care about having a lot of money or any of that. We both know that's not where it's at. But we've struggled for so long, honey. God knows we could use a break. Even if it just means not having to sweat the bills for awhile. You know ... kind of a reprieve. But Maddy, listen ... I think it's going to be better than that. I've got a feeling we're gonna kick some ass now!"

And we did.

The readers kept coming. As I pushed north in the Caravan, more and more of them turned out at each signing. My belief in the book strengthened a little more with each session. I was so UP that when the van's A/C crapped out again just north of Tallahassee, I simply blew it off and cranked down the window. For the first time in my life, repairing a vehicle would not be a major dilemma.

People everywhere were talking it up. 'Look What They've Done to Our Dream' was gaining momentum. Word of mouth was my biggest promoter. The first readers had loved it. They told their friends about it and interest in the book networked. Customers everywhere were beginning to put very serious dents in bookstore inventories. Things kept progressing better and better.

Then, on the last day of the tour, in the early afternoon, Fran Danforth phoned me at my motel room in "Hotlanta". She told me the first sales reports were coming in and already the Olympus brass was talking a second printing. She said they'd never had a first time novelist draw so much attention so quickly. And that was saying something because Olympus is a very old, highly-respected house that had signed many outstanding writers over the years.

As soon as I hung up with Fran, I dialed Maddy's work number with a quivering finger. There was no way I could wait until evening like I usually did. I had to share this phenomenal news with her now. I also figured, if I called her right then, I could crash immediately after returning from the evening signing (I had two appearances scheduled that day, the first at a Barnes and Noble in the afternoon, and the other later on at a Border's). I wanted to hit the rack early so I'd be fresh the next morning for the day-long drive home.

When I connected with Maddy, her first words were, "Happy birthday!" Then she told me she couldn't stand missing me, and she never wanted us to be apart again.

I promised we wouldn't be. I told her about Olympus' decision to run a second printing. Overwhelmed by this news and thoughts of my returning home the next day, she broke into happy tears. Almost overnight our lives were changing for the better. All the struggling just to get by, all the hard times, all those times I'd been out of work, and finally now we would actually have some (and I hate to use the term) disposable income. I also told her Fran had asked me to step up production on my other book when I got home, another novel I'd started eight months earlier, shortly after I signed the contract for 'Look What They've Done To Our Dream'.

After we hung up, I showered a second time and put on the same clothes I'd worn for the book jacket picture.

The rest of the day flew by. The afternoon signing went as smoothly as all the rest, and my final appearance that evening was going along just as well. Twelve days of motels, characterless chain restaurants and unfamiliar faces were coming to an end. Just thirty minutes remained at the final signing. The line of people in front of me was waning, maybe a dozen folks still waited to meet me as I autographed a book for a heavy-set older women. Somewhere in her sixties, she spoke the way stroke survivors do, her slurred words struggling to escape the left side of her mouth. "Ank you, Mithda Cathidy. Dith copy ith for my thithter, she'th thick in da hothpital. I jutht hope she'll enjoy it ath much ath I `id."

My heart went out to this woman. Her voice was so damaged, so ruined, just like my mother's was after her second almost successful suicide attempt in 1991. From the way this lady dressed, it was obvious she didn't have much. A twenty-two-dollar book purchase had to be an against-her-better-judgment decision. She was who my book was about and I connected with her instantly as if she were my aunt. It was easy to tell that she, like I myself, had gone to the University of Hard Knocks. I saw it in her weary, distorted face, in her small, unremarkable eyes. Her sad, arched brows, frozen in defeat, told her life's story, memoirs of constant pain that only years of unrelenting hardship can inflict. And that cockeyed half-smile, man, that just ripped at my heart. I talked to her for a minute or so, then we thanked each other and she left.

I watched as she lumbered toward the cashier under the heavy weight of her body and disability and all the rest. She laid the book on the counter and I saw the clerk read the note I'd written alongside the bar-code. When the clerk told her that the book "was on Mister Cassidy", she turned around slowly and glanced back at me, bashfully. I could tell she felt kind of funny, but nevertheless happy. She gave me a little wave and smiled a shy, appreciative smile. I smiled back warmly and nodded. She was me and I was her, and we both knew it. I knew this just by looking at her, and she knew it by what she had read in my book. We both had been living in the same cruel world. I hoped that my small gesture would, even if only for a few minutes, make this cold place seem a little warmer for her.

The next person in line had waited patiently during the thirty or so seconds this encounter took. She now took a book from a stack and laid it gently on the table before me. It took this small activity to bring me back to where I was, what I was supposed to be doing. When I looked up to greet this customer, my heart stalled, halting mid-beat as if a cold steel weight had been dropped on it.

I was looking at Theresa Wayman!

Chapter 29

Good God, her beauty stunned me. She was still more attractive than should be legal. Professional looking now, yet at the same time very sensual, if you can imagine that. Her hair was shorter but, other than a few random gray strands here and there, it was still the blackest black you've ever seen. Cut diagonally on the sides, it angled down her face sharply just below her high smooth cheeks, and it was lustrous as a wet seal's coat. I could see the overhead fluorescent lights reflecting in it and could tell it was freshly brushed. The small lobes of her ears peeked out and (although I don't like gold for what it's perceived as) the quarter sized hoops that hung from them added to her elegance. Even in the store's unforgiving lights, she was all but flawless. The only discernible lines on her breathtaking, heart-shaped face were thin as delicate hairs, barely noticeable alongside the most provocative eyes anyone had ever seen. Eyes that spoke. Eyes that now said happy things and sorrowful things at the same time. Eyes that seemed relieved, immensely relieved, to be resting on mine.

My brain traumatized, nearly paralyzed, the only words I could muster came out barely louder than a whisper. "Myyy Goddd ... Theresa!"

My condition just short of shock now, I raised a nervous palm to my chin. Twenty-four years had passed since she'd last graced my eyes, thousands of dawns and just as many sunsets, countless roads, a million miles and more than a few dark alleys. And now here she was, my Theresa, standing before me at a bookstore in Atlanta, Georgia.

Like a mother speaking to a small child, her lovely smile widened and she said, "Still the softie, aren't you, Dean Cassidy?" But despite her inborn, smooth confidence, I detected a deep hurt and even a hint of awkwardness in her voice. She was as moved as I was.

"Well ... I ... what do you mean?" I asked.

Trying to come across as nonchalant, not doing a very good job of it, she said, "I saw what you did for that lady just now. You know what I mean." Then her eyes narrowed and her face became very serious. "How have you been, Dean?" she asked, the cracks in her voice so big you could fall into them.

There it was. She HAD cared! Just like I had all this time. What we shared as teenagers had been much more than just some fleeting crush to her also.

"Theresa, I don't … I don't know what to say." I glanced at my Casio, then the small line of people standing behind her. "Look," I said, "I'll be done here in about twenty minutes. What do you say … "

"Sure … I'll wait."

She was visibly relieved that the ice had been broken. Her tone lightened some when she said, "I didn't come here to buy a book, Dee Cee. I have one. I've already read it." She put a manicured finger on the copy in front of me, gently caressed my name on the cover, and said, "It moved me like nothing I've ever read. And, I'm not saying that because I once dated the author."

I smiled from a soft spot deep within my heart, the same spot Theresa had occupied since the night I met her. Then I murmured so nobody could hear. The words spilled out before I could stop them. They also hung in the air. I said, "My heart was in it, Theresa … and … and so were you."

"I know that, Dean." Our eyes embraced for a second or two. Then, suddenly, like she had snapped out of a deep trance, she straightened her jacket, looked this way and that, and said, "I'd better get out of the way here. My car's parked on the … the north side of the building. I'll wait there for you." Her smile was so warm I could feel my temperature rising. "And oh, yeah," she added, "I almost forgot, I'll be in a dark green Mercedes." Then she turned and walked away.

As the next customer in line stepped forward, a twenty-something John Lennon look-alike (the hair, granny glasses and all), I accessed Theresa from behind. Her dove-gray jacket and matching skirt fit like it was tailor made and probably was. Damn, she looked fantastic! Better than in any of my thousands of memories. And she still walked with that innate queenly gait. Man, was she still a sight!

The young long-hair before me watched her too, then looked back at me and just said, "Wowwww!"

I wanted to sprint after her. What if she changed her mind, just drove off into the Georgia night? I'd noticed a ring, she was married. What if she had guilt-filled second thoughts about coming to see me?

But it wasn't that way. After I finished up, thanked the store manager and squared away for the book I'd given to that lady, I found Theresa still waiting in the parking lot. Sitting in her big Benz, parked in the glow of a towering mercury vapor light, she pensively watched the passing night-time traffic. As I approached, I couldn't help but to check out her expensive new car. She'd either married into money or had done alright for herself. Whichever, I knew that unless she had changed drastically, there was still a lot more to Theresa Wayman than her pricey car, jewelry and clothes.

Still dazed by her presence, I bent to her open window.   a loss for anything else to say, what with the awkward circumstances and all, I said, "Nice car." Boy was that an out-of-character comment.

"Yeah ... " she said, looking up at me now, "thanks. Can we go somewhere and talk, Dean?" She'd glanced at my left hand where it rested on the door. She'd seen my plain wedding band. Even if she hadn't seen it, she'd read my book. She already knew from the jacket bio that I was married. Her voice shrunk when she asked, "Would that be OK ... if we went somewhere?"

Looking into her eyes I nodded, told her I was staying at the Holiday, and that, sure, we could meet at the bar, have a drink.

Chapter 30

I can't tell you what exactly I was thinking, just that my mind was a whirlwind of anticipation when I pulled onto the bustling boulevard, smack in front of an oncoming Suburban. When I suddenly heard the blaring horn almost on top of me, I snapped back into the here and now, stopping short, half-in half-out of the lot. Luckily, the driver stomped his brakes in time. There was an elongated screech and instantly I smelled the cloud of hot molten rubber rising off the road. For the next mile or so the driver stayed glued to my bumper, sitting on his or her horn and with damn good reason.

I was still a wreck ten minutes later when I pulled into the parking lot at the Holiday Inn. Being early, and a Tuesday night, there weren't a whole lot of cars outside the lounge. I got a spot right next to Theresa's car. As I turned into the slot, my headlights illuminated the inside of her Mercedes and I saw it was empty.

I walked toward the entrance tucking the back of my shirt in a little deeper. Out of nervous habit, I swiped my comb through my salt-and-pepper mustache a couple of times. When I did this small ritualistic gesture it brought back one of my life's biggest memories, my first date with Theresa, when I was walking to her house, to be exact. I remembered how upset I'd become after checking myself out in that car window, discovering that ripe zit in my reflection. As anxious as I was at that teenage moment, it was nothing compared to how I felt now at forty-three, now that I was about to find out the answers to so many questions, uncertainties that had torn at my soul for well over half my life. Although through the years I had never stopped fantasizing about this moment, I never thought it was possible that I'd ever actually see Theresa again. Who would have dreamed? I would. Lord knows how many times I dreamed about it. But in all those subconscious wanderings, I always woke up before I could ask Theresa the first question, the biggest question: *Do you still care?* I would always wake to the black emptiness of night before the answer came and, for the past twenty years, to Maddy Frances in bed beside me. But it would be different this time. This was no dream and there were hundreds of southern miles lying between Maddy and me.

I looked up to the dark sky and I saw more stars than I had since a spring night in 1967.

The lounge was almost as dark inside as it was out in the Atlanta night. A good-sized oval bar was off to the right, maybe a third of its stools occupied; vacationers, business-types, probably a few locals but Theresa wasn't there. To the left the bandstand was deserted, though it was set with instruments and sound equipment. In front of it was a small wooden dance floor that could accommodate maybe ten couples. I looked beyond it, to the smattering of small round tables. Each was covered with red cloth and topped with a candle, flickering, red globe-candles that somehow, if for only a fractured second, brought my mother's tea cart altar to my mind's eyes.

Only three of the tables were occupied. At one, four women still dressed from the office were drinking, smoking cigarettes - one a cigar - and chatting away in earnest. At another table, a secretive couple sat too close and appeared too romantic to be married, although they both sported rings. Beyond them I spotted Theresa, sitting at a table back by the wall.

As I approached her, especially after seeing that couple, I felt a stab of guilt when she said, "Dean ... look at you ... you look terrific, a regular knight in shining armor." The knife in my gut turned a bit when she said that. How many times over the years had Maddy Frances called me that?

Masking my guilt the best I could, I sat down and said in a good-natured tone, "Oh stop, Theresa."

"No, seriously, it's obvious that you exercise, work out or something."

"Yeah, I try to keep moving." I took a cigarette from a breast pocket and holding it up said, "You don't mind, do you?"

"No," Theresa answered tentatively, "I don't mind." Then a melancholic smile lit her face. She leaned toward me, elbows on the table, resting her chin on two small fists, and she said, "Remember that old Zippo you used to have?"

This small recollection of our common past comforted us both. The stiffness of our reunion vanished that quick. Poof, it was out of there, making it easy to lead into the conversation we had both longed for, a talk neither of us thought would ever take place, and would not have if

Theresa hadn't noticed mention of my book signing in the Atlanta paper.

With a slow heave of breath I answered her question. "Yeah, I remember it OK. That was a long time ago, wasn't it, Theresa?"

She nodded slowly, wistfully, several times in succession and dropped her eyes to the gold rings on her wrist. She toyed with them for a moment before raising her exotic doe's eyes to mine. "Where do we start, Dean? Should we begin with who we are now or where we left off?"

"How about who we are now, then we can go back from there. Margaret Mitchell wrote 'Gone With The Wind' that way, from the end back to the beginning, and it turned out to be one hell of a story, didn't it?"

"It sure did, Dean, the best story ever."

At that moment we both fell silently into the warmth of each other's eyes. Together we went back twenty-five years to the balcony at the Keith's RKO theater. Theresa's lower lip began to quiver. Then the waitress came to our table. We straightened up like two school kids caught cheating on a test. The bottle-blond had obviously approached Theresa before I had gotten there.

"Are you ready to order now?" she asked in a syrupy, Southern accent. Theresa ordered some kind of fancy sounding red wine and I a bottle of Miller Lite.

The waitress left and I carefully punched out my cigarette so it wouldn't smolder annoyingly. I put my elbows back on the tabletop, my chin on folded hands and studied her for a few seconds. She did the same. Self-conscious of my own voice, I asked her a question I'd pondered for years, "How's life been to you, Theresa? From the looks of you I'd say pretty darn good. You still look magnificent."

"Yeah, Dean, magnificent," she said as she began twirling my cigarette pack on the table cloth. Then she looked at my face which must have been shimmering red from the candle like hers was. She picked up the cigarettes and slipped one from the pack.

"Do you mind?" she asked.

"Course not. Go ahead."

Holding it to her lips with one hand, she lightly laid her other on mine as I held a lit match. I wondered did she do it to steady me or did

201

she just want to touch me. I didn't want her to take her hand away. If she hadn't, I would have kept my hands cupped there even after the flame burned into them.

She took a drag, exhaled slow and long at the ceiling. Christ, she was sexy! Looking at the cigarette, assessing it, she said, "I haven't had one of these since ... since a few months after I last saw you." She studied me fondly, sniffled once and said in a somber tone, "Let me ask you a question, Dean. Do you think it's possible that life can be both wonderful and tragic?"

"Sure it's possible. Substitute the wonderful part with just OK, and I couldn't describe my own life any better."

The waitress came back with our drinks now. I leaned back in my seat and then forward again after she set them down. When she walked away, I said, "Tell me about the terrific part first." The time wasn't right to talk about us yet.

She took a dainty sip of wine, while carefully gathering her thoughts. "Remember how even in high school I was so hung up on the future, how getting an education and ahead financially meant everything to me."

"I don't know that I'd call it being hung up but, yes, I know those things were important to you."

"You sure know how to phrase things. No wonder you're a writer. Anyway, yes ... financially I`ve done better than I ever could have hoped. I ... I mean we have ... my husband ... Lauren ... and I, have everything you could want, two nice cars, a beautiful home and no mortgage! We've even got a terrific chalet, up in the Smokies, in Highlands. Do you know where that is, Dean?"

Son of a bitch! I thought. She-is-married! Sure, I'd noticed she was wearing rings, but I'm a guy, I didn't know if they were just for decoration or what. Hell, half her fingers had rings on them. I hadn't had time to study them.

"Yeah," I said, getting back to her question. "I've heard of the place, of course. I used to work for the post office, and some of the guys had places up there, Maggie Valley, Murphy, Highlands. A lot of people in South Florida go up there for the summer."

"It's unbelievable, Dean. Eleven acres on a mountain top with a view that would make an atheist believe."

I smiled at that. "Maybe you should try a little writing."

She laughed, a small girlish giggle, and playfully waved me off with her hand. I took another swallow of beer while she continued.

"I've even got a place in Florida, in the Keys, a stilt house on big Pine, on the bay side."

"Are you kidding? I'd kill for something like that. I love it down in the Keys." I was about to say 'We love it down there', that Maddy Frances and I had gotten married there, but not wanting to screw up our conversation's continuity, I withheld those truths and plenty more--for the time being anyway. It was just a temporary sin of omission, if you will, but it brought on another guilt pang. Again, I'd betrayed Maddy who was at home with my children, waiting for her husband. Again I took a swallow of beer, a much bigger one this time.

"I've also got a very lucrative stock portfolio," Theresa continued, "an IRA and full ownership of four Century 21 agencies here in Atlanta."

I let all this get to me. Theresa's success made me feel small. All I had to show for all the years that passed between us was two jalopies and a partnership with First Federal on a salt box house in dire need of new roof. And some partnership that was, eleven years in that house and we didn't even have 25% equity yet.

But, forget that. The inadequacy I felt now transcended mere finances. I had let this get to me. I'd let this news of Theresa's wealth reduce my own self-image, and that is the most important thing a person has to hold onto. I felt like slapping myself in the head but I caught myself. .

Nevertheless, it was a colossal understatement when I said, "Sounds like you've done OK."

"Yeah, I've done OK, alright, so OK that I'm on my third marriage. Dean … I've failed horribly at what's most important. I've been so caught up with making money, I never had time for any of my husbands. And now … this time … I'm married four years and it's not working out. He … my husband, Lauren, is senior vice- president of a large plastic manufacturer here in Atlanta. His job takes him away a lot, probably like seventy percent of the time. And me, I'm always on the go. You can't imagine what running four very busy C-21 agencies is like. We're talking twelve hours a day, seven days a week. Lauren and I spend less time together than people in commuter marriages do. Dean, every time our paths cross, I feel further estranged from him. I don't love him, Dean. I don't think I ever did. I know I didn't. I didn't love the two before him either."

She leaned over the table. Her deep brown eyes had moistened and now I could see the candle's red reflection shimmering in them. Somehow, even though I hadn't been with her, it hurt deep inside knowing she had been so miserable all those years.

"I was hesitant all three times, Dean. It just never felt like … like I guess what you might call fairytale love. I began to question my feelings, my emotions, my expectations. Maybe love just couldn't be like I thought it should be. Maybe I was looking for an emotion too profound. Maybe I was too idealistic. I don't know. Anyway, I went ahead and made three drastic mistakes."

The waitress brought over fresh drinks. Theresa dropped her eyes to the designer purse on her lap, began fumbling with it so the waitress wouldn't notice her eyes all welled up. After the waitress cleared away our empties and went about her business, Theresa dabbed at her eyes with a Kleenex.

"What about you, Dean?" She sniffled. "Tell me where you are, where you've been."

I lit another Carlton and searched my mind a few seconds. I wanted to get the chronology right. How do I start? Where do I start? Hell, I figured, I'll begin with now too.

"Like I said, Theresa, I've been married nineteen years, to a good woman … no, an exceptional woman. It's the first time around for both of us. We have a seventeen-year-old son and a daughter who's fifteen. Good kids, both of them." I took a swallow of beer and then a hit off my smoke. "I can't get next to my daughter, she won't let me. She's moody … and snippy. But still, like I said, she's a good kid and my wife insists she'll grow out of it." After saying that, I felt another well-deserved guilt-jolt, this time for intentionally avoiding Maddy France's name.

Some guy was on the bandstand now testing the sound equipment, a high pitched nails-to-the-chalkboard squeal, then, "testing, testing, testing."

"You know how it is," I continued, "you always expect your relationship with your kids to be better than it was with your own parents. When it doesn't quite turn out that way, you feel like you've failed. I could have … should have put in more time with my kids when they were small, given them more time and attention. But I was always caught up in my own problems. Don't get me wrong, the kids love me and all, but it's nothing like I thought it would be." I paused, looked down at my fingers, then my wedding band. "How about you Theresa, any kids?"

This question struck some kind of chord.

Her eyes saddened even more. Her chest rose as she filled it with a long breath, then, along with her words, she released it ever so slowly. "No … " she wavered her head, looking through my eyes into my mind, " … I don't have any children, Dean. And I feel so incomplete because of that. I would have loved to have children but there are two reasons why I didn't. Number one is because my career consumed most of my waking hours. And number two, the biggest reason, the real reason, is because I could never have a child with a man I didn't love."

Those last words hung in the air, suspended like promising white clouds. Sitting in silence beneath them, I wondered, *What did she mean by that last sentence?* I squirmed in my seat a little before breaking the uneasy quiet.

I went on to confess what a financial struggle my life had been. The unending string of nothing jobs, the constant stress of never having enough money even with two incomes. At first, Theresa listened intently, she was so interested in what had become of me. But about halfway through this second half of my life story, I began to feel as if I were talking to myself. Yeah, those beautiful eyes were still caressing me but her mind was somewhere else.

So, mid-spiel, I stopped short my biography. With a hint of agitation rising in my tone, I asked her, "Theresa, have I lost you? Have you been listening to what I've been saying the last few minutes?"

"Yes … " she said as if I'd awakened her from a funereal dream, as if she had been thinking of something far more important than what I was telling. " … I mean, no, Dean. I'm sorry. I was drifting off, thinking of something, something I've been carrying for a long, long time."

I was stunned at how somber she'd become, just like that. It was as if someone had thrown an emotional switch inside her. The only times I'd ever seen her look and sound even close to this sad were the night she introduced me to her mother, during the camera fiasco on prom night, and that night I broke her heart in an ice cream parlor. Sure we'd had a few drinks by this time, but only a few, it wasn't the wine that had made her eyes so watery and her heart so heavy. It was a force much stronger than that. Something deeply rooted in Theresa Wayman's psyche, something that had been forged into it over time. It was obvious she was about to unload something very heavy when she next said, "We need to back this conversation up a few minutes, Dean, to when I told you I didn't have any children."

"OKKK. Yeahhh?"

"Well ... " she said, clearing her throat, straightening up in her chair, " ... this isn't easy for me to say and it won't be any easier for you to hear either ... but here goes. Dean ... I was pregnant once ... back in 1968."

"Ohhh, Jeeesus, Theresa." My heart bottomed out. I was absolutely blown away.

"Yes, Dean ... the baby was yours. But relax ... don't get yourself all upset ... you don't have a child walking around somewhere that you've never seen, your life isn't about to become any more complicated than it already is."

Mechanically, without dropping my line of sight from her, I felt around the table for my cigarette pack.

"Talk to me, Theresa! What happened? What happened to the baby? You had an abortion, didn't you? Your mother forced you into it, didn't she?"

"No, no," she moaned wearily, dropping her head, shaking it. "I didn't have an abortion." She paused, gripped my hand tight as if she was trying to transmit the rest of her story without having to tell it. Her other hand was still wrapped around her wine glass and she began making pensive little circles with it on the tabletop. She watched the burgundy liquid oscillate beneath the glass's rim, but all she saw were visions of 1968. At the end of this short silence she started caressing my hand and she raised her eyes back to mine. They were so sad, so teary, all pink and glassy. When she finally spoke, she did it slowly, pacing herself, wanting to get it all just right. "It was born premature, Dean ... He was, I should say. He was such a tiny little boy, just under two pounds. He never had a chance. It happened ... the miscarriage ... in Raleigh, North Carolina. That's where my mother had moved us to.

God, I was so screwed up! It was just too much for me to handle at eighteen. And, Dean, all the while I was crazy from missing you. When we split up, my whole life stopped, no, it ended. I've never gotten over you since, and I never will."

There it was. She'd said it!

She had missed me as much as I'd missed her. I hadn't been living some foolish fantasy after all. Elbows to the table, we embraced each other's loving gaze, basked in it. Like I said before, neither of us were real high from the drinks, just relaxed, the slightest buzz, that heightened sense of awareness that so many writers strive for before sitting down to ply their trade. Once again, like so many years before, we were at the very center of this whole crazy universe. No, beyond that now! After travelling another twenty-odd years by ourselves to get here, this was even sweeter, deeper. Our own heavenly private cosmos and we were about to take refuge in it. We were Adam and Eve with the apple. Forbidden as it was, we were both thrilled to have it.

Our faces gravitated toward each other until our lips met over the candle. We could feel its warmth on our faces but it was nothing compared to the heat in our lips. She tasted delicious. I couldn't believe this was happening. We were home again. Finally! I smelled the lovely familiar scent of her flesh, of my youth. It wasn't a long kiss, just a brief meeting of lips, but it was drenched with passion and longing, passion and longing that had been pent up inside us both for more than half our lives, oh so powerful emotions that I can't here, with paper and ink, possibly describe.

When our lips parted, our eyes fondled each other's tenderly as Theresa went on with her story.

"My being pregnant was why we left College Point so suddenly. I made the mistake of telling my mother and she went absolutely ballistic. I was so messed up emotionally I didn't know which end was up. I was broken-hearted about you … the affair you had. Dean, we were sooo close. We had something special. We were very fortunate. We shared something most people in their entire lives never experience. And then … that night in Jahn's … poof, just like that, it all ended. I lost my soul that night. It left my body and never returned. "

"Theresa, that was one irresponsible, disastrous mistake, I have no excuse, other than I was a kid and…"

She waved me off. "I know that now. I've known that for a long time. But then I was mad. I wanted to punish you, just for awhile, not talk to you, not see you, but I truly planned to go back to you. But, when I found out I was pregnant, well, then I couldn't even think straight. The weight became too much for me to carry. I had to unload some of my fear. That's why I told my mother. But then she started laying all these guilt trips on me and I became even more confused, no, worse than that, I became unsure. Unsure about you, about us. I started doubting the legitimacy of what I thought we'd had together."

She reached across the table and once again laid her fine, delicate hand over mine. It no longer mattered that her rock and wedding band were in full view. They meant nothing at this precious moment. We felt like we had never been apart, like the past twenty-four years never happened. The two of us were together again, at long last, like we were always meant to be. All the old karma was still there, and then some. Her touch--that kiss--had set off an exchange of emotions, an energy so powerful that I'm sure we literally glowed inside that dusky bar.

I know it sounds cold, but to this point in the evening I'd only thought about Maddy Frances a couple of times. And they'd been just transient thoughts at that, brief concerns of her at home waiting for me and my crossing forbidden lines. But, as I said, both these considerations had been fleeting at best, both of them quickly, easily, and totally eclipsed by Theresa's intoxicating presence. As I looked deeply into the haven of her oh-so-familiar intriguing eyes, all I saw were the irreplaceable wonderful times we'd shared at a time when the task of living was much simpler.

I wanted to take Theresa in my arms, carry her away, off to a mountain, her mountain, any mountain, to the woods, a warm uninhabited island, her place in the keys, anywhere. I wanted to stay with her, never leave. Never go home.

Now knowing that I had impregnated her, that there had been a child, a love child, only fortified our already rock-solid communion of our souls. This revelation, in my eyes, legitimized our reunion, made it OK, appropriate, necessary. Our intimate connection felt so right it was like I was married to Theresa, not Maddy Frances. Knowing now that Theresa had once carried my child, our child, made anything destined to happen between us this night just that, destiny. Anything we might do would be natural and, in our hearts, justifiable.

All of a sudden the band cranked up. Talk about bad timing! I don't remember what they played but it was something loud, funky, fast and, to us, rambunctious, raunchy crap that trespassed, no, ravished this most intimate moment, this most significant conversation of both our lives. Theresa glowered over my shoulder at them, then shook her head and said, "I don't believe this." Nevertheless, competing with this music, she went on to tell me some of her life's longest-hidden, most heart-rending secrets. That she had to damn near shout such things seemed nothing short of blasphemous. But she did.

"After we got to Raleigh, my mother started taking me to a psychologist. He made me quit smoking, drinking coffee, alcohol, all stimulants, including you. He said that was most important, that I got over you, and that he could help me do that. With all my problems, if you'll excuse my French, that bastard actually made advances toward me, right in his office. Then, when I told my mother what he'd done, she wouldn't believe me. I had to keep seeing that sleaze. Dean, it was horrible."

The lounge had become crowded by now. Couples paraded by our table on their way to the dance floor, waitresses hustled this way and that, and the volume of other conversations around us also rose in competition with the blaring music. I could see that Theresa had had enough, and so had I. Ever so naturally, her voice devoid of any pretensions, she asked me, "Can we get out of here, Dean? I can't compete with all this. We've got so much to talk about. There's so much I want to tell you." Then in the form of a question, "Maybe ... maybe we can go to your room."

"Sure. Let's go," I said, uncertain of where we were headed, not caring as long as I was with Theresa.

I stood up, then chugged down what was left of my fourth beer ... or was it my fifth?

Chapter 31

It only seemed right that I should put an arm around Theresa's trim waist, a hand on her hip, guide her to the two glass doors that opened out to the motel lobby. But it didn't seem so right, more like taboo, that with each step she took, the sensuous rock of her solid hip beneath my palm delighted me so. Then, when we stepped out into the lobby, to make matters worse, or better depending on how you look at it, Theresa slid her arm around my waist. Arm-in-arm now, had it not been for the sound of our footsteps on the marble floor to remind me, I would have sworn we were floating toward that bank of elevators. Listening to our steps echoing across the expansive, tile floor, I rationalized that holding each other like this was just an innocent gesture of fondness, and that the kiss in the lounge had been justifiable too.

On the way up in the elevator, we were alone. We talked about what had become of our parents. I could see she was affected deeply when I told her my father had passed on just a few months after our break up, right about the time she had the miscarriage. The grimace that immediately took over her face told me she felt some guilt about the untimeliness of both those events. She gave her heartfelt condolences and, at the same time, tightened her grip on my waist. She knew all too well what I meant when I told her my mother was still alive but still dying of the same delusional disease. When Theresa told me her mom was still around but convalescing from a stroke she had suffered nine months earlier, I couldn't help feeling sorry for the woman, despite her evil ways.

When we got up to my room, I unlocked the door and stepped aside. Theresa flipped on the light and entered the room, looking around, accessing it while I followed wondering, *How does this work? Where do we sit - at the table, in those little chairs, or on one of the beds?* Theresa would answer that question for me. Still scoping out the room, she slipped out of her jacket, folded it neatly and laid it on a chair nonchalantly, as if she was home. As she stepped out of her patent leather black heels, she said, "I must have spent a thousand nights in rooms like this, you know, with business trips, conventions and all that."

Then, as she prepared to sit on the edge of the one bed that was still made, she asked, "Do you mind, Dean?"

All dummied up for a second, I shook my head, a semi-urgent "no", before managing to say, "Nooo! Sure! I don't mind. Go 'head, Theresa, relax!"

Damn, I felt awkward. It had been twenty years since I'd last been alone like this with any woman other than Maddy Frances. I was beginning to feel guilty too. But the guilt, that most noble of emotions, quickly faded to the outer fringes of my psyche when I noticed that, from sitting, Theresa's skirt had risen halfway up her thighs. That was distracting enough, but when she crossed her legs and I heard the small sound of her sheer nylons rubbing together, it really did something to me, turned me on like a four-stack power plant running at full capacity. Being alone with her like this, watching her, delighting in her every feminine gesture and movement, had suddenly given this previously benign reunion an entirely different feel.

"Little warm in here, isn't it?" I said, stepping toward the window to turn on the AC.

"Yes, it is," she said, pivoting on the mattress, gracefully lifting her legs onto it, tucking her small stockinged feet beneath her bottom. Again the rustling of nylons, again my stomach flushed with this strange enchanting heat. Then she leaned back against the headboard, tossed her head back and, elbows to the ceiling, began lazily massaging the back of her head.

Good God, she's still so tantalizing, and, without even trying!

I sat on the other bed facing her, the messed up one I'd laid down on during the afternoon. I fished my smokes from my breast pocket and held the pack toward Theresa.

"Sure...why not?"

I lit two, leaned across the nightstand-wide gap between the beds, handed her one, then sat stiffly against my own headboard. I could see her in the dresser mirror which meant she could see me also.

Theresa took a long hit off the Carlton. She dropped her eyes for a moment to scrutinize the cigarette as she slowly exhaled the smoke and said, "Ya know ... I'm enjoying these way too much tonight. If I didn't watch myself, I could easily go back to smoking." Shaking her head at her cigarette, she said, "Sorry, I don't care what they say, once you give it up you always miss it, maybe a little less as time goes by, but you still always miss it. At least I do. I've never gotten over them completely, Dee Cee, just like I've never gotten over ..." She paused there, mid-sentence, raised her eyes from the cigarette and looked back at my reflection in the mirror, " ... just like I've never gotten over other things in my life."

Did she mean what I thought she meant? You know how women are, you just don't know. I couldn't be a hundred percent sure. But I was sure of one thing; that I was actually blushing. Forty-three years old and I blushed. I know I did. I felt the heat in my face when it flushed. I hoped like hell she hadn't noticed. If she had, she spared me the realization. I smiled stupidly at the mirror. What she'd insinuated made me feel damn awkward but, at the same time, damn good. She had to be hinting about me, didn't she? Whether she was or not, I hoped her words would dissipate in the air along with the cigarette smoke when I said "Well, cigarettes aren't the best for you, but I smoke the lowest tars on the market and I enjoy the hell of them. I suppose you could call me a judicious smoker, been keeping it under half a pack a day for more than fifteen years now. The way I figure it, if eight or nine a day are going to kill me, then bring it on. This life thing hasn't been all it's cracked up to be anyway, at least not for me, for the most part."

Letting my innuendo pass now, she said, "The way you look, Dean, you'll probably make it another forty years!" Then she turned her head my way, a little quarter roll against the headboard and she looked behind the nightstand lamp. I did the same. Seeing me first hand now rather than my reflection, she said, "I'm serious, you look great. You're a sight for sore eyes, Dean Cassidy."

All four of our sore eyes locked. They forged together for a quiet moment. There was no more skirting the issue now, it had risen to the surface. I didn't know quite what to say. Theresa bailed me out. She broke the silence, but all the forced gaiety left her voice when she said, "Happy birthday Dean."

"Jeez, how did you ever remember that?"

She didn't answer right away. Instead she began digging for something inside her handbag. When she found it, she held it behind her back and stood up. Then she came over, sat alongside me on the bed, and handed me a small, rectangular gift-wrapped box.

212

"Noooo! Theresaaa, why'd you do this?"

"Because I wanted to, now open it up," she ordered.

Obediently, I peeled away the wrapping paper and, as I did, like background music in the heaviest scene of a most dramatic movie, Theresa Wayman reopened her heart to me.

"I've always remembered your birthday, Dean, every year on the fifth of May. No matter where I was, or how busy, whether I was married at the time or not, I would take a walk ... a long walk ... always alone, and I'd think of us. Yeah, sure, I thought of you many times over the years, Dean ... God ... if you only knew how many times. But during my walks for some reason, the memories always came back clearest. It was weird. Every time it was as if my mind had somehow connected with yours, telepathy or something. Almost as if we were talking on the phone, reminiscing together, sharing the memories. I'd think back to the first time I ever saw you at that dance at my school, when you were fighting. I'd also bring back the first time you came to my house, the night you gave me the ankle bracelet, Regina's New Year's Eve party, prom night, shopping for clothes together on Main Street ... on Saturday afternoons. All that and more came back to me during those walks, but what came back the clearest was the first time we ever made love. No, every time we made love! It always had such meaning. Dean ... I know that because of our circumstances this kind of talk is probably way out of line, but I want you to know, I have to tell you, those times, they were the only times I've ever really made love."

When she said that, I felt the goose bumps flush beneath my sleeves. I wanted to cry, bawl like a baby. But I didn't. I held back the flood of emotions inside me. I opened the gift box and, when I saw what was inside, my heart stopped, my pulse suspended and I gasped.

Lying inside that tiny box on a bed of white cotton was another ID bracelet.

It was quiet then, just the hum of the air conditioner. I picked up my gift, looked it over real good. Silver, just like the first one she'd given me. Finely-incised lines dulled the face. This one was Florentine finished too. Both of us still speechless, I turned it over and read the inscription; "To Dean, all my love still and always, Theresa".

"Jesus, Theresa! Goddam! This is ... I don't know what to say." I lifted my eyes from the gift, looked back at her warm ironic smile, her loving

213

face, those deep dark tilted eyes, and then it came to me. I DID know what to say, right, wrong, proper or improper, that emotional dam within me burst. The words surged out. Nothing on earth could stop them now. "Dammit, Theresa, you've been with me too! All these years! If you only knew … " I paused there. My voice was breaking up and a vision flashed inside my head, a pitiful vision. A glossy black and white crime-scene snapshot of my suicide attempt in the garage. As I watched it, I thought, *you bet I missed you Theresa.* Then the tears found their way from my heart to my eyes, and I sobbed, "You've been with me every day, Theresa, at every dawn and every dusk. Up and down so many highways … and back roads too. I thought about you every night when I went to bed, each morning when I woke up, and thousands of the hours in between." Then, with tears streaming both my cheeks, I said, "Theresa … I thought … for sure … I'd never see you again!"

Struggling to hold onto what was left of her smile, she slid closer now, right up against me. She put her hands lightly on my wet cheeks, held me like that, and her small smile disappeared. The corners of her mouth dropped and quivered, and a tear fell to her cheek. Then she eased my face to her bosom. She wrapped her arms around my head and began rocking me gently. Reflexively, as if they had their own mind, my arms found their way around her also. Finally, at long last, I was once again embracing my Theresa. With my face buried so deep inside the refuge of her breasts, feeling the heat and the lovely softness against my cheek as if they were naked, I knew she still wore those sheer silky bras. This was the ultimate homecoming. The faint scent of lilac emanated from her cleavage, mingling subtly with the long lost, yet so familiar, smell of her flesh. We held this most intimate pose for a long time. And we cried together, our bodies twitching and convulsing as one as the sound of her sobs fed mine, and mine hers. And the whole time I could hear Theresa's heart beat a most lovely serenade.

When I finally drew my head away and looked up, we held each other's mournful teary eyes for a most tender moment. Then Theresa brought her face down to mine and, ever so gently, she fitted her delicious mouth onto mine. They opened together. And like it used to when we were teenagers, the tip of her searching tongue brushed along my gums, slowly, tantalizingly, then along my teeth before it finally joined my own tongue. When it did, we slid together down onto the bed. The air in the room suddenly seemed thinner. Our chests began heaving and rubbing together frantically, desperately, lustfully. Theresa slid her hand up between us and I felt the tremor in her fingers as they worked on her buttons. I peered for only a second through the two slits in my eyes and watched. Both of us on fire now, the buttons undone, Theresa jerked her mouth away, slid a little higher on the bed and pulled my head down to her breasts. Her blouse was wide open. I nuzzled my face in there, kissing, loving her cleavage, loving, kissing the soft white bulges that swelled above her bra's cups. Ohhh Lord, that lilac, the now intensified smell of her naked flesh, those dark nipples rising, hardening, about to explode from her sheer, powder-blue bra. Theresa purred, and she whispering things, things I couldn't discern, things muffled deeply beneath her passionate moans. Bliss! Rapture! Elation! Euphoria! Ecstasy! This was all of that rolled into one indescribable, titanic emotion.

Blindly, my face still buried in her fleshy pillows, I stripped the blouse from her shoulders, all the way down her arms in one blind, reckless motion. I lifted my face from her and, shakily but gently, slid the delicate straps off her bare shoulders. Easing my fingertips inside her bra cups, I lowered them, slowly. The paler flesh coming into view now, bulging even more, I stopped. I needed to be sure Theresa wanted this. I looked up at her. What I saw only verified what I had already known, that she was as intoxicated with passion as I. Her lips all puffy, their coating worn away now, she looked three times more sensual than I had ever remembered. She was smiling and, through a disheveled shock of black hair laid over her forehead obscuring one of her bedroom eyes, the other spoke for them both. It was full of lust. And love. It urged me on. I lowered her bra. This was it! After waiting half my life, I had returned to the gateway to nirvana!

But then, something happened! I heard a voice, from somewhere deep within me, a resonant, commanding voice that spoke irrefutable words, words that somehow found their way to my lips, words that, even as they spilled from my mouth, I could not believe I was actually saying. "Theresa ... I'm sorry ... so sorry, but I can't do this."

Filled with carnal desire, she shoved that lock of hair from her eye and rose to her elbows. Full of hurt and questions, her eyes strained to read my face and eyes for a clue to why I had put an end to this. Both us, just beginning to catch our breath, froze like that, trying to see into each other's mind. She looked for the cause of what I had just said and I looked for the effect. Neither of us said anything. We held that pose for a long painful moment until finally, totally exhausted, Theresa let her head fall to the pillow.

Now the words didn't come so easily. I started to say something, I'm not sure exactly what, but Theresa stopped me. She put a fingertip to my lips. She wanted me to know I didn't have to say anything. Her voice, deflated as if the wind had been knocked out of it, said, "It's OK, Dean. I understand." My eyebrows rose and arched, the way those of sufferers do when caught in the deepest throes of pain. Slowly, withdrawing her fingertip from my lips, Theresa said, "That was a big part of our magic, Dean, that we always understood each other so well it was uncanny. And I think I still understand you! No. I know I still understand you. And I know that, deep down inside, you don't want to make the same mistake twice."

She'd hit it on the head! Had we consummated this affair, it would have wrecked everything Maddy Frances and I had going for us. And I knew, now that I didn't want that. Nothing was worth losing Maddy. Shoot, I'd spent almost half my life with her. Sure I could have run off with Theresa. She would have gone with me. We could have ran off to her mountain, or her paradisiacal island, but I couldn't have hid! I would always be haunted, haunted by the knowledge that I had abandoned Maddy Frances, my wife, the woman who had so unflinchingly put up with me for so long, a first-class lady who for the past twenty years had loved me more than her own life, a near-saint who had loved me unconditionally while the whole time - what did I do? - I secretly fantasized, and hypothesized, and agonized over the very decision I had been confronted with this night. But now it was over. I had made my choice. And though that choice turned out to be very different than I had imagined all those years, it had been made.

Theresa and I quickly neatened up a bit, she in the bathroom, me in front of the dresser mirror. Standing alone, looking at my reflection, running a comb through my mustache, something dawned on me, a revelation so ironic that a chill coursed my entire body. I knew that after all that had been thought about, said, and done, something positive had definitely come from the misdeed an eighteen-year old boy committed a long, long time ago inside a squalid bedroom of a Queens housing-project.

A few minutes later, Theresa and I were downstairs in the parking lot. As we walked in silence to her big expensive car, I felt so bad for her. I felt so damn guilty. I realized that I had everything and she had nothing, that I had someone special, someone very, very special at home waiting to spend the rest of her life with me, and all she had was four booming businesses, a ton of money, three houses and another irreparable marriage.

A few steps later, we reached her car. She unlocked the door, opened it then turned back around. Theresa studied my face in the moonlight and I studied hers. We stood like that for a long moment, before she said, "I'm sorry Dean. I just can't help it." Then she threw her arms around me one last time, buried her teary face in my denim shirt and squeezed me tighter than I ever imagined she was capable of. I knew well and good that she didn't want to ever let go. I hugged her back long and hard, our bodies gently swaying together. It was our last dance and we knew it. Both of us tried to be strong, both of us failed. Though her voice was muffled in my chest, I heard her loud and clear when she said, "I love you, Dean Cassidy ... I always have, always will." And, with that, she began to shake and weep in my arms. I snugged her tighter and rolled my eyes toward the Georgia stars. Silent tears streamed my face and fell into Theresa's hair. Soon it was time for our dance to end and I looked down at her, and she up at me. There is no explaining the magnitude of hurt and the heartbreak we shared at that moment, no way of describing the excruciating sense of loss. I said to her, "I love you too, Theresa, and that I'll take to my deathbed. Weee ... you and I ... we were sooo right for each other. Hell, we're still right for each other. But we're still missing one thing, the one thing we could never get quite right, and that's timing."

Theresa didn't say anything. There was nothing to add. She just wiped her cheeks with her fingertips, stretched up onto her toes, kissed me hard and quick, then, just like that, she lowered herself into the car. More like fell into it. Then she started the engine, turned on the headlights and lowered her electric window. "Have a good life, Dean ..." she said, " ... you deserve it. You're a good man, the best, the only man

I've ever known." Looking like she was in deep physical pain, she paused as she struggled to muster up the strength for what she was about to say. "Dean, I hope that you and Maddy have a good life together, and that you stay together 'till you're both ninety, but ... if somehow that doesn't happen ... always remember, I'll be here ... in Atlanta."

With that, Theresa Wayman dropped her eyes to the gearshift, put it into reverse, and looked back up at me for the last time. There were new tears streaming her lovely heart-shaped face. She looked so small, so fragile, so broken and so very alone in that great big car when she said, "I know I can't have you, Dean, but still, I'll always be yours." And with that said, she managed one last smile, a painful half-smile, backed her car out of the spot and pulled away. My eyes followed her tail-lights as long as they could until the two red blurs were swallowed up by the river of night-time traffic out on the boulevard.

The rest of that night was the longest of my life. I didn't sleep well at all. I turned and tossed and wrestled with the pillows, the sheets and my thoughts. I had already made my choice, but that sure didn't stop me from scrutinizing it. My mind pulled back and forth, back and forth, between my two lovers. By the time my emotions had wrung themselves out enough to allow me to doze off, it was well after three AM and, even then, my sleep was not restful but broken, fractured in three places. Each time I woke to the same unfamiliar darkness, the incessant hum of the air conditioner, the same troubling considerations and the urges that opposed them. And each time the scent of Theresa Wayman was still on the sheets with me.

When I awoke the fourth time, I knew there was no getting back to sleep. With one hand I felt along the top of the nightstand in the darkness until I found my Casio. With what was left of my index finger's nail, I depressed the tiny 'light' button - 5:03 AM. Yes, I really do remember the exact time. I dragged myself out of that bed. I remember too that my legs were leaden, dull and achy with fatigue, and that the rest of me didn't feel anywhere close to renewed. Nevertheless, I needed to get going. I had to get some distance between me and this place, these sheets, and Atlanta's Century 21 agencies.

Minutes later, in the lukewarm Southern darkness, a foam cup of steaming coffee in one hand, I climbed into the van behind my suitcase and cranked her up. The old Caravan coughed and sputtered as we rolled slowly through the parking lot because, just this once, I hadn't taken the time to warm her up. I didn't have the time. I wasn't about to wait for anything. I wanted out of "Hotlanta", pronto.

But, anxious as I was, when I idled out of that lot, I just had to steal one last glance at the place where Theresa and I had said goodbye. As I rolled past the lounge, in unison my stomach tightened, my shoulders lurched, and I sniffled a few times. Despite the lead in my chest, I forced my head around, tightened my jaw, jutted it over the steering wheel and motored out onto the all-but-deserted boulevard. Once in the marked lanes, I drove as fast as I legally could. I made jackrabbit take-offs after every red light and quickly ate up the four or so miles to I-75. As I climbed onto the highway entrance ramp, something very strange happened. Although I hadn't seen any C-21 agencies along the way, I suddenly felt a small but very warm glow inside because I knew they could always be found

Had my mind not been full of Theresa, I would have savored the peaceful feeling I always get when driving in early morning along uncrowded Southern highways. But it was and I couldn't. Still half-dazed from sleep and the lack of it, I couldn't fight off the thoughts of Theresa that still jammed my mind, remembrances of last night, in the bookstore, in the lounge, in my room, and our heart-wrenching goodbye. The few thoughts I was able to compose on my own were very, very disturbing. Things like, *I can turn around right now, get Theresa, finish out my life with her.* After all, wasn't she my high school sweetheart, my first love, the woman I'd dreamed about so many times, the lover I damn near killed myself over?

But I didn't turn around. I pushed south and, as the day wore on, as the miles and miles of hot asphalt rolled beneath my wheels, those hauntings slowly thinned. Gradually my ability to process my own thoughts returned, and strengthened. As it did, something became clearer and clearer. I realized that the farther I was getting from Theresa, the closer I felt to Maddy Frances. By mid-afternoon that Wednesday, May sixth, 1992, as I was cruising down Florida's Turnpike south of Orlando, something came over me, a feeling, a spooky feeling that had come on as suddenly as a panic attack. Out of the clear blue I got this intense, urgent feeling that I had to call Maddy Frances right now, a scary, palm sweating, soul-jarring premonition that for some reason I might never hear her voice or see her again.

A long twenty minutes later I pulled into a rest stop at a place (and I kid you not) called Yeehaw Junction. When I eased my legs out of the van, they felt as if they'd come all the way from Atlanta on horseback. The bright, scorching Florida sun beat heavy on me as I pushed my tired body, one step at a time, across the parking lot to the entrance of the characterless state facility. Once inside, I got change of a few bucks from a cashier who, when she fished it out of the register, acted as if it were coming out of her own dwarfed salary. I thanked her anyway, dragged myself across the tiled floor through a buzz of faceless travelers to a bank of pay phones along a wall. I dialed Maddy's work number.

You can't imagine how relieved I was to hear her voice. And did she flip when she heard mine. You would have thought the Publishers Clearinghouse entourage had piled out of their van again, the cameras, balloons, giant cardboard check, the whole schmear.

"Ohh, Dean," she said, "I'm so glad it's you! When will you be home? I don't think I can wait another hour. I'm so excited!"

I told her where I was, that I had left early that morning, made good time and that I'd be home around dinner time.

Then, all the excitement leaving her voice, she said, "Honey, I don't e-v-e-r want to be apart like this again. Do you hear? I mean it!"

"Me either, Maddy. Me either. It's just something I had to do."

"I know. But it was horrible."

Just as quickly as it had deflated, her voice puffed up again, and she said, "Anyway, Dean, I'm so glad you're coming home. God, I don't believe it, I'm so excited I almost forgot to tell you the latest fantastic news. You're not going to believe this. Are you ready?"

"What? What is it?"

"Fran called me last night. She didn't want to bother you at the motel, it was late and, knowing how tired you must be, she was afraid she'd wake you. Anyway, take a deep breath, honey. Brace yourself. You're not going to believe this. It's the best thing that's ever happened to us, well almost!"

"Come on Maddy! Tell me! What is it?"

"Alright, here goes. Fran – got – word – yesterday that 'Look What

220

They've Done To Our Dream' is going to be on the best seller list. It's going to be number eight on this week's New York Times list. DEAN, you can quit your job! Fran said that Olympus is going to send you a contract for the new book you're working on, AND ... THE NEXT TWO AFTER THAT! And Dean, that's not all. She said, there will be, and I quote, a SIX-FIGURE ADVANCE. You've done it, honey. You're a writer!"

My legs jellied beneath me. A chill coursed every cell in my body. I had to put my free hand on the tile above the phone to steady myself. "Maddy...you're serious, aren't you?"

"Of course, I'm serious. We're home free! God, I want to see you so bad I can't even think straight. That's it, I know what I'm going to do. I'm going to ask Darwin if I can get off early. He'll let me. He knows you're coming home today, everyone here does. Oh, Dean, I love you so much. I'm the happiest I've ever been. I'm gonna go home and cook you a really nice dinner. What do you feel like?"

There she goes again, I thought, true to form. Good old selfless Maddy Frances, always thinking of me first, Dean this, Dean that, what do you want Dean?

"Maddy, listen ... don't put dinner on. Let's go out and celebrate, nothing heavy, I'm too tired, just a nice quiet dinner somewhere."

"Sure. That sounds great. I'd love to go out. What do you feel like - Mexican, Italian, seafood?"

Slowly, I turned away from the pay phone. I leaned my travel-stiff back against its partition. Massaging my temples, shaking my head side to side, I said, "Nooooo, Maddy Frances ... Listen to me. This time I want to know what you feel like."

THE END

221

8009601R0

Made in the USA
Charleston, SC
30 April 2011